NIC TATANO

I've always been a writer of some sort, having spent my career working as a reporter, anchor or producer in television news. Fiction is a lot more fun, since you don't have to deal with those pesky things known as facts. I grew up in the New York City metropolitan area and now live on the Gulf Coast where I will never shovel snow again. I'm happily married to a math teacher and we share our wonderful home with our tortoise-shell tabby cat, Gypsy.

Boss Girl

NIC TATANO

Harper*Impulse* an imprint of
HarperCollins*Publishers Ltd*
77–85 Fulham Palace Road
Hammersmith, London W6 8JB

www.harpercollins.co.uk

A Paperback Original 2014

First published in Great Britain in ebook format by HarperImpulse 2013

Copyright © Nic Tatano 2013

Cover Images © Shutterstock.com

Nic Tatano asserts the moral right to
be identified as the author of this work

A catalogue record for this book
is available from the British Library

ISBN: 978-0-00-758491-8

This novel is entirely a work of fiction.
The names, characters and incidents portrayed in it are
the work of the author's imagination. Any resemblance to
actual persons, living or dead, events or localities is
entirely coincidental.

Automatically produced by Atomik ePublisher from Easypress

For Myra, my love and source of inspiration.

CHAPTER ONE

I used to think I was Eve in a previous life. But then again, if that were true, I would have made the serpent eat the apple.

Doesn't really matter. These days, no Adam stands a chance against me.

Because I'm the new keeper of the Garden of Eden. Right now it's known as a television news network. I, Sydney Hack, a/k/a *Neutron Syd*, (Okay, okay, so I've fired a few people) have been running it for a year and a half.

I'm the Boss Girl.

And the ratings have not budged one inch with news anchored by the pageant fembots (those beauty queen androids.) If they don't move in six months, I'm out of a job.

That scraping sound you hear? Someone upstairs sharpening the guillotine.

Sydney Hack, white courtesy phone, please. Your career is calling.

Time for a pre-emptive strike.

So I'm changing the rules tonight. I'm going to start giving our target demographic, women over thirty, what they really want.

And what they want on their "to-do" list is on his way from the front door. He struts, as if in slow motion, a chiseled six-foot-two trophy buck with tousled black hair and a chin that could carve granite. I cross my legs and playfully rock a Kelly green four-inch heel on my toe and smile, calling my dimples and high cheekbones into service as he makes his way through the crowded, dimly-lit restaurant. The brass rails and colorful Tiffany lamps are suddenly painted in sepia tones as his powder blue eyes stand out like they were surrounded by black velvet. His five o'clock shadow is a light brushstroke of virility.

Members of my target demographic drool, posture dramatically improves as c-cups raise their hands for attention, and forks are suspended in mid-air over crème brûlée as he passes.

I can see it in their eyes as they note my bar stool is his destination.

He's ten years younger than her.

Why not me?

And I know he's the key to the ratings.

Damn, it's so simple. Robbing the cradle. Age inappropriate. Cougar newscast. Or call it whatever. Older woman, younger man.

I shove my long copper tangles back behind one ear, widen the eyes that have been dipped in the Caribbean (thanks to the kind folks at Eye-World, with several convenient locations to serve you) and stand to greet him, my heels taking my five-ten slender frame up to his level. I'm the long-stemmed Red Queen of the Garden.

Scott Harry extended his hand. "Good to see you again, Ms. Hack." His deep, smooth voice flowed, the edges of the words smoothed over as they segued into one another.

"Sydney, please," I said, sliding back onto the stool. "Our table won't be ready for a half-hour. Would you like a drink?"

"Never drink on a job interview," he said, smiling, dimples to match mine, then hopping up onto a bar stool. He leaned toward me, and the faint scent of his Polo cologne followed.

"The interview was this afternoon," I said. "This is the negotiation."

He tried to hold back a smile, but couldn't. The twenty-nine-year-old Ken-Doll didn't have a poker face. "So, you're making me an offer?"

"Well, I'm still considering two other candidates." I paused, watched the color drain from his face as if I had pulled a plug.

Gotcha.

I ran my eyes up and down his body. "But I like what I see." I turned my attention to my glass of bourbon and took a sip. "Your agent tells me you've been looking for an anchor gig for a while."

"The job market's tough."

"Well, to be brutally honest, your reporting skills aren't the best."

His head dropped.

Okay, he's ready to swallow the hook.

"But you're a decent enough anchor for our purposes." The head raised up, a hint of hope crept back into those powder blues. I downed the rest of the drink in one gulp and checked my watch. "Tell you what, Scott. I don't feel like waiting here thirty minutes for dinner, and the service is slow anyway. I'm thinking room service."

He furrowed his brow. "Huh?"

I reached into my beaded bag, pulled out a Montblanc pen, and grabbed a cocktail napkin from the stack on the bar. "Tell you what, if you want to continue our negotiations, here's my room number at The Plaza." I wrote 1634 on the napkin and slid it over to him. "If not, well, I'm sure you'll have a nice career in Indianapolis."

His face remained a twisted puzzle. "Ms. Hack… are you—"

Geez, the man needs a road map.

But, if the other head works and he can read a teleprompter, I'm good to go.

I slid my toe inside one cuff of his slacks, gently running it up his shin. "If you want the job, just bring yourself to my room. I need to check your… references."

I hopped off the barstool, smoothed my short green halter dress and headed out, zigzagging through the tables.

Watching my target demographic look at me like I was nuts.

I had them.

And I was pretty sure I had him.

Two hours later, his references checked out.

* * *

As an attractive 38-year-old woman, I didn't need focus groups or expensive research to know what women want in a newscast.

They sure as hell don't want a blonde pageant fembot who is prettier than they are.

And they don't want to feel past their prime.

So here's a newsflash for the next generation. I'm giving them news delivered by a woman who is one of them. Middle-aged, smart, experienced, attractive.

And for dessert on this news buffet, male eye candy.

But not just any confection. They want a late twenty-something with a body so hard you could give him an hour-long massage and a bottle of wine and still bounce quarters off his ass. A guy with a chiseled face and a smile that can melt a heart. Eyes that can look through the camera and caress a soul. Buffed shoulders that could easily carry you into the bedroom.

And they want that sitting on the anchor desk next to a woman…

Just.

Like.

Them.

They want to know a woman on the back nine still has a chance against the fembots.

Yes, we're still interested in sex. We're mature, not crypt keepers.

Our drivers' licenses may say we're over thirty, but the libido is still in high school.

For years, male news executives had their casting couch.

Now it's our turn.

And when you've got an anchor in your stable like Scott Harry, well, membership has its, uh… privileges.

Weekly.

The female-owned network that hired me as Vice-President of the News Division gave me carte blanche my first day, but thanks to the incredible ratings spike provided by Scott Harry in his first month, I've been upgraded to platinum.

The powers that be want me to take the woman-on-top co-anchor theme national, opening chapters in our other three affiliates in Los Angeles, Chicago, and Dallas. (They don't know about my current "benefits package" regarding reference checking, and as long as the ratings stay up, they won't care.)

Thank goodness I was smart enough to hire women as News Directors for those stations.

All between 35 and 40.

All intelligent, attractive and single.

May as well give you a line-up card as I lead the gals who will change the face of the news business into our conference room, for those of you scoring at home. And if you're not, you should be. (If there were a drummer in my office, I would call for a rim shot after that one.)

"Tawk to me, Syd," said Rica, coffee-with-a-little-cream eyes searching my face for more information and somehow getting female-only telemetry that I'd gotten an infusion of Y-chromosomes the night before. "Did'ja have a pahty afta woik?" she asks, in an accent so sharp it makes fingernails on the blackboard sound like classical music. One perfectly plucked eyebrow goes up like an extra question mark. The girl does love details.

If a pastrami sandwich could talk, it would sound like Rica Carbone, who is the youngest at thirty-five and runs the chapter on the left coast. This petite, raven-haired Brooklyn *paisan* could slice Tony Soprano in two with her death stare, and has enough confidence in her body that she once marched up to a jukebox and played *Brickhouse*. Every man in the bar thought the lyrics fit perfectly as she strutted back to the table smiling like she not only ate the canary, but the canary thanked her for it on the way down. Everything on this woman's Pilates-whipped body points east and west without any Lycra scaffolding, with no indication of various parts heading south anytime soon. All that and she's a brilliant journalist to boot.

"Yeah, she's got someone new," said Jillian, using one hand to curl the ends of her straight, strawberry blonde, chin-length cut in towards her face. "Her skirt's on backwards." I snapped my neck down to check. "Made you look," said Jillian. "At least that answers the question."

Damned reporter's tricks. You'd think I'd know better.

Trust fund debutante Jillian Charles is the black sheep of her family. Because she actually has a job. With no desire to pitch Krugerrands with her Massachusetts Ivy League neighbors, Jillian actually went to a state school (such a *scandal* in the gated community!) and likes getting her hands dirty. She's an inch shorter than I am, but all legs and none of it fat. I think her age (thirty-seven) matches her inseam; meanwhile, not a wrinkle on her gently freckled face and no Botox receipts on her tax return. Beneath those soft blue eyes lurks an executioner who enjoys the sight of heads tumbling down the steps of the Mayan temple, which is a handy trait to have in a Chicago News Director.

"So, c'mon Syd. Y'all don't keep us waitin'. Dish." The whiskey two-packs-a-day Southern accent you just heard comes from Neely "Vodka" Collins, the former hard-boiled reporter from New Orleans who doesn't smoke but believes that Russian alcohol is to a liquor cabinet what WD-40 is to a toolbox. If you run out of either, you'll get rusty and won't be able to screw anything. She looks like Demi Moore, sounds like Demi Moore if Demi Moore had been cast in *Gone with the Wind*, and therefore logic dictates that she hangs out with younger men like Demi Moore while running our station in Dallas. Neely first went against the grain in the eighth grade, shoving a sixth grader into a coat closet and giving him a free tonsillectomy. Her long, dark hair and innocent emerald eyes might lead a guy to think she's the girl next door, but there's nothing but lust embedded in her vocal chords. Like a good Irish Catholic she goes to confession every week, the old-fashioned way, in a booth, and must take a legal pad with her. I can only imagine her saying, "Bless me... Father... for I have... *sinned*," giving *sinned* three syllables with that scratchy drawl and having some priest on the other side breaking into a sweat while she enjoys torturing one of the few men in the state of Texas who can't load his gun.

"I've got good news. Take a seat," I said, as I grabbed the burgundy leather chair at the head of the long, mahogany table. Floor to ceiling windows on an entire wall turned the room into a greenhouse, which had the air conditioning blowing full blast. The gals sat down, all away from the sunny side of the room, backs toward the dark green wall that was covered with colorful posters of network shows. I grabbed a remote, swung my chair around, and fired it at the flat-screen monitor that hung on the wall behind me.

"We want details about last night, not more newscast airchecks," said Jillian.

"You're getting both," I said. The picture cleared and the face of Scott Harry filled the fifty-inch plasma screen.

"Hot damn," said Neely, though *damn* came out "day-umm."

"Damn hot," said Jillian.

"Fuhgeddaboudit," said Rica. (Which, depending on your inter-pretation of the term, can mean either *hot damn* or *damn hot* in Brooklynese.)

The video cut to a two-shot as Scott shared the desk with Caroline Jensen, a veteran brunette anchor in her early forties with laser beam ice-blue eyes.

"*This* is what's getting you a ratings spike?" asked Jillian.

"*Madonne*," said Rica.

"I don't think I've ever seen a major market anchor team where the man is that much younger than the woman," said Neely. "How do the demos break out?"

"They're a hit with women 18–34," I said. "And 34–49 is off the charts. Check out our sweeps series on beach safety." I flicked the remote and the video cut to a shot of Scott Harry walking on the Jersey Shore in a bathing suit, talking about the importance of sunscreen.

"You don't need sunscreen if he's providing the shade," said Jillian. The other two still had their jaws hanging open like the mouth-breathing shoppers at Wal-Mart, as the shot tightened up for a high-def look at Scott's pecs.

"Are the guys watchin'?" asked Rica. "Not that it really matters."

"Incredibly, they're holding steady," I said. "They apparently don't miss the pageant fembots. And considering our network's prime-time line-up, it's nice to see people switching over to catch our news product."

"Yeah. *Trailer Park True Confessions* isn't exactly a great lead-in," said Jillian, cocking her head toward a poster that featured a rusted Camaro and a cheap blonde woman whose roots had been dyed brown.

"Enough with the ratings," said Neely, who was staring holes in the monitor. "Just how did you manage to hire this young buck for our fledgling network?"

I muted the sound and turned back to them. "His agent told me he couldn't get arrested by the big networks and he'd do anything to get to New York. So I appealed to his sense of ambition. Then I checked his… references."

Jillian cocked her head to the side. "Syd, are you saying—"

"That's part of my new hiring manual," I said.

"What made you pair him with Caroline Jensen?" asked Neely.

"Do you want to watch women who are younger and prettier?" I asked.

"If you could find women who are younger and prettier than us, no," said Neely, sticking her nose in the air.

"And what do women our age want?" I asked.

Slowly, all three began to nod.

"So, this is our new playbook?" asked Jillian. "Find our own versions of Scott Harry and partner them with a competent middle-aged woman?"

"Exactly. Your guys don't ever have to report, just read. I don't care if you find them at a modeling agency. Hey, the men have been hiring that way for years. If I had a nickel for every beauty queen anchoring on local television I'd be rich. And there are plenty of talented women out there who have been put out to pasture by the old boys club."

"Do we get the same… benefits package… as you?" asked Neely, playfully batting her eyes. "I mean, do we get to check… *references*… during our job search?"

"Of course," I said. "You don't want your audience buying a product you haven't tried yourself, do you?"

* * *

Nine months later our network, Consolidated Broadcasting, had raised several eyebrows in the industry.

The four top affiliates of a network best known by its programming for the *sophistication challenged* (a politically correct television term for rednecks) were showing remarkable ratings growth in local news.

Jillian had turned the Windy City on its ear with her hire (after what she calls an *exhaustive* search) of twenty-eight-year-old J. T. Farrell, a sandy-haired, blue-eyed anchor from East Deliverance, Arkansas who had put himself through college as a male stripper. When pictures of Farrell wearing nothing but a collar and cuffs were leaked to a local tabloid (amazing how that happens, huh?), photos of his perfect six-foot physique (with a discreetly added black bar) were splashed under the headline **Chicago Bare**. Overnight ratings jumped twenty percent that day, while "Farrell nude" became the top Google search in the metro area.

Jillian paired Farrell with forty-one-year-old Jennifer Lorton, a spunky brunette with devilish green eyes framed by a few character lines. Lorton had been out of the business for three years but got with the program real quick, knocking out a three-part series titled "Sex in a Flash" that featured three local forty-something women and their trophy bucks while discussing the effects of hot flashes on the libido. As a reward, Jillian threw Lorton a bone (sorry, bad choice of words, but accurate) by delegating the *reference checking* duties of the current search for a weekend anchor.

I'd really thought Rica would have the hardest problem, Southern California being obsessed with youth and all. But the real Silicon Valley surprised me.

Since Angelinos are used to such hard-hitting journalistic fare as "Smiling Naturally White Using Botox" and "Regaining Your Balance After Large Implants", one would think they'd have little use for a female anchor who actually qualified for a ten-year high school reunion. But apparently Hollywood's aging actresses (those over twenty-nine who found roles hard to come by) saw the debut of Rica's new anchor team as a watershed moment. Rica found a Meg Ryan lookalike named Carolyn Baynard, who is in her mid-forties but remarkably well preserved. She's also the master of the double entendre ad-lib, which, when directed toward her co-anchor, sends a clear message to the viewer that the man sitting next to Carolyn is her catch of the day. (The other part of the subliminal message is, "Honey, this could be you.")

Carolyn's co-anchor arrived with a built-in promotional campaign. Rica bypassed the viewing of résumé tapes and those pesky journalism requirements, Los Angeles being what it is, went directly to an advertising agency and tabbed well-known underwear pitchman Dirk Anderson. Southern Californians couldn't go a mile without seeing a billboard that featured his ripped abs being caressed by tighty-whiteys that left nothing to the imagination. Thirty-year-old Dirk had amazing chemistry with his co-anchor, and the two were an immediate hit. On one occasion Carolyn said, "Dirk Anderson is on *assignment* tonight," paused, raised one eyebrow, and had every woman in LA wondering if the guy was under the anchor desk.

His five-part series, "Boxers or Briefs" was simply a no-brainer. But teaching Carolyn how to shop for men's underwear using a tape measure and a balloon was a stroke of genius.

Rica, of course, said his references were perfect, and that he made the gum fall out of her mouth when she had an orgasm. (I'm still not too clear on Brooklyn sex metaphors, but she smiles when she says it.)

Neely took a page out of Rica's book, but reversed things a bit, since Texas is, after all, the beauty pageant capital of the world, as well as the setting for weird cheerleader crimes. For her female anchor she chose former NFL cheerleader Dawn Mullaney, a sultry brunette Texan in her early forties who had retained a body that still cried out for hot pants, boots and a halter top. So Neely got them for her, then sent her to try out for a cheerleading squad with women half her age. Her dance moves had every cowboy wondering if the hitching post outside the barn would be better served standing vertically in the bedroom.

Since Texans like things bigger, Neely reached down into a tiny market and came up with Iowa sportscaster Nick Hallinger, a twenty-nine-year-old former linebacker who had blown out his knee during his rookie year with the New York Giants. At six-foot-five and 240 pounds, Hallinger looked as though he could bench-press Toyotas, but his kind blue eyes and wavy dark hair led you to believe he'd save a stray kitten.

Then Neely took things a step further, deciding to ditch the traditional anchor desk and have both anchors stand during the entire newscast. Dawn barely came up to Nick's shoulder, and between his impressive stature and her killer legs, they looked like the top of a wedding cake. Dawn made it a habit to always sign off first at the end of the newscast, then turn and look up longingly at her co-anchor who told viewers, "Have a great night," before looking down and smiling at Dawn.

As always, a local tabloid managed to dig up pictures of Dawn on a cheerleader swimsuit calendar and Hallinger during a bare-chested weigh-in from a bowl game (there are those damned leaks again!). Under the headline **Rah-Rah and Ga-Ga**, the photo splash made the anchor team hotter in Dallas than jalapenos.

So at this point you're probably thinking, "Hey, Syd saved her job with great ratings and women over thirty all over the country are rethinking their sex lives." And you'd be right.

But given enough ointment, there's always a damned fly.

It's Scott Harry, the trophy buck who helped save our New York affiliate.

He's in love.

And you won't believe who the object of his affections is.

* * *

"He's in *love?* With *you?*" asked Jillian.

I bit my lower lip and nodded slowly. The endless sound of slot machines provided audio wallpaper as I turned my attention back to the casino buffet breakfast. I shoveled a forkful of pancakes soaked with syrup into my mouth and savored the rush of the sugary sponge. The conversation stopped, I looked up, and saw three women who had stopped eating begging me for more details with their eyes.

"You can't just drop news like that and go back to your breakfast," said Neely.

"Details," said Rica. "Now."

I swallowed, took a sip of water, and looked around to make sure we were out of earshot. Sin City was crawling with television executives for the annual convention, and news like this sure wouldn't stay in Vegas. Two huge old women with fanny packs, who had bathed in *Jean Naté*, occupied the nearest table and were totally focused on their food, shoveling it in so fast that sparks were probably imminent from their knives and forks, so I figured we were safe.

"Okay," I said, lowering my voice a bit. They all leaned forward. "Last week he shows up at the hotel room after the Friday late newscast, just like always. Only this time he's got a dozen roses."

"Sounds like a real gentleman," said Neely.

"He also had a ring," I said.

"Oh, shit," said Rica. "An engagement ring?"

I nodded.

"What did you do?" asked Jillian.

"Well," I said, "let's just say that after I told him our working relationship was just that, he would have needed a tub of Viagra and a forklift."

"He really believes that you're romantically interested in him?" asked Jillian.

"Scott Harry is not exactly Stephen Hawking," I said. "One day I was talking about how you remember where you were on important days in history, like on 9/11 or the day Kennedy was shot. And he says, *'Ted Kennedy got shot?'*"

"Good God, what a complete moron," said Neely, who then added the Southern disclaimer. "Bless his little heart."

"What exactly does that mean anyway?" asked Rica, turning to face her.

"What?" asked Neely.

"The *bless his little heart* thing," said Rica. "You always say that."

"It's considered impolite in the South to say something bad about someone else," said Neely, "so you just add *bless his little heart* at the end and it cancels out the insult. Why, how would you say it?"

"He's a friggin' idiot," said Rica, just before taking a bite of a bagel.

Jillian started frantically waving her hands. "Can you two stop with the North and South stuff? We're dealing with some serious shit here. Syd's eaten two plates of pancakes because she's not getting any Y-chromosomes, and her main anchor is hopelessly lovesick while trying desperately to remember what the hell he was doing when Ted Kennedy was shot."

"If this convention were in Dallas, they'd turn that into a country song," said Neely.

"So what's his current status?" asked Jillian.

"His performance has slipped," I said.

Neely furrowed her brow. "You already told us he couldn't—"

"*On air*, for God's sake," I said, shaking my head. "He looks like a lost puppy."

"So waddaya gonna do?" asked Rica, spearing a sausage with her fork.

"He's got a two year contract," I said. "His ratings are great. There's really not much I *can* do."

* * *

You see trophy wives all the time in New York. The couple always looks the same. Rich old fart who could raise a "separated at birth" question with a Sunsweet prune, and a twenty-something vapid blonde on his arm. He only wants sex, she only wants money, bada bing, bada boom, let's draw up a pre-nup. She multitasks in the bedroom, either counting the cracks in the ceiling or the days till she can bail with enough for a Palm Beach condo.

Old joke about trophy wives:

Man walks into a bar and sits next to a really attractive woman. "Would you sleep with me for a million dollars?" he asks.

"Absolutely," she says, suddenly sitting up straight on her barstool.

"How about a hundred bucks?" he asks.

She gets indignant. "What kind of a girl do you think I am?"

"We've already established that," he says. "Now we're just haggling about the price."

So now I sorta know how a man feels, except, being a woman,

I'm not as shallow. (Stop laughing. Stop! Okay, you got me.) While I need a trophy buck, actually sharing the rest of my life with someone who could moonlight for Chrysler as a crash dummy isn't on my to-do list.

Scott showed up at my townhouse after the late Friday newscast like nothing happened, the wrong head in control. He apparently (like any man would) thought that all I needed was a reminder of how much he belonged on my list.

Then I would come to my senses.

While my senses suffered the usual high-speed blowout on the sexual Autobahn, and the Zorro outfit he wore was a nice new wrinkle, I regained my faculties during re-entry.

"You look like you enjoyed that, Ms. Hack," he said, looking down at me while propped on one elbow.

I let my body melt into the five hundred thread count Egyptian cotton sheets as my brain synapses continued to fire sparks. "That's an understatement." I closed my eyes, my face still flashing like a firefly, hoping he would just shut the hell up and let me—

"You can have that every night for the rest of your life."

Annnnnnd.... Cue the cold shower!

I slowly opened my eyes and saw the puppy dog with the granite body just inches from my face, about to kiss me. I sat up before he had the chance. "Scott, I thought we already resolved this."

"I thought you might miss me in Vegas and change your mind."

"No, I haven't changed my mind."

He leaned over to the cherry end table and picked up a glass that had a touch of scotch left in it. "Maybe you need some time to think." He downed the rest of the liquor.

"Maybe you need to remember who hired you." I leaned back against one of the four posts of the bed, which had moments before served as an impromptu stripper pole. "I'm your boss. Why do you call me Ms. Hack in the bedroom if you think I love you?"

"I thought it was part of the dominatrix thing you had going."

Dear God...

"So that's all I am to you? A piece of meat?"

Oh, man, I wish I'd had a camera rolling. Coming from a man that would have been the sound bite of the year.

Hey, great idea for cable… an entire network with older women and younger men.

But back to our regularly scheduled sexual encounter….

"In return you get to anchor in the number one market in America."

He threw back the covers, grabbed his underwear from the ceiling fan blade, and started to get dressed. "You've been leading me on."

"I've done no such thing, Scott. When I interviewed you, I told you that if you wanted the job you should come to my room."

"I thought you were attracted to me."

"I am, physically, but not in a romantic way."

The hurt in his eyes grew and he turned away. He finished getting dressed and started to head for the door. He stopped a few feet from it, picked his car keys off the dresser and turned to face me. "I want out of my contract," he said.

"Not gonna happen," I said.

"We'll see."

* * *

"So let me get this straight," said Jillian from the speakerphone. "Young man who has trouble spelling IQ is offered a job anchoring in New York City. But wait! There's more! As an added bonus, he got to sleep with his hot, red-headed boss to get the job. And there's a problem?"

"Apparently," I said, wishing they were in my office instead of just voices on the weekly Thursday conference call.

It was Neely's turn. "Correct me if I'm wrong, but wouldn't most men jump at the chance for mind-altering sex on a regular basis while bypassing the usual dinner and courtship stuff?"

"Courtship? That still exists?" asked Rica.

"In the South it does," said Neely, turning on the drawl. I could almost see the dreamy, faraway look in her eyes.

Rica laughed. "In Brooklyn, courtship's when a guy says, 'Meter's running. You wanna have sex, or what?'"

"Then most men are from Brooklyn, 'cause that's what they want," said Jillian. "No holding car doors open, no cuddling, no *so, what are you thinking?* questions, just clean-out-the-pipes-air-out-the-brain-blast-furnace-sex with a woman who looks like she needs a bail bondsman and a public defender."

An image of a black leather miniskirt and red platform heels that Scott liked flashed through my brain, along with a picture of a blast furnace blowing his hair out of place. I shoved it to the back burner for later.

"And guys say women are hard ta figure out," said Rica. "Fuhgeddaboudit."

"So what should I do?" I asked, looking at the speaker like it was some sexual magic 8-ball.

"*Screw* him," said Rica.

"She'd *like* to keep doing that," said Neely. I heard chuckles all around and couldn't help but smile.

"You know what I meant," said Rica.

"So what's the situation this week?" asked Jillian.

"He's not speaking to me," I said. "Though yesterday he went from brooding victim to looking like he's up to something."

"Think he'll show tomorrow night?" asked Jillian.

"We'll find out soon enough," I said.

* * *

Actually the answer swatted the front door of my townhouse around five in the morning on Friday. It arrived in the form of a New York tabloid, complete with a front page picture of Scott Harry and a headline that made my jaw hang open like a trophy bass.

Ho.

Lee.

Shit.

I dashed back inside the heavy oak front door, slammed it, and pressed my back against it like I was hiding from a firing squad. Then I quickly unfolded the paper.

It got worse.

Cougar Boss Turns Scott Into Dirty Harry

By Cassandra West

Apparently the news business is no longer couched in secrecy. It's simply a couch.

Of the casting variety.

That's the story from local anchor Scott Harry, who claims that he was hired by News Director Sydney Hack in return for sex. Harry adds that weekly trysts with his boss are a requirement should he wish to keep his job.

"I've spent every Friday night with Ms. Hack at her home since I was hired, and I only got the job after sleeping with her," said Harry, who has pumped up ratings for the station since his arrival but has grown tired of the arrangement. "I recently asked to be released from my contract, but was told that providing sexual favors was part of my job description."

The attractive, copper-haired thirty-something Hack, known as both *Neutron Syd* or *The Red Queen* in the broadcasting industry, raised eyebrows when she hired twenty-nine-year-old Harry and paired him with middle-aged Caroline Jensen, creating what is often referred to in journalistic circles as *The Cougar Report*. Curiously enough, the biggest ratings increase for the station occurs in the middle-aged female demographic.

Hack could not be reached for comment.

"Yeah, you can't get a comment if you don't pick up the damn phone," I said aloud.

Just as the phone rang.

*   *   *

It was so quiet I could hear my pumps crunch the royal blue carpet that led to the CEO's office.

I could also hear my heart pounding in my head as I opened the glass door to the reception area.

"Ah, Ms. Hack," said Kendra, the young Asian receptionist who had been busy opening mail. "You're expected. Go right in."

"Thanks," I said.

Then Kendra did something I didn't expect to see at a career wake.

She smiled at me.

Okay, I've never done anything to this woman. She can't possibly be happy that I'm getting fired.

I knocked softly, opened the heavy mahogany door and entered the executioner's den. Thankfully the CEO was on the phone and I got a stay for a few minutes.

"Yes, thank you," said Madison Cartwright, the founder of the network. The slender forty-year-old blonde smiled at me and extended an open palm toward the chair in front of her desk. I took a seat in the red leather chair and hung on to the arms for dear life as she continued the conversation. Her pale blue eyes matched her silk blouse, both lit up by the bright sunlight that poured into the corner office through windows that offered a terrific view of the Chrysler. "Stroke of genius, if you ask me," she said, twirling a slim silver pen in her long manicured fingers. "She's here right now. I'll call you a little later." She hung up, brushed her shoulder-length hair back and looked at me. "Sydney, I'm sorry I didn't get to meet with you Friday but I had a family emergency." She slapped her hands face down on the desk. "All I can say is that I sure never expected something like this from you."

"I'm really sorry, Madison," I said. "I should have—"

"Actually I'm glad you didn't tell me because I'm terrible at keeping secrets." She leaned forward and lowered her voice, even though the office door was closed. "So tell me, how'd you get Scott to go along with it?"

Now I'm really confused.

"Go… along…"

"Syd, the phones have been ringing off the hook. Half the women calling are congratulating you and the other half want to know how to get into news management." Then she held up a printout that I recognized as the daily ratings chart. "And the overnights for this past Friday are through the roof."

"So, you mean, you're not—"

"What? Mad? Are you *kidding*? We're the talk of the industry. You proved that women don't have to be put out to pasture at forty." She flipped the ratings printout to me. "The young women love him, the old women love him, and they all love you for giving him a mature co-anchor and letting them know the rules can be the same for women as men. You've empowered us, Syd. You turned back the clock to the 1950s so we can make up for lost time and chase the cute men around the desk. Frankly, I'm wondering why the hell I have a female assistant."

I exhaled for perhaps the first time in three days.

"Just one more thing, Syd."

"Yes?"

"I know you were the one who found Scott and all, but I was wondering if—"

"Yeah?"

Madison's smile grew, bringing out her perfect cheekbones. "Maybe one Friday when you're out of town. Would you be willing to… share?"

I was done with Scott, having "given" him to Madison. So back to checking references.

The leading candidate to anchor our new five o'clock newscast weaved his way past the tables, leaving a trail of hanging female tongues in his wake. The dark gray pinstripe vest draped from Jason Deller's broad shoulders, while his slim hips carried him through the room.

Here we go again.

I sat up straight on my bar stool, crossing my left leg over my right to take advantage of the slit on that side of my royal blue dress.

Just in time for the six-foot-three slice of prime beef to notice.

He extended his hand as he reached the bar. "Sydney?"

"Yes," I said as I shook his hand.

"What's a nice News Director like you doing in a place like this?" he asked.

Good. Sense of humor.

"It's a good place to relax after work," I said.

His cobalt blue eyes stole a glance at my legs, then locked on my own, looking right into my soul and almost putting me in a hypnotic trance. He smiled, revealing dimples that ran like trenches along his rugged twenty-eight-year-old face that bristled with a three-day growth. A shock of coal black hair cascaded over his forehead. He hopped onto the bar stool next to mine and swung it around to face me. His knees gently brushed mine, sending an electric charge through my body.

Damn, he makes Scott Harry look like a Boy Scout.

"You're not what I expected," he said.

"I hope that's good."

"Oh yeah."

"And you look good in clothes," I said.

His face flushed a bit as he shook his head. "I can't believe you actually saw that Off-Broadway disaster."

"Hey, Shakespeare in the nude wasn't all that bad."

"Right. That's why I'm still waiting tables uptown after playing opposite *Lady McBare*."

"Did you have a problem doing nudity on stage?"

"Nah. I just needed the work. At least I got discovered by you, right?"

"Right."

"I'm frankly surprised you'd actually consider an actor to be a news anchor."

"Well, we've had an actor as President and one was the Governor of California. It's all about being able to communicate. What's the difference?"

"True." He looked off to the side for a moment, then turned back to me. "I do have one question that we didn't cover during our phone conversation."

"Shoot."

He bit his lower lip, then fired away. "I've read the tabloids about your… hiring practices. And the regular weekly—"

"Let me answer your question with a question," I said.

"Okay."

I leaned forward and slid my hand on the smooth bar toward his so that our fingers lightly touched. "Hypothetically, mind you. If you were to be offered a job, a great job that paid really well, and one part of the interview process was to take care of the sexual needs of your future boss, how would you respond?

"Hypothetically?"

"Of course."

He shrugged. "Well, that depends."

"On what?"

"On who the boss is. If the boss is some twenty-five-year-old ditsy blonde looking for a commitment, then I'm not the guy. Romance can't be part of the picture. If it's some wrinkled sixty-year-old prune, forget it." He looked around, then leaned closer while putting his hand on top of mine. "The boss would have to be, say, a very attractive tall redhead with a great pair of legs and spectacular eyes. It would also be nice if she were a little older than me. I like women who are... seasoned."

Well, rub some spices on me and toss me on the grill.

"So," he continued, "to answer your question. If I were to be offered a great job that required me to have sex with my hot boss, and no romantic strings attached, well..."

"Yes?"

"I'd jump on it."

Gulp. (I don't even want to describe the image that flashed through my head, but let's just call it the really Off-Off-Broadway nude production of *Taming of the Shrew*.)

"Really," I said, feigning surprise. "You wouldn't consider it any sort of sexual harassment?"

"Oh, please. Hell, I'd let her be in charge in the bedroom too. Great job, free sex, where do I sign? Hypothetically, of course."

"Of course," I said.

"You know, the service at this place is really slow," he said, looking around at the lack of empty tables. "I oughta know, I used to work here. And the food's not that great either."

"True." I reached into my beaded purse, pulled out a ten-dollar bill and tossed it on the bar. "You know, I think we should continue our conversation elsewhere. I have a room at the Plaza."

"They have excellent room service there."

"They do. Are you hungry?"

He licked his lips, hungry eyes looking directly into mine. "I think I will be in a couple of hours."

He hopped off his stool and extended his hand. I took it and slid off the chair, then stood straight and tall, inches away from his face, breathing in his musky cologne.

"Oh, I do have one more question," he said.

Uh-oh. "Sure."

"All I have to do is read and look good, right? No reporting in the field, no journalism stuff, no writing. I mean, I'm an actor, not Edward R. Murrow."

"That's the deal. You're not a real news anchor, you just play one on TV."

"Okay."

"You only have to remember one thing, Jason," I said. "It's not brain surgery. It's just television news."

CHAPTER TWO

If you get the punchline to this joke, you probably understand the mission statement of the Consolidated Broadcasting Network's entertainment division:

What do a Mississippi divorce and a tornado have in common?
Somebody's gonna lose a trailer.

As networks go, Consolidated Broadcasting is not what you'd call the purveyor of highbrow programming.

If your idea of a big night is a six-pack and a bug zapper, you're part of our target audience. Congratulations!

(Of course if you're reading this, and your lips don't move when you read, you're obviously not. I am presuming the only books in the homes of CBN viewers are sitting next to a box of Crayolas, so I feel pretty safe in sharing our secrets.)

CBN prime-time shows have simple formulas. Every show needs at least one, and preferably more, of the following:

—Women with multiple tattoos, a bad dye job, and a lit cigarette at all times.

—A male star with so many body piercings it looks as though the phone rang and he answered the staple gun.

—A home with wheels, that may, or may not, change locations due to a storm. (The network once actually created a spin-off series in this manner when the Georgia mobile home of one secondary character sailed away in a hurricane and landed on a beach in Boca Raton.)

—A truck, vintage Trans-Am, or Camaro, preferably having one door of a different color than the rest of the vehicle. One part of the car should be held together with duct tape.

—At least one character with missing teeth. If there is just one missing tooth, the character should use the space to spit tobacco juice.

—The word "confessions" or "naughty" in the title. (Both were used in one series titled, "Confessions of Naughty Trailer Park Queens.")

And if you live in a state in which you can be arrested for driving without a gun rack, we want your eyeballs every night after you bring home the bacon and fry it up in a pan.

Well, that *was* CBN's strategy.

Until today.

Since even the sophistication challenged haven't been tuning in and the network could possibly have fewer viewers than PlayStation at any given moment during prime time, the powers that be at the network have called a meeting to discuss the future. Two days ago Madison told me, "Changes are coming, but in a good way."

That's usually the equivalent of a Sicilian kiss in broadcasting, so for the past forty-eight hours I've been hitting the liquor cabinet like Neely on a weekend bender, while looking around corners for hit men with dark shirts and white ties lurking in the shadows. Even though Madison assured me that I was in no danger, you always worry in this business that someone is going to send you a dead fish wrapped in a newspaper. You're only one bad ratings book away from decapitation.

But then Madison threw a curveball at me, and told me to summon the gals to New York for an eleven o'clock meeting. Again, no other information.

So we're here, at one end of the conference room, ten minutes early, trying to place bets on a: what the network is going to do in prime time; and b: what this meeting has to do with the news division. (Well, three of us are here; we're waiting on Rica, whose plane was late, but she'll be here shortly.) Jillian has been driving herself nuts, speculating, while burning through calories at an alarming rate. Neely took the more casual approach.

"Hey, a free trip to New York is just another excuse to get together with you guys," she said, sipping a bottle of sparkling water.

"What time's happy hour?" asked Jillian, drumming her fingers on the table, as she grabbed another jelly donut from the large basket in the middle of the table. (The girl can eat all day, by the way, and never gain an ounce.)

"If we're not having lunch with corporate, it's in about an hour," I said.

"By the way Syd, how's your new hire working out?" asked Neely.

"Jason? Terrific. He picked up the prompter really quick," I said.

"Not what I meant," said Neely, as Rica blew through the door carrying her briefcase.

"Made it," she said, as she dropped her valise on the floor and brushed a few strands of hair from her face. "Did I miss anything?"

"Just more endless speculation about our possible futures," said Jillian. "Where the hell else can we work and get the benefits package we've got?"

"Anything new since I left LA?" asked Rica.

I shook my head. "Nada. You know as much as I do. But I'm betting—"

The giant wooden doors swung open and Madison Cartwright entered the room, followed by an entourage of sharply dressed women in their thirties and forties that I recognized as the corporate staff.

With one exception.

They circled the table and all took their seats as Madison

stood at the front of the room. The exception, a sharply dressed striking brunette in her middle thirties, sat in the chair to her immediate right.

"You recognize her?" whispered Jillian, just before shoving the remainder of the donut into her mouth.

I shook my head.

"Thank you all for coming such a long way on such short notice," said Madison. "I know that you've all been trying to figure out what's in the works for the past few days, and I'm sorry to have been so vague, so I won't keep you guessing any longer. Let's start with the entertainment division. You may have noticed that Carlie Hammersmith, the head of prime-time programming, is not here. She tendered her resignation this morning."

Jillian leaned into my ear, so close I could smell the strawberry jelly on her breath. "I told you heads would roll."

"But fear not," continued Madison. "The rest of you are not in any danger of losing your jobs. In fact, quite the opposite. You're all about to play bigger roles in this network. To tell you about that, I'm going to turn the meeting over to Amanda Bain, who has been named our new head of the division and will totally revamp the prime-time line-up, which will hopefully give you a much better lead-in for your local newscasts. She has fifteen years experience with the major networks in Hollywood, and I know she'll do great things for us. Let's give her a big welcome."

The slender brunette with Carolina-blue eyes stood up and was greeted by polite applause. Her shoulder-length straight cut curved in around her chin and framed her thin, oval face while dusting the shoulders of her deep red business suit. (Well, the suit part was business. The very short skirt was pleasure.) Her dangly hoop earrings looked more appropriate for a night on the town instead of a day in the boardroom, but they worked with the outfit.

"She's one of us," whispered Neely, noting the woman had a body like a Sports Illustrated swimsuit model, though she wasn't terribly tall, maybe five-five. She took off her jacket and draped it on the back of her chair, revealing a tight, eggshell silk blouse. The outfit screamed "woman in charge."

"And she brought her own party hats," Neely added.

"Oh yeah," I said, noting the chilly air and her lack of a bra had provided two impressive points to the front of her blouse.

"She could dial a phone with those things," whispered Rica.

"Like you couldn't," I said.

"Thank you so much," said Amanda, who took Madison's place at the front of the room as my boss stepped aside. "Madison is right about one thing, and I hate to throw stones at my predecessor, but our prime-time programming couldn't be any worse. So I'll get right down to it. I'm sure you'll all be happy to know that the days of redneck entertainment at CBN are over as of today."

A mild cheer erupted with more applause. "I like her already," said Jillian.

"Damn," said Neely, "I guess that cliffhanger of *Bubba Does Boca* will never be resolved."

She smiled, looking around the room and making eye contact with several women. "I know, I know, tens of viewers will be disappointed." We all laughed at the old joke about ratings and the tension we'd felt about our jobs began to dissipate. "CBN is about to undergo several major changes in the coming weeks, some of which will be made public, some which must be done in secrecy. I'm going to need help from each of you to make that happen. But first, I must say that none of this would be possible if it were not for the incredible vision of Sydney Hack."

Huh? Whaaa...

She turned and looked right at me. "Sydney, we haven't been formally introduced yet, but I must compliment you on the way you turned things around in the news division for this network. Your work is nothing less than inspiring, and it takes a lot for someone in a news department to inspire someone from Hollywood. Anyone who can grow the ratings with that disastrous prime-time line-up as a lead-in is a genius. What you've done is the basis for the changes that we are going to start implementing today."

Twelve pairs of eyes looked at me for an answer. I just smiled and nodded. "Thank you," I said. "You're very kind."

"Don't be modest, Sydney," said Amanda. "Your changes have given us the road map to take this network in a new direction. One that is going to change the face of broadcasting and kick our competitors' asses. One that is going to make the entire country rethink the way business is done, one that will change the way men and women look at relationships. The premise is very simple, and one I know you are all going to like. Here's the deal, and it will be written in stone. All of our prime-time shows this fall are going to mirror the current theme of our local newscasts."

She paused a moment, letting it sink in. "Got it?" she asked.

Heads began to nod.

Oh.

My.

God.

(That crazy idea I had for a network the other night in the bedroom while Scott was pulling his laundry off the ceiling? Should have copyrighted the damn thing.)

"In other words," said Amanda, "the shirtless, tattooed men who have starred in CBN's shows are being replaced with very attractive, smart, professional, sexually aggressive women over thirty who don't see age as a boundary in a relationship. Every show in prime time will be female-driven. Every single one. There will still be good looking, shirtless men of course," she said, pausing as the women in the room laughed, "but they'll be playthings. They'll also be classy, well-educated, have full sets of teeth," she paused as the group laughed again. "And they'll also be…" She stopped and looked around the room and put her palms up. "Anybody?"

"Younger?" I said.

She pointed her finger at me and smiled. "You got it, Sydney.

Welcome, women of CBN, to a network where women are *always* in charge."

Several "woo-hoos" went up around the room as the group exhaled all tension collectively. No one was getting fired, except the people who had produced the God-awful stuff we'd been running in prime time.

And my grand little experiment was about to take on a life of its own.

"Oh, one more very important thing," added Amanda. "We're going to be known as the Consolidated Group from now on. And you'll see why down the road."

Neely gave me a gentle elbow. "I can understand why *you're* here Syd, but what are *we* doing here?"

"I'm glad you all seem so receptive to the idea," said Amanda. "And I think America will feel the same way. When the fall rolls around, you won't be able to recognize this network. Everything will be new. Every single show now on the air has been cancelled, and most will be yanked off the air immediately. We're basically rebooting, rolling out a new network, which is another reason for the name change. And that brings me to the second part of our plan, which entails synergy with the news division." She turned toward me and smiled. "And that's why we needed you here, Sydney, along with the news directors of our major market stations."

Neely, Rica and Jillian all sat up straight and leaned forward in unison, as if on cue.

Then Amanda dropped the bombshell.

"We're going to launch a 24-hour cable network based here in New York. And I'm asking the four of you to run it."

* * *

"Oh, we're definitely having an agenda on this network," said Amanda, who speared a forkful of grilled salmon that was drenched in bourbon sauce.

Aw, shit. There goes paradise.

"Republican or Democrat?" I asked, suddenly losing my appetite at the prospect of tormenting the American public with political scream-fests. The petite sirloin that had just arrived was still spitting at me, sending out a call to my growling stomach.

She shook her head as she chewed her salmon. The brightly lit midtown restaurant was still crowded at two o'clock, and loud, filled with too many business people talking either to each other, on their cell phones, or both. The bar was elbow-to-elbow with men who were maintaining their liquid diets during lunch, while watching a rare Mets day game and cheering the occasional good play. Amanda flagged down a young waiter and pointed to her empty wine glass. He nodded at her, smiled and disappeared into the kitchen where he was swallowed up by the sound of clanging plates and silverware. Finally she took a sip of water and gave me my answer. "Nothing so pedestrian as politics, Syd. Let the other networks go right or left and alienate half the audience. Our only agenda is *women*. Women over thirty are the target demo specifically, but women overall. Remember, young women will eventually become older. In the back of our viewers' minds, subliminally, must be the concept that men are simple playthings, just accessories that any woman can have, like a designer purse. Just as the shoes must match the dress, the younger man must match the older woman. No knock-offs, either. The men must be the real thing, the dream guy, not something they'd settle for to avoid a life as a spinster with a houseful of cats. All you have to do is time-warp yourselves back fifty years to the days of weather bunnies on the news, when women stayed home and did all the cooking and cleaning, and men routinely slept with their secretaries. Then just reverse the sexes. It's that simple. And that's what I want from you. That's what our viewers will want from the network once they get a taste of it. We're going to turn the damn country upside down in the bedroom, and the boardroom.

Let the world know women have had enough, that we're taking over, and we're changing the rules for good. It's a seller's market, and we're the only store in town. If you're a man, and you want sex, you play by *our* rules. And we take what we want."

"You know," said Jillian, stabbing a bit of her blackened chicken salad and pointing her fork at Amanda, "I think I like her."

"Fuhgeddaboudit," said Rica. "I'm in love."

An attractive young man walked by our table while his eyes made the rounds. He locked on Neely, who smiled back at him. Then she turned back to Amanda. "So, what you're basically saying is that women are the new men," said Neely.

"Oooh, I love that," said Amanda, grinning wide. "And there needs to be an underlying tone in the broadcast as well. I mean, you still need anchor teams like the ones you have in your stations, but the stories all have to reflect our agenda. You can't just do a regular style newscast. The product has to have a lifestyle feel to it. Viewers need to sense that women are in control of everything and that men are—"

"Oooh, oooh!" Neely put up her hand and waved, chewing fast, making us all wait till she swallowed. She gulped, took a swig of water, and almost jumped out of her chair. "I've got it! Men are the new women!"

"Yes! I think I love that even more," said Amanda. "Neely, we might have to turn you loose on the promotions department."

"So basically it's all women, all the time," I said.

"Twenty-four seven," Amanda said as she nodded. "If I turn on our news network at four in the morning, I want to see a hot middle-aged woman with... what did you call them?"

"Trophy bucks," said Jillian, through a mouthful of lettuce.

"Right," said Amanda. "And I want to see a story talking about the lifestyle that is possible for a woman who takes charge. Viewers need to come away with that notion when they're done watching."

"Oh, Amanda," said Rica, "I meant to ask you something. What are we going to be calling the news channel?"

Amanda's face lit up. "Well, I was saving that for down the road, but since you guys are going to be running the thing..." Her eyes sparkled. "This is the best part, and it's going to leave no doubt as to our agenda. We're the Consolidated Group Report. But we're just going to call the channel CGR."

Oh, you gotta be kidding. "C...G...R?" I asked, speaking each letter slowly.

She smiled and nodded. "Yeah. Get it?"

"Not exactly a brainteaser for the *Jumble*," said Rica. "If you're a woman who can't figure that out, you shouldn't be watching anyway."

"I like it. It's really sort of in your face," said Jillian.

"Subtlety is not my strong suit," said Amanda. "In business or in life."

My appetite switch turned back on. Suddenly I was ravenous and attacked my steak, savoring the hot, juicy rare beef that had been seasoned with fresh peppercorns and topped with garlic butter. I saw in Amanda a woman who was supremely confident in what we were about to do, and I liked her immensely. We all did. She was obviously very smart and had a plan that made sense, incredible as it was. If it actually worked, it really would change the face of broadcasting.

That face wore eye shadow and bright red lipstick. That face was over thirty and might even have a few character lines. It would speak words that told the world who was in charge.

But I couldn't help but wonder.

Had Madison briefed Amanda on our benefits package and reference checking?

"Amanda," I said, wiping my mouth with my white cloth napkin and dropping it back in my lap, then folding my hands. "I need to ask you about—"

She put up her hand and stopped me. "Syd, I don't care how you hire people or anything about any... arrangements... you might have. Yes, I've read the tabloids. Madison told me how the system works. The point is, it works very well. I could care less if you turn your offices into Caligula's palace as long as you deliver the product we need. No one's going to give it a second thought if ratings are good. Put anyone that you like on your to-do list."

I relaxed and sank back into my seat. I could see my girls all doing the same.

Hello, Jason? Yeah, we're still good to go for tonight...

A young, attractive waiter with light brown hair, deep-set blue eyes and a strong chin arrived with a bottle of wine and began to refill Amanda's glass as she quickly glanced down the length of his body and back up again. "Would you all like to see the dessert cart?" he asked. "The tiramisu is fantastic."

Amanda lightly put her hand on the man's hip, then tilted her neck so she could get a better view of the man's tight backside. "What I want isn't on the menu," she said, staring up into his eyes. She reached into her purse, pulled out a business card, wrote a number on the back, and handed it to the waiter. He looked at it, turned it over, and smiled.

"I get off at nine tonight," he said.

"Apparently, so do I," said Amanda, who locked her eyes on the waiter's.

Whoa. And I thought we were slick.

Eyes widened and jaws dropped around the table as the young man nodded, dropped the check on the table, mouthed "see you then" and walked away.

"Oh, you're smooth, Hollywood," said Rica.

"Long flights wipe me out," said Amanda, swirling her wine around in the glass. "A little... exercise... always perks me up. He looks like a good workout buddy."

"You know what they say. No pain, no gain," said Jillian. "Go for the burn."

Now I was the one who wanted details. "So Amanda, are you—"

"I wouldn't call myself a cradle robber," said Amanda, "but I do primarily date younger guys, and I tend to think of men as

Kleenex."

"One blow and y'all are done?" asked Neely, laying on the accent pretty thick. Everyone laughed.

"Neely, you really do have a future in promotions," said Amanda, shaking her head as she finished her wine.

"By the way, what exactly was your job in Hollywood?" asked Jillian.

"Well, I wore many hats," said Amanda, "but I spent seven years as a casting director. It has its… perks… when men really want the part." She took a sip of wine and glanced at her watch. "I assume all your questions about business practices have been answered?"

"Actions speak louder than words," I said.

CHAPTER THREE

ONE MONTH LATER...

Getting all the girls to move to New York in May wasn't a problem, though we all had to work on Rica a bit when it came to finding new living accommodations. Jillian and Neely both settled in on the Upper East Side near me, each renting a townhouse. For whatever reason, Rica actually considered moving back to Brooklyn. Neely finally hit her with a dose of her own medicine one night and yelled (or tried to yell) "fuhgeddaboudit", which was so long and drawn out it didn't carry the same punch as it did coming from a New Yorker and sounded more like a Southern belle come-on to a man searching in vain for a condom. ("Sweetie, just fuhgeddaboudit and get on top of me before y'all start floppin' around like a catfish.") Rica finally relented and agreed to live in Manhattan, on the condition that Neely, as she put it, "Leave my slang alone, and I won't try to say *y'all*." Though Rica's *y'all* sounded more like a plea for help from an adenoidal patient in the office of an ear, nose and throat specialist.

Living arrangements taken care of, now to the hard stuff. Building a news department from scratch, I've done. Building a twenty-four-hour network, well, that's another story. Thankfully Madison and Amanda had taken a lot off my plate, renovating our new home while coordinating the things like sets and equipment. They told me to focus solely on hiring air talent.

(Oh yeah, I forgot to mention that in television news, people in front of the camera are referred to as "talent", regardless of whether they possess any. Often they don't, but then again this isn't rocket science. I can't remember the last time I heard the word "journalist" in a newsroom. So in reality, it really is a lot like Hollywood.)

We put our four pretty heads together and figured we'd need two dozen full-time anchors to cover all the shifts and allow for sick days, mental health days, vacations, etcetera.

Twelve mature female anchors with experience.

Twelve trophy bucks to sit next to them, read, and look good. In case you hadn't guessed, no experience necessary. (Don't look at me in that tone of voice. The pageant fembots have been operating under those rules for years.)

And once the word got out that we were staffing a new network and had two dozen openings, the floodgates of the United States Postal Service, FedEx, and UPS opened in a nanosecond.

Every former female anchor who had been put out to pasture at thirty-five dusted off a résumé tape and overnighted it to me.

Every male anchor over thirty who thought of himself as distinguished or authoritative or experienced sent a tape. Which meant just about every man in an anchor position in the United States.

Jillian took care of sorting the mountain of tapes that filled the mailroom. She promptly threw every tape from the men over thirty in the trash. Men under thirty were put aside. The reverse was true for the women. By the way, I'm always amazed at the way women, especially those with pageant or modeling experience, apply for jobs. They don't seem to understand, we are hiring people to work on television, yet they send eight-by-ten glossies, bikini shots, modeling portfolios. Geez, do they think we're gonna hire people based on their looks alone? (Okay, don't answer that.)

Anyway, we weren't close to being done. We now had to start

sorting out the hundreds that were left. Though I'm using the term "sorting" in a way you've never encountered.

(At this point you're about to see how incredibly shallow news executives are. We make guys at a singles bar look deep and thoughtful. And we learned all this from men, so please, don't blame us.)

We took all the tapes (actually, they were mostly DVDs with a few scattered VHS cassettes) to the conference room, ordered pizza and beer for the evening, and began our own personal gong show.

What, you're thinking we're going to sit down and watch twenty minutes from every job applicant and evaluate their journalistic abilities? Rate them one-to-ten on things like interviewing skills and mastery of grammar?

Pfffft. Ah, grasshopper, you have much to learn before you may roam the earth.

You could have the interviewing skills of Mike Wallace, but if you look like Jabba the Hutt you're gonna get gonged. Of course, every News Director in America will deny this because they'd get sued out the wazoo, but if it comes down to a choice between a credible Quasimodo and a woman who looks like she could suck a golf ball through a garden hose without smearing her lip gloss, the woman who can pass the oral exam wins every time.

The rules of a television news résumé tape gong show are similar to those of a courtroom, in which lawyers have peremptory challenges when choosing a jury. If an attorney doesn't like a prospective juror, said attorney can send that person packing without justifying the reason. But lawyers have a limited number of jurors they can dismiss without cause. In teevee land, any manager can veto an unlimited number of candidates for an unlimited number of reasons.

And we always have cause.

And it's always, always, always superficial.

Too fat, too old, too young, too wrinkled, bad teeth, bad hair, wrong color hair, not enough hair, big ears, Samsonite under the eyes, no chin, too many chins, no neck, pockmarked complexion, too flat-chested, too top-heavy, too bottom-heavy…

Got it? Ready?

Now a gong show has to be a well-oiled machine if you're going to deal with hundreds of résumé tapes in a short time. So I'm at the front of the room, about to feed tapes or DVDs into the machines, while Jillian and Rica sit on opposite sides of the table poised to fire away, gongs at the ready. Neely has set up three large cardboard boxes on the credenza at the other end of the room and is stationed next to one of those five-foot giant plastic blue dumpsters on wheels. She has labeled the boxes "hot damn!" "doable" and "exponentially cute."

Two steaming pizzas loaded with every imaginable topping sat on one corner of the table and made the room smell like an Italian restaurant. The scent of garlic hung in the air along with the anticipation we all had of finding twelve Mister Rights. (We would take care of the women tomorrow. And we're just as brutal on our own gender, lest you think we're gonna hold anything back. But now that the rules have changed, we have actually gonged the pageant fembots without looking.)

It was going to be a long night. I twisted open my bottle of ice cold beer, grabbed a slice of pizza and took a bite of the hot pie before tossing it on a paper plate. Rich sauce did battle for my taste buds with sausage and mozzarella cheese as I grabbed the first DVD. "You guys ready?" I asked, talking through the pizza.

I got three nods and grunts from the girls who were as impressed with the pizza as I was and were shoveling it in.

(Note to television viewers: the hardest video to get isn't some politician cheating on his wife or a corporate CEO taking a bribe or even a UFO landing. The toughest video to get is that of women eating. Take a camera to a shopping mall, park it in the food court, aim it at the tables and the eating magically stops among females. If you left the camera there, all the restaurants would go out of business. Take the camera away, and you've got the scene in this conference room. Four women chowing down like they were about to be contestants on *Survivor*.)

I shoved the DVD into the slot and unfolded the corresponding résumé as I waited for the disc to load. "Leading off... Todd from Wichita," I said. The monitor filled with the image of a mid-twenties man who already had the beginnings of a second chin to accessorize his lovely receding hairline. I glanced at his paper résumé. "Three years as a reporter, one as an anchor."

"None on a to-do list at this network," said Rica. "Gong."

The other two nodded. I ejected the DVD, put it back in its plastic box, and slid it down the table. Neely grabbed it like she was pulling a cold draft off a bar counter and deftly deposited it into the trashcan in one sweet motion.

"Next up, Carl from Idaho." Tape in machine, man with noticeable overbite appears on screen.

"Gong," said Jillian, before five seconds had elapsed.

"Looks like he could eat an apple through a picket fence," said Neely.

I slid the DVD down the table. Neely grabbed it and made an exaggerated slam dunk with it into the trash.

I shoved a VHS cassette into the VCR. "Next up, Walter from Peoria."

"C'mon, Walter!" said Jillian, shaking one fist like she was warming up the dice at a crap table. "Momma needs to check some references."

Walter's moon face and bug eyes filled the screen and told us why he was still in Peoria.

"I don't need to check 'em that bad," said Jillian.

Neely made a cross with two fingers like she was warding off a vampire and leaned her head back. "Gong. Good God, y'all, that face could stop a clock."

"Bless his little heart," added Rica, without missing a beat. Even Neely laughed. I slid the tape down the table and she grabbed it with two fingertips, held it at arm's length like some lab experiment from a bachelor refrigerator, then dropped it in the trash.

"Not off to a very good start," said Jillian, slugging down her beer.

"Fear not," I said. "We have hundreds more from which to choose."

"It has occurred to me," said Neely, leaning on the end of the table with both elbows, "that this would be even more fun if we had an honest to goodness Chinese gong."

"If you can find one, I'll authorize the expense," I said, sliding another DVD into the machine. "Mario from Colorado."

I reached for another slice of pizza as I heard the disc whirring in the machine.

I didn't hear anyone call for a gong.

"Hello there, Mario," said Jillian, with a little lust in her voice.

The monitor was filled with a lean, rugged face that sported dark brown hair and eyes to match. The man's voice was pure dark silk pouring from his mouth, a deep baritone you wouldn't expect from someone under thirty. Kind of a Sylvester Stallone type, without the accent.

"No gongs?" I asked.

"He's a possible," said Jillian. "What's his story?"

I glanced at his résumé. "Three years anchoring in middle-of-nowhere Colorado."

"Put him in a box," said Rica.

"Which one?" asked Neely.

"I think he goes under *doable*," said Rica.

"Agreed," said Jillian.

I slid the tape down the table. Neely grabbed it and gently put it in the appropriate box.

Rica turned toward Neely. "Would you explain *exponentially cute* again?" she asked, as I popped another DVD in the machine. "I'm still a little confused."

"It's a guy who is beyond cute," said Neely, sipping her beer. "Cute to the tenth power. Not scorching hot, but incredibly good looking with an underlying boy-next-door appeal. If the boy next door regularly showed up in your bedroom wearing a Chippendales outfit, carrying two cans of Reddi-wip and a riding crop."

"And *hot damn* is the same as *scorching hot*?" asked Jillian.

Neely nodded. "One and the same. Top of the line."

"Michael from California is next," I yelled, trying to bring order.

A blonde, blue-eyed anchor in a pastel suit filled the screen. He looked more suited to a surfboard than to a news desk.

"Eh, doable," said Rica.

"I was thinking exponentially cute," said Neely.

"Doable," said Rica and Jillian in unison, as I slid the tape the length of the table.

"Let's see if we can get two in a row," said Jillian.

"Say hello to Bill from Bristol, Tennessee," I said, as the tape rolled.

"Good face for radio," said Rica, about two seconds into the tape.

"Bless his little heart," cracked Jillian, getting into the Southern spirit of things.

"Edward from Florida," I said. The screen filled with an extremely tall, extremely skinny man.

"Looks like an advance man for a famine," said Neely. "Gong."

Twenty tapes later (including one which featured co-anchors that left some doubt as to which was the man and which was the woman and was followed by Neely's tomahawk jam of it into the dumpster) I finally popped in a tape and watched a glob of pizza almost fall out of Rica's mouth.

"Whoa," said Rica.

Twenty-seven-year-old Vance Hiller's face jumped off the screen and grabbed our undivided attention. With no anchoring experience, the tape featured the reporter out doing a variety of stories in the field, one of which included him in a pair of tight running shorts that revealed tan, sinewy legs. Tall, slender but well built, nearly black hair and piercing sea-foam green eyes which peered out of a face that was all angles and planes.

"Is he real or computer generated?" asked Jillian.

"Really, it looks like someone designed him," said Neely. "He's a virtual reporter. But I wouldn't mind checking his virtual references."

"Gongs?" I asked. (Kidding of course.)

"You outta your friggin' mind?" said Rica.

I slid the DVD down to Neely and she placed it in the "hot damn" box without any argument. She patted the box's first occupant for good measure.

By eleven thirty we'd gone through more than four hundred résumé tapes, two large pizzas, two six packs of beer, and had seen Neely toss tapes into the dumpster with incredible flair. (We all agreed her jump shot was impressive, but the behind-the-back swish into the trash with an anchor from West Virginia could have been a hit on YouTube.)

"Done," I said, plopping down in the chair. The dumpster at the end of the room was overflowing with DVDs and VHS tapes.

"So where do we stand?" asked Jillian. "What's the grand total of the guys who are left?"

Neely looked through each box and began counting. "There are half a dozen *hot damns*… four *exponentially cutes*…. and twenty who were considered *doable*."

(It should be noted there would have been twenty-one *doables* but Neely unceremoniously dumped the first surfer dude when she found another California anchor she liked better.)

"So," said Jillian, "Where do we go from here?"

"Fly them all in as soon as possible and get rolling on the interviews," I said.

"Hang on a minute, guys," said Neely. "I'm a little concerned."

"About what?" asked Jillian.

Neely picked up a DVD from the doable box and held it up. "There is a great deal of quality that separates the hot damns and the exponentially cutes from the doables," she said. "If I know I can have someone from the first two boxes, I don't really want anything from the other box."

"You know, she's got a point," said Rica. "If I'm stuck in the Peoria airport, then a doable is… well, doable. But if there's lobster on the buffet, I sure as hell ain't eatin' tuna salad."

Jillian nodded. "So if I've got this straight, we should ditch the doable box or our viewers will be stuck eating tuna fish instead of fantasizing about someone who is exponentially cute."

"I'm not even gonna try to figure that out," I said. "So just dump the box."

Neely took the box and sent twenty careers careening into the dumpster.

Which left us with ten guys we really liked.

To fill twelve slots.

Do the math.

We're hittin' the streets.

* * *

"I heard you had a gong show last night."

I looked up and saw that my first visitor of the morning was Scott Harry, who was standing in my doorway, hands in pockets. What a surprise, he didn't look happy. "Hi, Scott. What can I do for you?"

(Oh, by the way, gong shows are no secrets among the rank and file. As for Scott, I know exactly what he wants, but I'm going to make him say it. He wants to be part of the network, so bad he can taste it, but we're keeping him right where he is, taking care of local… and his spot on Madison's to-do list. However, I can't let him know that he hasn't a prayer of getting on the network, so the carrot must be dangled at a discreet distance.)

"I assume you're getting around to staffing the new network."

"Yep," I said, pausing to take a sip of my coffee, which had gotten cold. "Lots of people to hire and not much time to do it."

Oh, you should see his face. It's killing him. He looks like a man who's been constipated for a week only to find out all the laxatives have been pulled off the market by the FDA.

"I…uh…" Scott stopped and walked into the office, taking the seat directly in front of my desk. (The chair is a low-boy, by the way, two inches shorter than normal. A little psychological advantage.)

"Yes? Something on your mind?" (I wear my best "playing dumb" look. All women are born with this innate capability. It's embedded in our DNA, just like the shoe chromosome. The equivalent for men is the not-listening, bobblehead nod.)

His shoulders were hunched and his neck taut as he looked at me with his now patented "wounded doe" face, despite his lack of brown eyes. "I was hoping to be considered for one of the anchor slots on the network. I mean, I love working local, (forced smile) but this is a great opportunity."

"Don't worry, Scott, you'll be considered." (I'll have to ask Neely what the penance is for a blatant lie.)

Scott exhaled and the tension melted from his body. "Thank you. I mean, I hadn't heard anything. So I assumed—"

Watch this. "So how are you enjoying your time with Madison?"

Ah, such a joy to watch the color drain from his face like the last strawberry Slurpee coming out of the machine at Seven-Eleven.

"She's very nice. But… I miss you."

Aw, shit. And the day had started off so well with Jason and I doing our little Cirque de Soleil number before breakfast.

I got up and walked around the desk, leaning on the edge and extending my legs so that they nearly touched his. If he was going to screw with my day, I was going to torture him. "Scott, we've been through this. Several times. Our relationship is purely professional."

"I just—"

"What are you gonna do, Scott? Try another trip to the tabloids? Did you really think anyone would see a man who has to sleep with his hot boss as a victim? Every guy in New York thought you were an idiot to complain. And then half of those called me wanting a job here."

"It seemed like a good idea at the time."

"Just keep Madison happy." (And I know she's happy from her note that read, "Thanks for the leftovers.")

"Just Madison?"

"Yes. Madison is a great gal with a rockin' body and you should consider yourself lucky that I don't make you sleep with Carla the producer."

His face tightened and I could tell the image of the overweight troll in a state of undress was flashing through his mind.

"Now go," I said. "Do your job, keep Madison entertained, and we'll keep you posted on the network gig."

He got up, turned and shuffled out of my office without saying a word.

Men.

* * *

The term "meat market" is a throwback to the eighties, but never seemed more appropriate as we occupied the corner table in the back of one of Manhattan's trendiest bars. The electricity in the place sent a charge through my body, while various expensive colognes and perfumes made the room smell like a walk through the Bloomingdales fragrance department where the Stepford girls spritz you. In reality, our hunting expedition tonight wasn't much different than trying to pick someone up. The men and women in the bar were looking for someone attractive to sleep with, and I was looking for someone attractive to sleep with, under thirty, who could read a teleprompter and knew that Ted Kennedy had never been shot. I sipped my Bailey's and tried to unwind as the cream with a bite ran down my throat, but things were getting too exciting. Tomorrow New York's top modeling and talent agencies were going to fill our office with male models and actors. (I know,

I have such a tough job.)

"What time do we start tomorrow?" asked Rica, not looking at me but scanning the crowded uptown bar for any hot prospects. One attractive man in his forties smiled at her, but was repelled by the force field of her death stare. He bounced off, shook his head, and headed out the door, letting in the sound of New York's heartbeat: car horns and police sirens.

"Nine o'clock," I said. "We'll do a preliminary screening, then call back the ones we like for reference checks."

It was wall-to-wall people and noise but one man at the bar somehow managed to connect with Jillian across the packed watering hole. "Oooh, I just got a shiver," she said.

"Which one?" asked Rica, trying to follow Jillian's line of sight.

Jillian nodded toward the bar, her eyes still paralyzed by the man's stare. "Sitting at the corner talking to an older guy but looking right at me. Gray pinstripe vest. Dark hair. Light eyes. Five o'clock shadow."

Rica glanced around, trying to look through the wall of people. Finally she spotted him. "Damn, he's cute."

"He's even beyond exponentially cute," said Jillian, suddenly possessing Neely's dreamy-eyed look. "It's a whole new level of cute."

Rica turned to me. "Waddaya think, Syd? Should we go talk to him?"

I was about to answer "yes", when the man hopped off his bar stool and headed across the floor to the men's room. I finally got a good look at the total package and my smile faded.

He was short. And I mean *really* short. Five-three, five-four tops.

"Aw, dammit," I said.

"What?" asked Rica.

"He's just a little thing."

"So?" asked Neely. "He's an exponentially *cute* little thing. We just sit him on a Manhattan phone book and tilt the camera up at him when he's on set."

"You're missing something. That plays havoc with our plan to have our anchors stand during part of each hour," I said.

"No, *you're* missing something, Syd," said Neely, just as our waitress arrived.

"Another round, girls?" asked the tall, slinky brunette in the short black spaghetti strap dress.

"Make it so," I said.

The waitress, who looked around thirty, wrote our drink order on her pad, shoved a pencil behind her ear and was about to leave when Neely touched her arm. "Excuse me, can we ask you a couple of questions?"

The waitress shrugged. "Long as they're quick," she said. "I got a lotta tables."

Neely looked back at the men's room just as the man emerged. "How tall are you?" she asked.

"Five-eleven. About six-two in these heels. Why?"

"See that guy walking to the bar?" Neely pointed at him. "Real cute, dark hair."

The waitress craned her long, slender neck around the crowd and squinted. "You mean the little guy in the dark vest?"

"Yeah," said Neely.

"What about him?"

"Would you ever consider going out with him?" asked Neely. "I mean, being as tall as you are, do you find him attractive?"

"I'd do him in a New York minute," said the waitress, licking her lips. "He'd make a great Friday night snack."

"You don't have a problem with a man that much shorter?" I asked.

She shook her head. "Hell, I date shorter guys all the time. Most of the ones taller than me are pretty stuck on themselves. The shorter ones try harder, they're more polite. Better personalities and sense of humor. And they don't try anything funny 'cause I'm bigger than they are." Suddenly she put her tray down on our table, leaned forward, and lowered her voice. "Plus, I'll let you in on a little secret. *They obey*."

"Excuse me?" I said.

"They're so afraid you'll ditch them for a tall guy they'll do anything you want. I guess I feel more in control with a guy like that. It's sorta nice being the *man* in the relationship, if that makes any sense." She looked back across the room at the man, dark eyes suddenly steamy with lust. "But yeah, I wouldn't mind bending him across my knee and spanking that tight little ass."

Interesting mental picture I hadn't considered.

"Thanks," said Neely.

"What's the deal?" asked the waitress, picking up her tray. "You guys taking a marketing survey or something?"

"We work in TV," I said. "Just keeping in touch with how women think."

"Let's put it this way. They're all the same height lying down," said the waitress. "I'll be right back with your drinks." She turned and headed back to the bar.

"Syd, we are really missing something here," said Neely. "If we want to convey the notion that women are in charge, why can't a few of our female anchors be taller than their male co-anchors?"

"She's got something, Syd," said Rica. "A lot of women wouldn't mind takin' that guy home, even if he is a munchkin. And look at Jillian. She looks so possessed I'm gonna have to call a priest."

I turned and saw that Jillian was in some sort of schoolgirl trance, which I might expect from Neely. But Jillian, I'd never seen her this way. The cool, always in control girl looked like she was in the ninth grade suffering from her first crush. "Jillian? Earth to Jillian?"

"Huh?" she said.

"Have you heard a word we've been saying?" I asked.

"Yeah. Sort of. Not really," she said, still staring at the man.

I looked up at the guy who had returned to the bar. He shook hands with another man who handed him an envelope, then paid his bill, picked up his drink, and headed for our table.

"This oughta be fun," said Neely, cocking her heard toward Jillian. "Woman hit by Cupid's arrow. Film at eleven."

"Someone reel in her tongue before he gets here," said Rica.

I elbowed Jillian who snapped back into reality just as the man reached our table. He stood between Jillian and Neely but it was obvious he had his sights on Jillian.

"Hi, I'm Shawn Carlyle," he said.

Whoever said good things come in small packages must have been talking about this guy. Mid-twenties, perfectly proportioned, slim hips, broad shoulders accented by a tailored white French cuffed shirt. Turquoise eyes you could get lost in. Rugged square jaw, long dimples covered by a day's growth. And yes, a tight little spankable ass.

Yeah, I'm starting to see Neely's point.

Jillian was still too busy staring to answer, so I picked up the ball. "Hi Shawn. I'm Syd, and this is Rica, Neely and Jillian."

"So, girls night out?" he said.

"This is actually an extension of a business meeting that started this afternoon," I said.

"Oh, sorry, I didn't mean to interrupt," he said.

"No problem," Neely said. "We like to mix a little pleasure with business. We'd just wrapped up the business part anyway, so you can hopefully provide the pleasure."

"You guys all work together?" he asked.

"We run the news division for CBN," I said.

"That sounds like a neat job. I took a journalism course in college and it seemed like a lotta fun."

"So what do you do, Shawn?" asked Rica.

"I work on Wall Street," he said, eyes suddenly filling with a tinge of sadness. "I've been there three years since I got out of college and it feels like thirty."

Jillian still hadn't said a word, hadn't stopped staring, and her freckles were lit up like they were on fire. He glanced back in her direction and shot her a quick smile.

"Not happy with the career?" I asked.

He shook his head. "I just need to find something else to do. I'll be dead by forty if I keep this up. And honestly, my heart's not in it. Money's good, but I'm not happy. It may look exciting on TV, but the job just wrings you out."

"Well, you know," I said, "we're in the process of hiring a bunch of people for our new cable network. In fact, we start interviewing local candidates tomorrow."

"I read about that on Page Six. I already watch your local news. You guys do a good job."

"You like our news?" asked Rica, furrowing her brow.

"Yeah," he said. "You guys keep it simple. No agenda, no one trying to tell me how to think or how to vote. No one trying to shout someone else down during an interview. And the women on your station are credible, not a bunch of beauty queens. I mean, don't get me wrong, they're extremely attractive, but I get the feeling they actually know what they're talking about."

That click you just heard was Mister Edison turning on a thou-sand-watt light bulb over my head.

There's a young male audience for our product. Who knew?

The guy was not only extremely cute but smart. I wanted to know more. "Have you ever been in front of a camera?" I asked.

"No. Why?"

"Like I said, we're hiring a lot of people."

He smiled and looked down at the floor. "I'm sure I don't exactly fit the traditional anchorman profile."

"We're very untraditional, in case you hadn't noticed from watching our newscasts," said Rica.

"Well, yeah, I guess you are," he said.

"Speaking of untraditional, what made you walk over here?" Rica asked. "We're not exactly girls right out of college."

His hands went into his pockets as he slouched, and suddenly I saw a sheepish teenager about to ask a girl out. "Well, I knew it was a long shot, with me being... well... me. But I... how do I put this without offending you?" He pulled one hand from his pocket and placed it on top of Jillian's, patted it a few times, then stared directly at her. "The, uh, women my age aren't terribly… stimulating."

Jillian gulped. Her longing eyes faded deeper into a dream state, as her head tilted to one side. She still hadn't said a damn thing.

He pulled an envelope from his pocket and held it up in front of us. "Listen, I have an extra ticket to a new Broadway show this evening. It's a musical. My boss couldn't go and he just gave them to me. And…" he turned back to Jillian. "I just thought you looked like the kind of classy woman who might enjoy a night at the theater. No strings attached. I'll take you right home afterwards. But I insist on stopping for cheesecake after the play."

Cupid was still apparently holding down the mute button on Jillian, but a smile grew across her face. I was about to grab her head and move it up and down like a bobblehead doll when Neely saved the day.

"Jillian *loves* Broadway musicals," said Neely. "And we can vouch for her; she's very classy."

"Uh-huh," muttered Jillian, looking like a willing subject from a hypnotist's show.

The sphinx speaks!

"Tell you what, Shawn," I said. "We're pretty much finished up here with the business stuff so why don't you take Jillian to that play and on the way she can tell you about the opportunities at our network. Maybe you'd be interested."

He looked at Jillian. "That okay with you?" he asked.

The waitress was right. He was asking permission.

This stuff isn't in the tall girl playbook. How in the hell did I miss this?

"Yeah," she said, voice cracking.

He looked at his watch. "Okay then, we'll need to get going if we're gonna get a cab," he said, and extended a hand out to her. She took it, hopped off the bar stool and stood up next to him, towering over him in her four-inch heels. The top of his head reached her shoulder. He looked up at her like he'd just won the tall strawberry blonde lottery, then turned back to us. "It was nice meeting you all. Maybe I'll see you again."

"That would be nice. Good meeting you, Shawn," I said, as they turned and left.

"And you thought all our viewers were gonna be women," said Rica.

I watched them leave the bar, her arm around his shoulder, his arm around her waist.

More important, a whole bunch of guys in their twenties looked past the vapid, mini-skirted bimbos that filled the bar and stared at Shawn with envy.

So much for blowing off the male demographic.

* * *

The walk through the large reception area was like going through a buffet line of men. Models and actors filled every chair, while a few stood and lined the walls. I made my way to the meeting room just off the front door that we'd designated for interviews. A cloud of cologne filled my lungs. Our middle-aged, impeccably coiffed, blonde receptionist, the only woman in the room, was obviously enjoying the attention she was getting as two of the men leaned on her desk and were chatting her up.

Oh, this was going to be fun. A quick glance around the room told me there were plenty of possibles in this bunch.

I reached the door to the meeting room just as the receptionist buzzed me through, turned around and said, "Guys, we'll be starting shortly." They all straightened up as I headed through the door.

Inside, I found Rica and Neely already in place at the long maple table which dominated the room, enjoying coffee and donuts. The deep red walls were bare, faded squares showing the previous locations of prime-time posters that Amanda had thankfully ditched.

"Pretty nice-looking bunch out there," said Rica. "Not too shabby at all."

"I never knew New York had so many hot men," said Neely.

"Between Madison Avenue and Broadway, what did you expect?" I took a seat at the end of the table, next to a black metal cart on wheels that held a monitor, a DVD player and a VCR. "By the way, anybody seen Jillian?"

The door opened and she appeared on cue, newspaper under one arm while carrying a dark leather portfolio. "Morning, guys," she said, trying to hold back a smile as she made her way around the room and took a seat next to Rica at the far end of the table.

Rica immediately turned to face her. "So?" she asked.

"What?" said Jillian.

"How was last night?" asked Rica.

"Pffft," she said, with a wave of her hand. "The play was a disaster. We left at intermission." She then pulled a blank legal pad from her portfolio, placed it on the desk in front of her, and pretended to stare at it. "Terrible choreography. Just terrible. I can't believe they can get away with that on Broadway."

"What a bunch of horseshit," said Rica.

"What?" said Jillian.

"You know what we mean," said Neely. "How was your *Pocket Chippendale*?"

I smiled at Neely's dead-on description of Shawn, leaned back in my chair and crossed my arms as Jillian began to squirm in her seat. "Yeah, Jillian. Did you manage to speak the rest of the evening?"

"You guys leave me alone," she said, blushing. "And yes, we talked quite a bit. He's very sweet, incredibly smart. Perfect gentleman. And his references are impeccable. By the way, you should know that not everything about Shawn is proportional."

"Really," I said, raising my eyebrows. "What a pleasant surprise for you."

"You have no idea what you're missing, Syd," said Jillian. "You need a Pocket Chippendale of your own."

"That good, huh?" asked Neely.

She nodded. "Oh yeah. He tortured me for an hour on the couch and finally I couldn't take any more, so I just threw him over my shoulder like a cave girl, carried him to the bedroom and took him. You have no idea how empowering that is."

Rica's mouth dropped. "You actually *carried* him to the bedroom?"

"Sure. I'm really strong, and he's pretty light." She flexed her muscles, revealing well-toned biceps, and lowered her voice. "Me woman, you sex object."

"So the waitress was right?" asked Neely. "You enjoyed your little snack?

Jillian nodded. "Very much. And he obeys like a trained seal. Does whatever I ask. Worshiped me like a goddess."

"You *are* a goddess," I said. "Is he anchor potential?"

"Yes, and he's very excited about the benefits package."

"Can you keep him in line?" I asked. "You know about the problems I'm having with Scott."

Jillian shrugged. "If he needs a reminder, I'll just give him another spanking."

"You actually spanked him?" asked Neely.

"He was a bad, bad boy," said Jillian, eyes gleaming, while both eyebrows went up.

Rica started fanning herself with her pad. "Syd, can you turn up the air in here?"

I got up and moved toward the thermostat. "Okay, I guess we'd better get started with the interviews."

* * *

"It occurs to me," said Neely, pulling her chair up to the table, "that this is just like a reality show. We are lined up here at this table, facing a single chair in the middle of the room and we'll rank each contestant on a scale. The winners move on, the losers skulk out or throw fits. We ought to put a reporter in the outer office to interview them as they leave."

"I wanna play the British judge," said Jillian. "They always have some guy from London on the panel, who says something like, '*Your performance tonight was just ghastly*' with that accent, before they send the poor sap on his way."

"That might be a line you should save for the hotel," I said.

"I hope I never have to use it," said Jillian. "You guys ready?"

"Let's rock," said Rica.

I punched a button on the intercom.

"*Yes?*" said the receptionist.

"Start sending them in," I said. I turned to the girls. "Remember, the code word for *gong* is *doable*."

They nodded. The door opened and a tall, very beefy man in his mid-twenties entered the room. "Good morning," he said, brushing his wavy dark hair out of his eyes. "I'm Brian Fairfield. I'm an actor and model here in New York."

And you're a model for… let me guess… Michelin Tires?

"Good morning, Brian," I said, gesturing toward the chair. "Please have a seat and tell us about yourself."

He moved toward our table and handed each of us a manila envelope, then sat down. "I brought each of you a portfolio from my agency. I've been doing print ads for quite a while, though I did audition for a television commercial last week. I'm hoping to break into TV."

I slid the portfolio out of the envelope and opened it.

One side featured a full eight-by-ten headshot of the model, a beautifully lit photo that had obviously been air-brushed or Photoshopped or whatever. It didn't look anything like the guy sitting in front of us. The piercing blue eyes in the photo weren't nearly as dark in person. The other side featured three photos from different ads. He wore a tux in one, a bathing suit in another, and a sports jacket in a third.

He also looked like he'd gained a good bit of weight since the pictures were taken. The face was much fuller now, the beginnings of a second chin evidently having cancelled out the jawline that was so prominent in the photos.

"How old are these photos?" asked Rica.

"About three years," he said. "I, uh, haven't had a gig in quite awhile."

"Do you think reading a teleprompter is something that's... *doable* ... for you?" asked Neely, accenting the code word for my benefit.

"Sure," said the man.

"Thank you," I said, getting Neely's vote. "We'll be in touch."

The man's head dropped, he exhaled audibly and a sad look grew on his face. "Ohhhh… kaaay. Well, thank you for your time, I guess." He got up and left the room.

"That didn't take you long," said Jillian. "You could have at least asked him a few more questions."

"He'll be a doughboy in two more years," said Neely. "If he wants to break into TV he can get a gig selling crescent rolls. Why waste time with him?"

"I still like *gong* better," said Rica.

The parade continued, with plenty of hot damns and exponentially cutes sprinkled in the mix with those who looked closer to their driver's license photos than the ones in their portfolios. We got into the spirit of the chase by getting creative with the code word when we needed to gong someone.

From Rica: "I'm sure an anchor position might be doable if you spend three years behind the scenes. We do have some entry-level gopher jobs." (The guy left skid marks.)

From Jillian: "I'd be curious to see how you'd look if you dyed your hair bright red. Would that be doable?"

From Neely: "As we say in the South, if it's doable, it's worth doin' right."

By noon we were almost done and had at least nine viable

candidates. And that wasn't counting the people with actual television experience who were flying in later.

Then the door cracked open and the man who entered seemed to suck all the oxygen out of the room.

About six-three, with ripped arms straining at the sleeves of his baby blue, short-sleeved polo shirt, while his pecs tried to escape the fabric. Thick, dark brown hair, deep-set hazel eyes, square jaw, slightly crooked boyish grin that led you to believe he was up to something. If there was such a thing as a cross between hot damn and exponentially cute, this guy was it. "Hi, Denton Hale," he said. He handed me a DVD, résumé and portfolio, then grabbed a chair and took a seat.

"Denton, I'm Sydney, and this is Rica, Neely and Jillian." (Incidentally, you should know that even though I didn't expect any gongs, I do retain supreme veto power in extreme circumstances. Just in case one of them loses her mind.) I opened the portfolio and had to fight to keep my eyes from bugging out as the pictures jumped off the page. After about ten seconds I heard this clicking sound as Rica's fingers tap danced across the table and deftly snatched the portfolio and dragged it down the table, where Jillian and Neely leaned over to take a look at the man who didn't appear to have a visible flaw or an ounce of fat.

"Those are from my print ads this year," he said. "The DVD has my television work. Mostly exercise equipment infomercials and some voiceovers. You might have seen me if you're up in the middle of the night."

I popped the disc into the player and the monitor filled with Denton Hale extolling the virtues of a new home bodybuilding system. I assume he was pitching the thing, because I never actually heard the words. I was too busy locked on a glistening body that had been cut from suntanned marble by Michelangelo. I looked down at the girls and knew there would be a battle later on to decide who Denton Hale would get to bench press at the Plaza.

"So, why do you want this job?" asked Jillian.

"Because I'm tired of modeling and my roommate Jason Deller told me this was a fantastic place to work."

I bit my lower lip and smiled. "That's good to hear. So you're Jason's roomie."

"Yeah, we've shared an apartment for two years." Denton stared right into my eyes. "He loves working here. Seems very… satisfied." He smiled and I knew that he knew.

"Also very good to hear," said Rica, smiling at me. She turned to Denton. "So would you be willing—"

"Look, I understand the deal and I'll do whatever it takes. I'm smart, I work hard, and I follow orders. And if I have to follow, uh, *orders* from you four, (big sexy smile here) trust me, there won't be a problem."

"Okay, Denton," I said, suddenly feeling very warm. "We'll be in touch to do some test shots on the set… see how you read the prompter and all."

"I had a prompter on that infomercial."

"Then I'm sure it won't be a problem," I said.

"Do you have any questions for us?" asked Neely.

"Just one. If I get hired, which one of you am I going to be working under?"

Oh my.

"We'll, uh, figure that out as we put the staff together," I said. "Look forward to working with you."

"Same here," he said, getting up and heading for the door. "Have a good day."

The door shut and we all exhaled.

"Good God," said Jillian, looking at the portfolio. "The man's body is a playground. He looks like someone pasted an exponentially cute face onto a hot damn physique." She turned to Neely. "You got a category for that?"

"If the Pocket Chippendale is a snack, this guy's a seven course dinner," said Neely.

"I'm just trying to imagine Jason and Denton in one apartment,"

I said. "Can you picture the reaction of any woman who knocks on that door?"

"So how are we gonna decide who gets to check his references?" asked Rica. "Rock, paper, scissors?"

CHAPTER FOUR

"It's coming along a lot faster than we thought," said Amanda, as she and Madison led us through the construction. "And being ahead of schedule in New York is no small feat."

I followed with the girls, all outfitted in jeans and hard hats, past the carpenters and electricians who were putting the finishing touches on the new studio and offices. The smell of sawdust filled the air as we carefully tiptoed our way through the two-by-fours and power tools, while the sound of a bandsaw filled the air.

I heard a few of those power tools stop when we passed, as several workers decided it was time for a union break and that leering at us was more satisfying than coffee and a Krispy Kreme. Jillian, who seemed to be the object of their affections thanks to her mile long legs in skinny jeans and stacked heel boots, tipped her yellow hat at one guy drenched in sweat who had ditched his shirt.

"I'm amazed at what you've done with this old place," I said. The abandoned three story hotel had been a neighborhood eyesore, but the network's bottomless pockets were transforming it into a showplace. Exposed brick on the wall behind the set framed oval windows, some of which were filled with the original stained glass. The natural light that poured through the ones that weren't lit up the dust particles in the air. A long, royal blue set, with three giant flat-screen monitors in the background, popped against the freshly sandblasted red brick. A dark burgundy leather couch, loveseat and beveled glass coffee table sat off to the side for interviews, framed by bookshelves filled with actual books.

"This is going to be the best studio in the country," said Jillian.

"But it's more than a studio and offices," said Madison, heading toward a door at the back of the building. "Let's go upstairs."

Rica looked up. "Upstairs? I thought you knocked out all the ceilings for the lighting grid."

"We did," said Amanda. "But the architect found something we didn't know existed. There's a fourth floor."

"You found an extra floor?" I said.

"Not exactly," said Madison. "C'mon."

Amanda led us through a steel door at the back of the room and up three flights of stairs. Madison pulled a key out of her pocket and unlocked an ornately carved oak door at the top landing. "This part of the project is already complete." The heavy door creaked a bit as she pushed it open, and we all stepped inside.

"Apparently the original owner of the hotel was an artist and had a secret loft which isn't even visible from the street," said Amanda, who turned on the lights, revealing a living room furnished with a leather sofa and several antiques. Rich, deep library paneling ran from floor to ceiling, while a picture window offered a beautiful view of the Hudson.

"We turned it into an apartment," said Madison. "Though no one is going to actually live here."

They led us through the living room and down a short hallway into a bedroom that featured a cherry four-poster king-size bed, topped with a bold red comforter and a half dozen pillows to match. The adjoining bathroom had a huge sunken ivory garden tub and an etched glass shower. The room had enough black marble and brass fixtures to stock a Home Depot.

"Good Lord," said Neely. "This is fantastic."

"Talk about a crash pad," said Rica.

"Each of you will have access to the loft," said Amanda, who reached into her pocket and pulled out a batch of keys, then handed one to each of us. "Obviously you need to coordinate its use."

"How very convenient," said Jillian. "Our bedroom away from home."

"Nice when you need a between meal snack," said Neely. Jillian smiled at her.

"Oh, there is one more very important feature of the loft. This way, please," said Madison, who led us back into the living room. She threw a switch next to the door and the stairwell glowed red. I stepped outside and looked up.

"An on-air light," I said. "How appropriate."

"It's your electronic *do not disturb* sign," said Amanda. "If you're using the loft, please don't forget to turn it on. And it's even more important that you turn it off when you leave. Press the button next to it, and it will tell the secretary to notify the cleaning service."

Rica ducked her head out the door and looked at the light. "Sure beats a sock on the doorknob."

* * *

"My name is Todd Jones. I was wondering if you've had a chance to look at my tape."

The call was typical for a News Director, and one I usually avoid because if the job applicant is calling you, it means you haven't called them, which means you didn't like their tape, which means you're stuck trying to let someone down nicely. But the secretary was out sick and I made the mistake of picking up the outside line.

"We've already narrowed things down to our short list," I said, trying to sound polite. "If you haven't received a call by now then I'm afraid you haven't made—"

"Well, then could you offer me some feedback on my tape? At least tell me what you didn't like?"

Yes, of course, I remember every single tape we looked at. Of course if you were gonged, I might have caught a nanosecond glimpse of you before deleting you from my memory forever. And if Jillian tossed you in the trash before...

"I'm really sorry, but we looked at so many tapes it would be impossible for me to remember what yours looked like."

"You'd remember me. I'm forty-five and bald with a moustache. Very distinctive look for a news anchor."

"Sorry, doesn't ring a bell."

Long pause. "You didn't look at my tape, did you?"

The swish you just heard was a red flag going up. This was more than just a typical job call, the guy was on a fishing expedition. I needed to cut this short and be careful doing it.

"Sir, lots of managers looked at lots of tapes." (Actually true. We looked at the over-30s tapes from men and the under-30s tapes from women as Jillian threw them away.) "I'm sorry yours wasn't chosen. Best of luck in your job search."

"That's all I needed to know." Click.

Okay, now I know something is up. And Madison's appearance in my doorway with a worried look confirmed it.

"I just got a strange call," she said.

"I just got one too. Guy wanting feedback on his tape, but this wasn't the typical kid out of college making a follow-up call."

"What did he sound like?"

"Mature, deep voice. No accent, good diction. Said he was forty-five."

"I think I talked to the same guy. Said he was a freelance magazine reporter doing a story on the broadcast industry's hiring practices."

Uh-oh. "What did you say?"

"I told him I wasn't interested in being interviewed."

"Good," I said.

"Besides your three cohorts, who knows the hiring criteria for the cable jobs?"

"No one. Everything has been done behind closed doors."

"Well, keep it that way," she said. "We can't afford any leaks before the launch."

I looked through the glass panel of my office out into the newsroom. "I'm wondering if we already have one."

* * *

The "speed dating" theme of tonight's group dinner was Neely's idea.

Our two dozen new hires filled the hotel ballroom, dressed to the nines as they sipped drinks and mingled. The muted beige walls served as a backdrop to the array of colorful outfits worn by the women. The lone bartender, a sharp-looking blonde in her forties, was constantly in motion, mixing drinks as fast as she could for a group determined to get loosened up. Incredibly, she seemed to be able to mix drinks without looking, as she was riveted to the selection of men in the room.

Our twelve female anchors ranged in age from thirty-five to forty-four. All single, smart, experienced newswomen who could give a twenty-year-old a run for her money in a bikini. (By the way, we couldn't exactly hire married women or those with children for these gigs. We're not homewreckers. Plus, we can't have kids running around an R-rated workplace. We have morals!)

When we were done hiring, the final breakdown of the bucks came out this way: four hot damns, five exponentially cutes and one Denton Hale, who was in a class by himself. Neely created another category, since we hired one more Pocket Chippendale to go along with Shawn.

Little did the bucks know they were going to be part of a unique broadcasting experiment.

"This is going to be fun to watch," said Rica.

"I must say, I'd never have thought to put our anchor teams together this way, but it actually makes sense," I said.

"They've had an hour's worth of booze," said Jillian. "They should be in a good mood by now."

Neely grabbed a spoon from one of the tables and clanged it against her cocktail glass. "Okay, everyone. I'd like you all to take a seat at the very long table at the side of the room. Men on one side, women on the other. We're going to play a little game before we sit down to dinner."

The group headed for the table and began taking their seats. The bartender exhaled a sigh of relief and leaned forward to watch the festivities.

Neely moved to the head of the table and waited till they were all seated. "Now I know you've gotten to know some of your new co-workers this evening, but I want you to have a chance to meet every single person here tonight. So, here's how this is going to work. If you've ever seen speed dating, you'll understand the process. You'll spend three minutes talking to the person opposite you. When I ring the bell, the men will get up and move one chair to the right and the guy at the end of the table will move to the front. Everybody clear?"

They all nodded.

"Okay," said Neely. "Begin."

"You get the feeling she's done this kind of thing before?" asked Jillian.

Rica nodded. "I get the feeling she's working on a book titled *Throwing Sex Parties on a Budget*. She could be the new horny version of Martha Stewart."

"When choosing accessories for your tryst," said Jillian, nose in the air while speaking with an affected accent, "make sure your handcuffs are lined with a natural fabric, as synthetics may leave an unsightly rash."

When the first three minutes were up, Neely rang a bell she'd brought and the men did their rotation thing.

I leaned over toward Neely. "It occurs to me that there's a bit of a flaw in this system," I said.

"What's that?" asked Neely.

"When the music stops tonight, we're gonna be the only ones

without chairs." I said.

"You're assuming the other girls won't want to share," said Jillian.

"You're getting awfully adventurous since your little cavegirl foreplay episode with The Snack," said Rica.

Jillian just smiled and batted her eyes.

An hour later, every woman had gotten a close look at all the choices on the buffet.

"Okay," said Neely. "Now that you've all had a chance to meet, let's sit down and enjoy our dinner."

And the next thirty seconds told me that Neely was a genius. She didn't tell them where to sit, nor were there place cards on the tables. The group stood up and each woman worked her way through the crowd, seeking the man who had piqued her interest for three minutes or during happy hour. They all paired off quickly and moved to the three round tables that had been set up. No one was left standing, as this wasn't exactly like choosing up sides for sandlot baseball. Just like that we had our anchor teams. Gotta have that chemistry.

"That went smoothly," said Jillian.

The group had just polished off a decadent chocolate dessert and was settling down to coffee. Neely stood up and brought out a large brandy snifter that held a bunch of hotel room keys.

"I hope you've enjoyed our little get-acquainted dinner," she said. "But the evening is not over yet. If all the women will step up here, we have a little gift, which I'm sure you'll agree beats the hell out of welcome wagon coupons."

The women lined up and Neely handed out a hotel room key to each one. Each woman moved back toward the tables, chose a man, and headed out of the hotel ballroom to the elevators.

Neely slapped her hands back and forth like she was a baker brushing flour from them. "There. All done. Tomorrow we'll find out which teams have natural chemistry."

"We don't even get a consolation prize?" asked Jillian. "I at least thought the woman who grabbed Denton might want a little help."

"Yeah," said Rica. "Like you'd share."

"Sorry," said Neely. "One must make sacrifices for the greater good."

"I got your sacrifices right here," said Rica.

CHAPTER FIVE

I'm a little nervous this morning, because today is our network's Upfront, and the chilly theater is filled with newspaper and magazine columnists sharpening their pens and filling them with bile instead of ink.

The Upfront is the big hoo-ha that showcases what's coming on the network in the fall. They're called "Upfronts" because they allow advertisers to buy time "up front" before new shows go on the air. Advertising buyers get a sneak peek at what's in store for September and if they like what they see, they'll buy. If the print media creates some buzz for a show or two, they'll *really* buy.

In addition, General Managers and sales executives from affiliates show up from all over the country so they can shovel in the free shrimp and get a picture with a hot babe who said one line in a sitcom the previous year but looks fantastic in a string bikini. Reporters and columnists see Upfronts as a venue to vent at the industry that doesn't produce "quality" programming up to their impeccable standards and won't hire them. (And yes, that's the reason "critics" love to slam everything; because they aren't part of it all. In the media, those who can, do. Those who can't, criticize.)

Each network has an Upfront every summer. They rent a big venue, like Radio City, and bring in assorted stars; one or two from the most successful shows, and a whole bunch who are starring in new series they hope will succeed. "Names" always get preference over "unknowns", unless the unknowns have some sort of "IT" factor. (Hence the term, "IT Girl.") Occasionally someone from the news division pops in to tell how they strive for objective political coverage, and that usually gets the biggest laugh of the day from the audience.

Last year at the CBN upfront, Amanda's predecessor had the insanely stupid idea to bring the network stars out in character, which might have played well in Podunk, but not in Manhattan. Considering the themes of the shows, they looked like the front row at a Willie Nelson concert. Twenty-four legs, and about as many teeth. Then the previous head of the entertainment division went on about "an exciting new dating reality show set in Arkansas in which a man dates five women only to discover three are close relatives." The show, titled "Kissin' Cousins", thankfully died a grisly death after four episodes when it was discovered the man had previously fathered a son with seven toes on each foot, which, he proudly pointed out, enabled his kid to count to twenty-four by the first grade.

And now you know why the woman got canned and was replaced by Amanda.

Thankfully, the old CBN will be dead and buried in two months. Actually, Amanda has pretty much blown out the schedule and is running movies most of the time, all of which have a decidedly female appeal. But we're not talkin' romance-novel-damsel-in-distress appeal; all the movies feature strong female characters who can kick ass like Sigourney Weaver fighting acid-bleeding aliens. Meanwhile, Amanda has certainly given prime time a new look with some of the shows scheduled for the fall. And if these don't get our message across...

"Legal Briefs" features a former model who put herself through law school by posing for underwear catalogs. She graduates at thirty-five, hangs out a shingle, and starts her own firm. But she's short of clients and misses her old career. So she does an occasional photo shoot, one of which features her in horn-rimmed glasses and a thong sprawled out across a jury box promoting a line of unmentionables known as "no objections." The practice takes off and triples her workload, forcing her to hire hot young male attorneys right out of law school. Then, as Amanda put it (with one raised eyebrow), "Each episode ends with a new recruit practicing a closing argument on his job interview." (And, each media person attending found a thong with the "no objections" logo in the goodie bag. Talk about promotions on a shoestring.)

"Boy Friday" is a twist on the old 1950s term used to describe a woman who did just about everything around the office, while the men in the office did her. In this case the "boy" is played by David Harrington, who, as every woman in America knows, is the 22-year-old hardbody in those jeans ads that never show the jeans. He works for an advertising firm run by four attractive women in their thirties, and is frequently required to be a "stand-in" for "mock-up ads" that usually require him to take off his shirt, among other things. Of course, the women never tell him he's modeling for clients that don't exist. He's such a ditz! He also goes for coffee, just so the viewer knows who's boss.

"Injections" features a bunch of young, attractive male nurses who operate the immunization clinic at a hospital, which is, of course, also staffed by libidinous thirty-something female doctors who are committed to the principle that no hospital bed remain empty. Amanda is trying to create a national catchphrase with this one.

And finally, there's "Hung Jury" which is a legal dramedy. In this one, a sultry, oversexed thirty-something babe (are there any other kind on this network?) operates the hotel next to the courthouse which is used to sequester jurors. But little do the judges know that she's on the payroll of a sleazy defense attorney. The items on her "room service" menu are delivered and *voila!* Young, hunky male jurors amazingly have a change of heart and discover that the defendant is always innocent. Case dismissed!

That's all well and good, but I'm a bit twitchy because Amanda and Madison are going to introduce our new anchor teams after they're done rolling out the entertainment clips. While we're absolutely thrilled with the hires we've made, I'm still wondering how the media, and particularly the print media, is going to deal with it. Then again, as they say, there's no such thing as bad publicity.

It must be true. I mean, who would have guessed Scott's little trip to the tabloid would have paid such dividends and ultimately launched a cable network?

Jillian evidently noticed my anxiety and patted my hand as we sat in the front row of the theater. "Syd, relax. This is *our* day." However, I did not release the white-knuckle death grip I had on the red velour arms of the chair.

Neely was on my other side and chimed in. "Really, Syd. You should be excited, not nervous."

"Yeah, if the press doesn't like what we've done, screw 'em," added Rica.

Amanda wrapped up her presentation to great applause. I turned around to survey the crowd, and noted most of the noise was coming from the women in the audience. They obviously liked what they'd seen from the entertainment division as the clips were highly entertaining. I exhaled a bit of tension, and turned back to see Madison walk to the microphone.

"Good morning," she said, placing a script on the podium. "Today we're going to change the face of broadcasting. Literally. Did all you fine journalists write that sound bite down?"

The crowd snickered as Madison smiled. She could work a room like few television executives I've ever seen. "Today we're going to introduce the people who will revolutionize the way people in America get their information. The Consolidated Group Report, or CGR, as it will be known on the air, will not only keep you up to date with what's happening in the world, but will seek to make your lives a little better. And, I'm serious, I want you to write this part down, because this is actual news... *we're going to do it without a political agenda.* Frankly, my dear, I don't give a damn who is in the White House."

That one got a cheer, even from the men.

"CGR will not look like any network you've ever seen. Because our main agenda is women. But even if you've got a Y-chromosome, you'll still want to watch," she paused for a laugh, "because we're also going to tell you how to treat the woman in your life… and that might just make *your* life a lot better. And we're going to teach you some things you didn't know about women. So if you are a woman, or if you like women, we invite you to tune in and get everything you need without the bias, without the shouting, and without the death and destruction. Women of America, the rules have changed. *We're* in charge."

That got a big cheer from the gals in the audience.

"Now please welcome the women and men of CGR!"

She waved her hand to the side with a flourish as the twenty-four anchors marched onto the stage. Twelve gorgeous women in somewhat revealing outfits (all primary colors), each paired with a trophy buck in matching dark pinstriped suits and red paisley ties. (Yeah, I borrowed the idea from the game show with the models and the briefcases. So sue me.) I turned and stole a glance at the crowd, about four hundred people scattered around the Broadway theater we'd rented.

The men looked puzzled.

The women looked like they'd just bounded down the stairs on Christmas morning and found a hardbody in a Speedo and a Santa hat under the tree asking who'd been naughty and who'd been nice, and if your name happened to be on the naughty list you could stay.

The anchors went down the line introducing themselves to the crowd.

The lights dimmed, and a five minute promotional piece filled a giant screen behind the anchors. The video featured every member of the staff, and left no doubt as to which sex was calling the shots.

When it was done, the lights came back up and Madison took control. "I know you probably have some questions and we have time for just a few before lunch."

A bald, overweight, fiftyish man in the second row, who looked like he'd slept in his short-sleeved shirt, raised his hand and Madison called on him. "I'm not sure how to put this question without offending anyone…"

"Watch it, Brad," said a middle-aged female reporter sitting nearby. The crowd chuckled.

"But," he continued, "there seems to be a, how shall I say this… *common denominator* with your anchor teams."

"Really?" said Madison, wide-eyed and playing dumb for the women in the crowd, who were eating it up. "I hadn't noticed. What common denominator were you referring to?" She scratched her chin and searched the heavens with her eyes as the crowd snickered. "Oh, wait a minute, I think I see what you're getting at. All of our men are wearing the same outfit!"

Big laugh. Now she had them.

"I was going to say," said the reporter (whose face matched his shirt, by the way), "that you seem to have a lot of men who have less… experience than the women."

Madison shook her head and put her palms up. "Then I guess we're gonna have to teach them, just like in the bedroom," she said. She got applause and a lot of hoots with that one. When it died down she turned serious. "Now I'd like to ask *you* something, Sir. If we'd brought out twelve older, distinguished men with twelve gorgeous women right out of college, would you have even asked the question?"

The man slumped into his seat and folded like a pricked balloon.

"Hey Brad, when your IQ hits eighty, sell," said the female reporter.

When the roar of laughter died down, Madison continued. "Tradition has it, at least in broadcasting, that the man must be older, stronger, taller. That he must be in control. That he wears the pants in the household. We women know those are just ridiculous stereotypes. We are simply presenting America with anchor teams that mirror life the way it might be if we stopped taking those stereotypes seriously. No limitations on age or anything else."

Another middle-aged male reporter raised his hand while flipping through his press kit, which held information on all the anchors. "I see from the bios that some of your male anchors have no television experience. Care to comment on that?"

"Again," said Madison, "would you ask that question of a woman who goes directly from a beauty pageant to the anchor desk? We've all seen that a thousand times and nobody bats an eye. It's not about experience, but being able to communicate. Some of our male anchors don't have any broadcast experience, but they communicate quite well."

"Only when she lets me," said Shawn, pointing to his much taller co-anchor. Madison smiled, obviously appreciating the ad-lib, as Shawn's co-anchor reached her arm around his shoulder and gave him a pat.

God bless Jillian's little snack.

The middle-aged female ad exec sitting behind me leaned forward. "He's absolutely adorable," she said. "Does he come in a six-pack?"

"No, but he's got one," whispered Jillian.

A female reporter raised her hand. "I've noticed from the bios that a lot of the women have been out of the business for a while. Any particular reason?"

"Yeah, honey, we'd been put out to pasture by the old boys club that runs broadcasting and thinks your odometer turns over at thirty-five," said Kristin West, a spunky, flame-haired anchor in her late thirties who was paired with Denton Hale. "I honestly thought my career was over, and when high-def came in I was sure of it. So it was nice to hear that CGR values my experience and doesn't see my age as a negative. I hope this opens doors for other women to get back into the business."

"You know what people are going to call you girls," said the reporter. "I mean, all anchoring with such good-looking younger men."

"Yeah," said Kristin, hooking her arm inside Denton's. "Damn lucky."

Kristin beamed as the audience roared. Madison waited for the laughter to die down before wrapping things up. "One more question, and then it's time for lunch."

"Why didn't you hire any men over thirty?"

The question was shouted from the back of the room. I turned and caught a glimpse of a bald man with a moustache standing behind the last row.

"They were all tied up chasing young beauty queens," said Madison, to more laughter. "Now, let's do lunch everybody."

But I knew at least one question about age wasn't going away.

*　*　*

Four hours later, we were scattered across the first two rows of the now empty theater. "I think we'll have a pool," said Amanda, who sat in the second row and had her feet propped up on the back of a chair in the first row, "as to how many times the word *cougar* is used in a headline tomorrow. The print people love that term."

"I think we're a hit," said Rica, stretching out her legs as she looked out at the stage where men were busy removing the podium and monitor. "And The Snack had a great line."

"The *snack*?" asked Amanda.

"The nickname for Shawn," said Jillian. "A waitress hung it on him."

"He did well today," said Madison. "Really worked the room after lunch. The guy's a natural." She then turned to me. "Syd, you've been awfully quiet."

"Well, I'm concerned about the guy who asked the last question," I said. "The man who looks like he belongs on a Monopoly card? That's the one who called me yesterday."

"You sure?" she asked.

I nodded.

"What are youse guys talkin' about?" asked Rica.

"Syd and I both got calls yesterday asking about our hiring practices," said Madison.

"The guy who called me wanted feedback on his résumé tape," I said.

"We've all gotten those," said Rica. "I just blow 'em off."

"Well," I said, "this guy said he was forty-five and bald with a moustache, so I'd probably remember him."

"We tossed all the tapes of men over thirty without looking at them," said Neely.

"I know," I said. "That's the problem. We never looked at them."

"If you're worried about an age discrimination suit, don't be," said Amanda.

"Okay, why not?" I asked.

"Well, we just hired twelve women no one else wanted because they were too old," she said. "You guys just worry about the product, which judging from today's reaction, won't be a problem."

Yeah, we just turned the tables on the men. I just hope ol' Rogaine Boy doesn't turn them on us.

* * *

Well, we're officially "IT" as far as the New York papers and the entertainment mags are concerned. In capital letters. The nice thing is that the buzz should continue for a while, since we're not even on the air yet. Anticipation is a great American tradition in the media. And if you can deliver the goods, you're golden. If not, there will be another flavor of the month just around the corner. So for now, I'm enjoying our "IT" status.

Some of the clips I'm putting in my scrapbook:

From a New York Tabloid:

CGR doesn't need to buy any vowels to get the meaning of its acronym across. Staffed by a dozen very attractive middle-aged female anchors, all paired with much younger men who stepped out of a GQ ad, the agenda is clear.

The cougars are on the prowl.

From a television magazine (written by a female columnist):

If CGR is trying for a subliminal message, then subtlety got lost in the process. The pairing of beautiful thirty-something anchors with much younger men virtually slaps you in the face with the concept that the women are in charge at this network… and the female viewers at home can set the rules as well.

It's about damn time.

From a more highbrow publication:

If you're one of those people who likes to figure out the meanings of vanity license plates, then CGR won't pose much of a challenge. While the older-woman-younger-man co-anchor teams send a message that is blatantly obvious, the network needs to be commended for turning the rules of television news upside down and putting competent women who haven't just stepped off a pageant runway on the anchor desk.

But this is my absolute favorite, from another tabloid:

CGR Offers Prrrr-fect Mix on Anchor Desk

The promotional video for CGR that features its female anchors shows the very attractive women in typical newsroom situations. The sultry female voice coos that CGR's anchors are "more experienced" and you get the idea they're not talking about journalism when you see a long-legged, thirtyish beauty sitting on the corner of a much younger man's desk. Hair up, horn-rimmed glasses surrounding spectacular blue eyes, while her slit skirt rides up her thigh.

She's teaching him. She points to the computer screen, he nods. She hands him a sheet of paper, he nods.

C'mon, boy. Fetch!

He doesn't have any lines in the promo, but his nod screams, "Yes, Ma'am."

And you just know when her hair comes down and the glasses come off, class will still be in session.

"Not too shabby," said Amanda, as we all slid newspapers back and forth across the conference room table.

"I'm surprised some of the male reporters didn't take some shots," said Jillian.

"I think they were afraid to," said Madison.

"Men afraid of women," I said. "Has a nice ring to it."

CHAPTER SIX

Random thoughts and other observations one week from the premiere of CGR:

—Jillian and The Snack are a really cute couple. I mean, at first I thought they looked odd standing next to each other, but now they seem like the kind of pair that can stay together forever. He really won her over on their first "date" after the Broadway show. (Left early 'cause of bad choreography, my ass.) He comes by her townhouse to pick her up, notices she's wearing flats with a short skirt, and says, "Killer legs like that should never be without heels." The girl just melted. Down the road it wouldn't surprise me to see the two of them play house for a while, or at least go exclusive, and I'm not talking about a breaking news story.

—The cougar thing has taken on a life of its own in the tabloids, which seem to have daily stories on older women and younger men. They apparently know a good trend when they see one. One paper even started a column called "*On the Prowl After 30*" and every single entry focuses on getting a younger man. Meanwhile, a supermarket rag took the shot of all twenty-four anchors and put little cat ears on each of the women under the headline, "Clawing their way to the top."

—I wish I had some of Rica's DNA. The woman can communicate so much with that one all-purpose New York word and her incredible array of facial expressions, the scariest of which is the bar-room death stare that can stun a man like a Star Trek phaser. I'm convinced that if she landed on another planet, she'd be able to converse with aliens using just "fuhgeddaboudit" and the movements of her eyebrows. The Italian hand signals get the message across as well. I often wonder if Joe Pesci has a sister he doesn't know about.

—The Monopoly Guy worries me. I mean, after the Upfront I was really expecting some sort of legal action regarding age discrimination. Every time Madison drops by my office my heart skips a beat. But so far, nothing. Still, I feel like he's lurking out there, ready to strike. (By the way, you're not paranoid if they really *are* out to get you.)

—When Neely turns on that Southern belle thing of hers (not that she needs it with that body and that face), no other woman stands a chance. No man either. But what's interesting is that Vance's co-anchor, a stunning strawberry blonde named Alana Stephens, is also a down home sweetie from Tennessee. Vance always looks like the happiest guy in the office bouncing between those two.

—I still cannot believe this is about to become reality. I'll either be the Helen Gurley Brown of television or the laughing stock. Either way, it's been a great ride.

But I desperately want it to continue.

* * *

So we're doing some dress rehearsals, fine-tuning the lighting on the set, and taking care of all sorts of last-minute tweaking. I'm standing in front of the set, warming my cold hands under the hot lights, watching the dream take shape, feeling like I'm outside my own body looking at the scene. Everything's going smoothly and then our giant fly (Scott Harry) has to buzz like a friggin' kamikaze into the ointment again.

"So, I was really considered for the network, huh?"

I looked over my shoulder to see Scott standing right behind me, hands in his back pockets, the wounded doe looking like someone had run over his dog. I turned back toward the set. "You were, Scott. We feel you're just as valuable with local. We're all part of the same team, you know."

"I have more experience than most of the people you hired." He moved next to me and cocked his head at Denton and Shawn, who were sitting on the set taking turns practicing reading the prompter. "Hell, half of them haven't paid any dues at all."

(Dammit, he's never gonna let this die. How many shopping days are left till the end of his contract?) "We can't play musical anchors with local, Scott. You've built a solid audience and we might lose that if we make a change so soon after you started."

"Well, I don't think you ever had any intention of considering me. I think you were just blowing smoke up my ass."

I finally turned to face him and folded my arms. "Anytime you wanna go back to Indianapolis, Scott, just let me know. I'm sure LaGuardia has several non-stop flights a day."

(There are several ways to prick the ego balloon in this business. Reminding people where they came from is the best one.)

His head dropped and he started to turn away, but got in one final shot. "I'm surprised no one has sued you for discrimination."

And just like that, I think I found my leak.

* * *

For a while we were a bit torn about the scheduling. Couldn't decide if we should start the broadcast day with a hot damn and have an exponentially cute do the evenings, or vice versa. Jillian and I thought it was better that viewers wake up with a hot damn, while Neely and Rica argued that they're better off going to sleep with them.

Deadlocked like a hung jury (did the fact that we have twelve hot men in the stable cross your minds when you read that term?) we asked Madison to cast the deciding vote. She, instead, made the decision easy for us. "We start our first broadcast day at five in the morning. Just put your best guy there. First impressions mean everything."

That's why Madison is running this network. Stuff that drives me nuts is so simple for her.

So Vance is the face that will watch you getting dressed every morning. (Don't laugh, when the guy anchors it seems as though he's looking right through the screen.) And if you're the man of the house (the actual one) you can drool in your corn flakes over his co-anchor, Alana Stephens, who has incredible chemistry with Vance, both on and off the set.

Speaking of drooling, the billboards featuring Vance have probably created a whole new generation of mouth-breathing women. (This is not counting the ones who used to watch "Kissin' Cousins" or those currently shopping at Wal-Mart.) Amanda's promotional team (all women, natch) has come up with some ads that have become water cooler talk all over the city. My favorite billboard features Vance half dressed, shirt open to the waist, giving you a little peek at his abs. A red necktie is draped around his neck while boxer shorts reveal his tanned, toned legs. He's carrying a tray into the bedroom, which, along with a plate of bacon and eggs, has a single red rose in a crystal vase. His face tells you he's already enjoyed his breakfast, and he's looking at it. The fore-ground features a bed with one long gorgeous leg sticking out of gold satin sheets and the back of a strawberry blonde head. The haircut and hair color and shapely leg match Alana (probably because that's her in the ad). A nylon stocking hangs precariously off a lampshade on the end table. The copy on the bottom of the billboard simply says, "Have breakfast in bed with Vance on CGR. Weekday mornings from five till eight." Neely has a mock-up of the ad in her office, much to Jillian's dismay.

On the other side of the coin are the billboards promoting the women. One features anchor Kimberly Sands in a living room, shoulder-length brunette tangles dusting the shoulders of her royal blue business suit. She stands next to a recliner, one leg with a four-inch heel on the arm of the chair as she glares at the younger man sitting in it. He is handing over the television remote to her. The ad reads, "CGR. *We're* in charge. You're not changing the channel."

My favorite is a magazine ad, and I think Amanda bought space in every major publication in America. This one features Kristin West, the redhead who will be co-anchoring with Denton, and this ad truly plays games with your imagination, which, of course, is what it is designed to do. Dressed in an oversized blue pin-striped man's dress shirt she's sitting up in bed, legs folded underneath. We assume she's straddling a man from the look on her face as she glances down. But all you can see are rumpled sheets and the top of a man's head on a pillow. "Mornings on CGR," the ad reads. "Our women are on top of things."

And Amanda wasn't kidding about Neely having a future in promotions. A television promo running on our broadcast network features all twelve of our female anchors getting dressed in various men's outfits, wearing everything from three-piece business suits to a football uniform (complete with eye-black under the anchor's eyes) to a construction hard hat. All the women wear serious looks while the CGR logo sits in the lower right-hand corner. You don't hear a single word as the women get dressed for battle. Then, with five seconds left in the commercial, a strong female voice brings the message home. "Women. We're the new men." (The phrase, "Men are the new women," will apparently stay behind closed doors for now, but Amanda says it's on the back burner at the ad agency.)

CHAPTER SEVEN

We're all at DEFCON ONE today. Tomorrow, in twelve hours, we launch, just like a missile. (Hence, the military reference. Except we hope that nothing blows up.)

I shouldn't be nervous, and I have no reason to be. Rehearsals have been flawless, the product looks spectacular, the sets really pop on high-def, we've got a ton of slick pieces in the can by every member of the staff, and the technical crew is getting along extremely well with the talent, which is no small accomplishment. Usually jealousy creeps into the mix with the behind the scenes people, but the anchors are treating them as equals. Some of the anchor teams act as if they've been working together for years. Chemistry is one of those things you hope for. It's not an exact science, but it's lightning in a bottle if you can catch it. I'm chalking it up to Neely's speed dating dinner.

Still, I'm popping Tums like M&M's. (The bottle says I can only take ten per day and I hit that mark at two this afternoon, so I'm switching to Bailey's. The cream will settle my stomach, though it is doubtful my impromptu antacid regimen will end up in a medical journal.) I won't be able to relax until the ship has left the harbor tomorrow morning at five and is safely out to sea.

But the girls are in a lot worse shape. I can tell by looking at their faces as they file through my office door and plop down on the couch that sits on the side of my desk.

We should have put a revolving door on the loft for all the use it has gotten within the last two days. (I can only imagine the cleaning service printing out its monthly bill and wondering why a television network goes through so many sheets and pillowcases.)

* * *

I'm sure you've gathered by now that if I'm still up at three-thirty in the morning it's because the man sharing the bed with me needs his references checked yet again.

In this case, the only thing getting any action around me is the coffee pot.

The girls were already in the studio when I arrived, bleary-eyed and yawning but still excited, as the beehive of activity swarmed around them under studio lights already turned up full. Production assistants carried scripts, cameramen checked their shots, and the director headed back to the control room to rehearse one last time.

"Morning," said Neely, as I joined the group. She held an over-sized coffee cup and was noshing on a cruller. The smells of the sugar and the vanilla-flavored brew filled my nostrils and made me hungry.

"Looks like a real TV station," I said.

"I still can't believe this is actually happening," said Jillian. "This could be one of those watershed days for women."

"It could," I said. I looked around and didn't see our first anchor team. "Where are Vance and Alana?"

Rica pointed up. "Loft," she said, with a mouthful of bagel.

Now I was wide awake. "Now? They don't have time for—"

"Good morning, Syd," said Alana, her heels clicking on the freshly waxed gray marble floor as she headed in my direction.

"Hi Syd," said Vance, waving at me and wearing a big smile as he headed for the set with a script in his hands.

"Congrats on getting this off the ground," said Alana. She

extended her hand and I shook it. "I must tell you I'm honored to be one of the anchors kicking this thing off."

I was more concerned with her preparation. "You guys were in the loft? Isn't that cutting it a little close?"

"We were just up there for five minutes," said Alana. "Vance was very… well, he was in a nervous state. We just played a little doctor. He asked me to open wide and say ahhhh, and I swallowed the entire tongue depressor."

The Southern euphemisms for sex never cease to amaze me. But coming from a strawberry blonde with a cute little pug nose and devilish green eyes, it fits.

"Not an easy accomplishment in five minutes," said Neely, who oughta know. (She looks down and suddenly loses interest in the cruller.)

"Well," I said, calming down, "thanks for taking one for the team."

A puzzled look grew across Alana's face as she touched up her lips. "Sydney, my dear, it's not like it's an unpleasant experience. Boy needed a little release, that's all. He'll pay the bill for cleanin' out the pipes this afternoon."

* * *

Lest you think we're just like men when it comes to management, let me clear things up.

We never micro-manage.

I've worked in stations where a manager hovered over anchors in the newsroom, hovered over the director in the control room, hovered near the set during a live broadcast. These "helicopter managers" never fully earn the respect of their employees because employees know they're not trusted to do their jobs. And when you've got a boss hovering over you and you can hear the beating of the rotors, you're more likely to make mistakes. Stand up too quick and the blades take your head off. You can't breathe normally if you're always walking on eggshells, and that just sends your creative muse into vapor lock.

That's why at two minutes till five, I'm in my office with the girls. Madison is at home watching, and Amanda is doing the same from her hotel room. (They both have the company of bucks from the night shift, but we know they'll take a break at five. This is too important to just record and watch later.) We've hired good people who are smart, and we're trusting them to do well. We don't need to look over shoulders.

"You guys wanna hear something funny?" I said, as I flicked on the giant flat-screen monitor in my office. The screen cleared and was filled with one of the many promotional spots we'd done for the channel that had been running for the past three weeks. A countdown clock ticked away the seconds in the corner and showed we were less than two minutes from the kick-off.

"What?" asked Jillian, getting comfortable on the couch.

I picked up a sheet of paper from my desk as I dropped into my leather swivel recliner. "I was checking the overnight ratings just to see what the competition is doing these days, and we actually have been showing up."

"Excuse me?" said Neely, furrowing her brow.

"We're already getting a one share just running promos and that countdown clock," I said.

"You mean to tell me," said Rica, pointing at the screen, "that enough people have been actually watching this stuff to show up in the ratings?"

"We get a two share after midnight," I said. I grabbed my coffee and sent some hot caffeine rocketing into my veins as I flipped the paper in the direction of the couch.

Jillian caught it and shook her head in amazement as she looked at it. "Interesting. More than half the viewers are men."

"Women over thirty, the final frontier," said Neely. "We're America's last untapped resource."

"Considering your escapades of the past few months, I wouldn't refer to us as *untapped*," said Rica.

"Ten seconds, guys," said Jillian, pointing at the monitor.

The room went silent as the clock ticked down to zero.

The screen went black for a moment, then faded up on the CGR logo.

Bold orchestral music that was loaded with energy filled the air, then faded down a bit. "Welcome to your theater of information," said a mature but spunky female voice. "Now, live from New York, *this* is CGR."

The logo dissolved into a two-shot of Alana and Vance seated at the set, both wearing warm smiles and looking a lot more awake than we felt.

"Good morning everyone, I'm Alana Stephens, and welcome to CGR."

"And I'm Vance Hiller. Thank you so much for joining us on our first day."

"We're embarking on something very different," said Alana, her dazzling eyes jumping through the high-def plasma. "And we hope you'll stay with us as we bring you something that's never been attempted in broadcasting; a new way of looking at things."

"And CGR isn't just for women," said Vance. "There's plenty of good information here for guys as well, so stick around."

One hour later it was clear we had nothing to worry about. The first sixty minutes had been flawless, and left no doubt as to the agenda of the network or who was in charge.

"They look great," said Neely.

"The whole product looks great," said Jillian, just as my private line rang. "The set is spectacular."

It was Madison. "If the girls are there with you put me on speaker," she said, and I did. "I'm really proud of you guys," she said. "It looks better than I ever imagined. This is a terrific start."

"Thank you," I said, and the girls chimed in.

"I'll be there in an hour," she said.

"A little early for you," I said.

"Scott's not exactly in the mood anymore."

Well, so much for the perfect start to my day. "I'm sorry, Madison."

"Whatever. He went home just before five."

And I'm sure he'll be all smiles when he gets to work.

* * *

By six that evening I wasn't sure how I was ever going to come down off the lift the day had provided. Although I was probably going to follow Alana's lead. A few minutes after her shift ended at eight this morning she walked into my office, face flushed, leading Vance by the hand, and said, "Loft. Keys. Now." I knew the look as the natural high all anchors have coming off the set, which makes it impossible for people who work the late newscast to get to sleep before two in the morning. Anyway, an hour later she wandered back, licking her lips as she tossed me the keys. "Breakfast of champions," she said, as I put the keys back in my desk.

"I'd better put the cleaning service on standby," I said. "I think it's gonna be a busy day for the loft."

She shook her head. "Not necessary this time. Vance went off-script."

"Huh?"

"My feet never touched the floor, much less the bed. Vance won't need to go to the gym today after keeping my hundred and fifteen pounds in the air for half an hour. I just joined the mile-high club without getting on a plane."

There are those Southern euphemisms again. Who would ever guess that an anchor going off-script would mean he would nail his co-anchor against the door like Sonny Corleone?

Despite Vance and Alana's flying circus, the usage of the loft would necessitate a quick trip to *Bed Bath and Beyond* by noon, where we discovered you cannot buy five hundred thread-count sheets in bulk. Meanwhile, my phone had been buzzing with congratulatory calls, most from women I hadn't heard from in years who saw the bandwagon rolling and wanted to jump on it for a ride. Or jump on the men we'd hired. (Sorry, too late on both counts.) The sales manager dropped by to tell me that advertisers were lining up after sampling the product, while Madison had been fielding more interview requests from every local newspaper and a dozen entertainment publications. Amanda dropped by to invite us all out to the most expensive restaurant in town.

We had officially achieved "IT" status in less than twenty-four hours. (Of course, you can lose it just as quick in this business. The higher the mountain, the longer the fall.)

The anticipation of the public had been rewarded.

In fact, it looked like we'd delivered even more than promised.

* * *

I woke to the smell of brewing coffee and frying bacon. I opened my eyes and saw a whole bunch of newspapers neatly stacked on the pillow next to me.

"Ah, you're up," said Harrell, our fill-in anchor, as he entered the room carrying a glass of freshly squeezed orange juice. He wore a pair of gray boxers and nothing else as he sat on the edge of the bed and handed me the glass.

"And you've been shopping," I said, patting the newspapers while sipping the ice cold tart citrus, swirling it around my mouth to kill the fire-breathing dragon.

"I ran down to the newsstand." I looked him up and down. "I did put on pants, if that's what you're wondering."

"Very nice of you, though I'm sure no one would have complained." I cocked my head toward the newspapers. "Did you read 'em yet?"

"Waiting for you." He smiled, then reached over, grabbed the tabloid on the top of the stack and handed it to me like a fragile heirloom. "Figured we could read the reviews together." He pointed at the headline and slapped his face in feigned amazement. "Oh look, we're on the front page!"

I sat up, stretched my eyes open, and was greeted by a one hundred forty-four point validation of what we'd done.

Cougars Roar in Cable Debut

I ripped open the paper and found the story on page three, as Harrell slid into bed next to me to read along. I moved closer, stealing his warmth and breathing in his Aramis cologne. Then he put one long arm around me and held both ends of the paper while I rested my head back against his chest. (If everyone read the morning paper this way, no one would ever get to work.)

CGR is the Cat's Meow

By Jessica Hale

Back in the 1970s, when women began to seriously infiltrate the television news business, there was a common rallying cry among the men who controlled it.

"Keep the broads out of broadcasting."

Well, CGR has taken the industry full circle. The new 24-hour cable network that promotes itself as a "theater of information" has a decidedly female slant, and one that belongs to women of a certain age.

These "broads" are experienced, authoritative, credible, and oh yeah... extremely attractive women over thirty. Each paired with a younger (in some cases, much younger) hunk who is easy on the eyes. The gals do the heavy lifting on CGR, taking care of any stories that might remotely resemble hard news; the fluff, lifestyle, and gossipy pieces go to the men. The traditional gender roles are totally reversed, while political correctness doesn't exist. Double entendres between the anchors are

commonplace, making you wonder if there's more than just a working relationship among the anchor teams.

And it makes for addictive viewing. Especially if you're a woman.

"Sounds like we've got at least one loyal viewer," I said.

"So," said Harrell, "I'm easy on the eyes?"

I looked up at him. "Ridiculously easy on the eyes," I said. I turned, picked up the next paper and handed it to him, then settled back in my trophy buck recliner with my glass of juice. "And other body parts as well."

We pored through the papers like kids opening toys on Christmas morning. The reviews were all basically positive, though a few deducted points for our blatant sexism. The word cougar crept into just about every piece that was written. Only one snooty newspaper took dead aim, focusing on the CGR acronym with the phrase, **"Was SLT already taken?"**

"I think," said Harrell, "that you may be the first female television news executive ever accused of being blatantly sexist."

"Hey," I said, turning to face him. "I love a good compliment."

He started to nuzzle my neck, but the phone rang. (Phonus interruptus.) The Caller ID told me I needed to answer. Harrell grabbed the cordless and handed it to me. I took the phone while he wrapped his arms around my waist. "Hello?"

"Syd, it's Madison."

"Hi, Madison. Did you read all the reviews?"

"Yes, and they're great. But I need you to come in as soon as possible."

The serious tone in her voice told me this wasn't good. "Problem?"

"Not over the phone, Syd. Just get here as soon as possible." She hung up.

I leaned back and gave Harrell a kiss. "Gotta go."

"What happened?"

"Don't know. But there's some fire that needs to be to put out and I've got the extinguisher."

Paradise sure has a short shelf life.

CHAPTER EIGHT

Madison and Amanda were already in the conference room with a female suit I didn't recognize. The woman was holding some papers that had a light blue cover.

Which either means you just bought a house or you're being sued.

"Syd, great job yesterday," said Amanda. "I can't be more pleased with the product or the response. Some terrific reviews in the papers."

"Thanks. What's up?"

"We're being sued for discrimination," said Madison.

I knew it! The Monopoly Guy had been waiting for the right moment.

"What a surprise," I said.

"Oh, Syd, this is Stacy Heller, one of our corporate attorneys," said Madison, who didn't look as concerned as she sounded on the phone.

"Pleasure to meet you," said the lawyer, extending her hand across the table. She was a fortyish, pert brunette in a light gray suit and a lacy beige silk blouse buttoned all the way to her neck. Her hazel eyes shone bright with sincerity through her bone frame glasses. "Loved the premiere yesterday. It was a great success."

"Thanks, you're very kind," I said. "Will we be in business long enough to enjoy it?"

"Don't worry," said Amanda.

"You said that when I mentioned this the first time," I said. "Now it's real."

"What do you know about the plaintiff?" asked the attorney, who scanned the legal document. "Todd Jones."

"Not much, really. He apparently applied for one of the anchor jobs. Forty-five-year-old guy who looks like he should be handing out *get out of jail free* cards."

"Did you ever see his tape or look at his application?" she asked.

I shook my head. "He's way too old so we never saw his tape. We sorted out the applications and didn't consider any men over thirty. Of course, we didn't consider any women *under* thirty. So don't be surprised if some twenty-two-year-old bimbo jumps on us as well and starts some class action."

"Madison tells me you talked to him on the phone. Do you think you were being recorded?"

"I do now."

"Can you recall the conversation for me?"

I recapped the call for her, short as it was. "We're screwed, aren't we?" I asked.

"Not necessarily," said the attorney. "You broke down a lot of barriers. You hired a lot of women no one else would touch because of their age."

"And a lot of men with zero experience," I added. "Plus, there are a few… tiny little details concerning our hiring practices and, uh, other duties our employees have."

The lawyer looked at Amanda. "Something else I should know?"

"Go ahead. Tell her," said Amanda.

Now I know how Neely feels when she goes to confession. "Okay. Well, in no particular order, all the men had to be extremely good looking and agree to have sex with us so we could, uh, check their references before hiring them. The ones we signed sleep with their co-anchors on a regular basis. And we have a secret loft on the top floor that sees more hook-ups during the day than a cable installer."

The lawyer pulled off her glasses and her eyes grew wide. "You're serious?"

"You can't make up stuff *this* good," I said.

She turned to Amanda and Madison. "You *knew* about this?"

"Not only do we know about it," said Madison, trying to hold back a grin, "we're part of it."

"The fringe benefits around here are incredible," said Amanda. "And I'm only here a few days each month."

The attorney's mouth hung open. "So that story I read about Scott Harry a while back was all true?"

More nods.

"And you have a room upstairs that you use during business hours?" she asked.

"The sheets are on fire," I said.

"Damn, I'm in the wrong business," said the attorney, shaking her head. "I thought making out in the law library when I was a clerk was pushing the envelope."

"So how is *that* going to play in a court of law?" I asked.

"I wouldn't be lying to say that kind of testimony puts us in uncharted territory."

"You've gotta settle with this guy," I said. "Discrimination is one thing, but this other stuff can't come out in open court."

"It won't come out as long as he sticks to the age issue. He doesn't work here, so he doesn't know about your... benefits package. But let me worry about the legal implications," said the attorney, who looked remarkably calm despite our outlandish revelations. "We do have several good cards to play."

"And those would be?" I asked.

"First, the word *news* is not associated with CGR. It's called a report, not a newscast. The slogan is *theater of information*. Again, the word *news* is not included. This is no more a newscast than *Entertainment Tonight* and they *really* don't hire unattractive people for that program either. It's a television show, pure and simple. And like any other television show, it has stars, and you're entitled to be subjective in your hiring practices."

"But we only hired women with news experience," I said.

"Doesn't matter," said Amanda.

"We do have one more card up our sleeve," said the attorney.

"What's that?" I asked.

"There will be women on the jury."

* * *

I'm not sure of the exact origin of the term "the shit has hit the fan" and I don't really care to look it up on Wikipedia. In real life, should a pile of actual shit hit an actual electric fan, it would leave an actual mess.

In New York, the shit hits the fan in the form of a giant headline in a New York tabloid just about every day. The tri-state area has a never ending supply of manure.

So when I read the phrase **"Too Old For Sex"** in a typeface generally reserved for the end of a war, you might as well have cleaned out all the stalls at Belmont Park and dumped the horseshit into my central air conditioning unit.

My bleary eyes cleared instantly as I ducked back into the safety of my townhouse. I felt my knees weaken, so I sat on the cold brick floor. There he was, the Monopoly Guy, looking at me from what little space was left on the front page under the headline.

And then, I opened the paper and saw myself without looking in the mirror.

Right there on page three, my picture side by side with the cue ball, under another lovely configuration of bold type.

SEX DISCRIMINATION:

"I couldn't get hired because she didn't want to sleep with me."

99

I dropped the paper in my lap as I buried my head in my hands. Ho-lee shit.

I didn't want to read the article, but I had to.

And I knew it was probably going to be worse than the headline.

I kept my head in my hands, slowly spreading the ring and middle fingers of each hand to make room for my eyes, like some crazed fanboy doing a double Vulcan salute at a Star Trek convention.

Sadly, I wasn't dreaming. The article was still there slapping me in the face.

By Harry Kartleman

The two-day-old CGR cable network is off to a flying start, both on the air and in the courtroom. Or is it the bedroom?

A forty-five-year-old man has filed a discrimination suit against the network, contending that his age and appearance knocked him out of consideration for a job. Todd Jones, a former anchor who applied for one of the many slots at the new network, claims that CGR's big kahuna, Sydney Hack, did not even consider his video résumé tape because he was over thirty and unattractive.

"Look at the guys they hired," said Jones, a bald, stocky man with an old-fashioned handlebar moustache. "All young hunks under thirty. Half of them have never even been in front of a camera. And you're telling me they're more qualified than I am?"

But this isn't just any age discrimination suit. More damaging to CGR are the charges of the internal machinations behind the scenes and the manner in which its current anchors were chosen. Male anchors reportedly are required to provide sexual favors to their co-anchors on a regular basis. In addition, midday trysts are burning up the sheets in a secret hideaway on the top floor, known simply as "The Loft."

Jones contends those men who were hired were required to

"have their references checked" on a casting couch.

CGR attorneys called the lawsuit "frivolous" and "without merit."

Hack, you may remember, was accused of sexual harassment earlier this year by local anchor Scott Harry, who still remains employed by the network's local affiliate. She has raised eyebrows in the broadcast industry by pairing middle-aged women with younger men at the network's local affiliates. The moves have resulted in an increase in ratings for every station.

I segued quickly from upset to pissed off.

My eyes narrowed as I tried to bore holes with my stare at the Monopoly Guy.

Okay, buddy. You want war, bring it on.

Meanwhile, it's time I plugged that damned leak.

* * *

I finished reading the entire legal document and slapped it on my desk. "I knew it. The stuff in the newspaper isn't mentioned in the lawsuit," I said, as we huddled in my office with the door closed and the blinds drawn. "This had to come from the inside. No one on the outside knows about the loft. No one else could know the term *checking references*."

"Gotta be Scott," said Rica. "He's the only disgruntled employee around here. Everyone else is too new to be jaded."

"Or too damned happy," I said.

Jillian and Neely both nodded. "Can we let him go?" asked Jillian. "When is his contract up?"

I shook my head. "Not soon enough and not an option. If we fired him right after the newspaper article it will look too suspicious. We've got a window in a few months, so we *could* let him go then. But if we haven't settled this thing by that time we can't get rid of him or he'll testify against us. We're stuck with him for the time being, like it or not."

"We could demote him," said Rica. "Take him off the anchor desk."

"Nah, he's a terrible reporter," I said. "That's only gonna hurt the product and piss him off even more. Besides, his ratings are still strong."

The conversation stopped for a minute as we struggled to find a solution.

"There *is* one sure-fire way to find out what he's up to," said Neely, looking directly at me. "We need to be nice to him. And Syd, I know you don't want to hear this, but you're the only one who can do it."

My face tightened as if I'd eaten spoiled food. "Oh, no, you are not suggesting that I—"

"I'm afraid so," said Neely. "The only way to get any information out of him is in the bedroom, and your body is the truth serum."

"Great idea, Neely," said Jillian.

"Great idea, Neely," I said, mocking Jillian in a nasal tone. "Sure," I said. "Great idea from *your* point of view. You're not the one who'd have to sleep with him."

"Aw, c'mon Syd," said Rica. "You used to rave about the guy before he played the commitment card. And he's not exactly chopped liver."

"Really," said Jillian. "How many women have to use the centrifugal force of a ceiling fan to collect their laundry after a date? It's not like we're asking you to engage in combat duty."

"It has to be you, Syd," said Neely. "I mean, I'd nail him, but he's not gonna open up to me."

"You'd nail anything with a pulse," said Rica. "Maybe you ought to give the plaintiff a call and then he'd go away."

They were right about Scott. Much as I hated to admit it. "Ironic, isn't it?" I said.

"What?" asked Rica.

"Scott's the guy who started it all, and I just thought he was perfect the first time. Now the idea of having sex with him makes my stomach turn."

"Shit," said Jillian. "We really *are* turning into men."

* * *

I flip open my compact one last time, and I'm glad to see the look in the mirror.

My game face is on tonight, and I'm not talking about make-up. And when that's the case, men don't stand a chance against me.

I am the Red Queen, cruising for my prey in the company limousine. I don't need hot lights or bamboo shoots under the fingernails to break a man. The strategy to get information out of Scott is simple.

Wear one incredibly hot outfit and screw his brains out until the sexual aftershocks make him look like he's been hit with a taser.

I could even take the subtle approach, hinting that I might have made a mistake with our relationship, that I miss him, that we might have a future together. (One of these days, I gotta go to confession with Neely. I'm probably up to about a hundred Our Fathers by now.) A lotta alcohol, a lotta sex, and he'll come clean.

I was going to wear Scott's favorite ensemble, but Neely said I needed something different to blow him away. (Not that you need clothes to do that.) So I borrowed some stuff from Jillian, which she says is a personal bedroom preference of The Snack. Electric blue sequined halter minidress, about mid-thigh; skin-tight black boots that just cover the knee. Red hair teased out like it was 1988. Fire engine red lipstick, forest green eyeshadow. I'm one hundred and thirty-five pounds of pure toned fantasy and Scott doesn't have to pay a dime. Even though, as I ran my hand across the soft black leather upholstery, I *felt* expensive.

The men on the sidewalk rubbernecked like they were driving on the Long Island Expressway as the driver held the door open and I exited the limo, extending one long leg with the promise of better things to come. (A burly guy walked into a trash can, causing me to laugh and break character for a moment as he hopped around and grabbed his banged knee. He looked back at me and yelled, "Your fault, lady!")

Okay, game face back on, I walked up the steps and rang the bell. There was a serious chill in the air, and for just a moment I cursed the hemline of the dress.

But just for a moment.

The door opens, and Scott's jaw slowly falls open. "Whoa," he said, eyes wide.

(Had he said, "Syd, what the hell are you doing here?" or "I didn't order a girl," I knew I'd be in trouble.)

"Hello, Scott," I said, keeping my voice low and sultry.

"I… uh….Madison was going to—"

"Madison and I swapped," I said, walking inside. "I hope that's okay. Actually, it doesn't matter if it's okay with you because it's what *I* wanted tonight."

"Uh… yeah, of course it's okay." (Big smile begins to grow, among other things. He's half dressed, by the way, in boxers and an unbuttoned shirt.)

"It's cold outside," I said. "I need to get warmed up." I close the door behind me. I dip my head and look up at him through my eyelashes while throwing my lower lip into a pout as I run both hands underneath his shirt and up his chest. "I've not been very nice to you lately, Scott, and I wanted to apologize. And I've been having second thoughts about… things. I hope you'll let me make it up to you and give me a second chance. I'd like to see where this relationship goes." I run my hands down his chest onto his stomach and he inhales quickly. "If you'd like to start over."

Oh, his eyes are filled with fireworks. "Of course, Syd. You know the door is always open for you. I was always hoping you'd come back."

Sixty seconds and I've already set the hook.

(See, this is the difference between men and women. Women

wouldn't fall for this crap. But one short skirt, big hair, some dominatrix boots, and a man's brain goes into vapor lock.)

"Thank you, Scott."

He started to button his shirt. "I'm, uh, not quite ready. You're a half hour early."

"I know." I took his hand and stopped him. "I wanted an appetizer before dinner. Just a quick bite before we go out. So don't bother getting dressed now, you'll only have to do it again."

* * *

An hour and two drinks in the limo later, Scott was well on his way to letting down his guard. My half hour of torture in his bedroom might have violated the Patriot Act, but it sure sent a clear message.

So now we're seated at a corner table of one of Manhattan's classiest restaurants. (Well, okay, not that classy… I mean, they let me walk in here looking like a high-priced hooker.) The place was filled with quiet conversation and understated violin music, and very little in the way of incandescent light. The well-heeled patrons sported thousand dollar suits and dresses that could pay down the national debt. My blue sequins shone like a beacon in a sea of gray pin stripes and New York black. We were sipping drink number four as the waiter served a decadent white chocolate concoction on bone china so pure you could read a newspaper through it.

The sweet chocolate sent a rush into my veins while I ran my leg up Scott's shin. "You know what I'd like to do now?"

His quick inhale was audible. "No, what?" he asked. He was ready to go home, but I pushed the torture a little farther.

"Shoot some pool."

His face twisted like a dishrag. "Excuse me?"

"Just for a while. I love to shoot pool and I haven't done it for such a long time." I ran my finger across the china, scooping up the last of the chocolate, before swallowing the finger and slowly

105

pulling it out. "But maybe we could ride around for a while in the limo first. I've got it for the entire night."

The smile magically returned. "Okay. Pool it is."

God, this is easy.

* * *

To say I was overdressed for a pool hall is putting it mildly. I'm sure the only time they've seen sequins in this place was when the gay pride parade route went past the front door and one of the participants needed to use the restroom.

But, 'tis all part of the plan. Actually, this part was Neely's idea. In her words, "While the perfect Southern woman has biscuits in the oven and her buns in bed, she must be able to stop traffic in a party dress and, at the same time, excel in at least one male activity. Men love women who like to do guy stuff. It's the ultimate turn-on. If you can do it while dressed like a whore, game over." So, since bowling in sequins and heels is out of the question, and I'm actually pretty decent with a cue stick (hey, hold the jokes, okay?), we were shooting a few racks in what would be considered an upscale billiard room. Beautiful mahogany inlaid tables with red felt, colorful Tiffany lamps throwing soft rectangles of light on the tables, no cigarette smoke, a few of the men fresh from the corporate wars with ties loosened around starched white French cuffed shirts. The constant clacking of the billiard balls mixed with the conversation at the packed bar. Every time it was my turn I picked a shot that forced me to stretch and lift one leg off the floor while leaning over the table in Scott's direction. (The first time I did this the guy at the next table missed his shot so badly he sent the cue ball flying off the felt and crashing through the mirror behind the bar.) Every time I chalked the cue I twisted it, then rounded my lips and blew off the residue very slowly.

And the fact that I'd won three games of eight-ball in a row, while not getting any chalk on my cleavage, had him impressed.

Of course, he might have been a bit distracted and missed just about every damned shot. (Neely has *got* to get a publishing deal.) He was sipping a beer, which meant he had downed six drinks and been serviced twice like a car at an efficient ten minute oil change shop.

I sank the eight ball in the side pocket and slid the cue stick back into a rack on the far wall. "Okay, I got my pool fix," I said.

"Ready to go back to my place now?" he said, looking like an excited puppy about to wet on the rug.

"Sure, Scott. Rack 'em up. Take me home."

Cue the ring card girl. Round three was coming.

* * *

Scott lay back, totally spent and still half in the bag after drinks number seven and eight. (I'd only been sipping my drinks all night, never actually finishing a single one, so I was still several million brain cells ahead of him.) I leaned up on one elbow and looked down at him while tracing his jawline with one long red fingernail. "So, is my apology accepted?" I asked. "Or must I continue to get on my knees and beg forgiveness?"

He was having trouble staying awake. "Good God, Syd, you've been incredible tonight."

"Wanna go again?"

"You kidding? I think I'm out of bodily fluids."

I laid my head on his chest, looking at him while I ran one hand across his hairless six-pack. "Well, you just re-charge those batteries and maybe I can take care of you for breakfast."

He stroked my hair and looked up at me, deep into my eyes. "It's nice to have you back. I'll try not to push you this time."

"Forget it, Scott. Ancient history. Like I said, I've been a little abrupt with everyone. I think the stress with the launch just caught up with me." I paused for a moment, then threw my first fishing line in the water. "Then, just when I thought it was over we get sued."

Okay, Syd, pay attention. If the boy is ever gonna spill, he's going to do it now.

"I was really concerned about you when I read the paper," he said. "And since we're in apology mode tonight…"

The eyes grew sad and looked away. Okay, this was it. *There's the wounded doe!*

Lock and load, babe.

He looked back at me. "I wanted to say I'm sorry for going to the tabloid."

Aha! Three orgasms and a ton of booze really is the new truth serum!

"*Really* sorry," he added. "It's been bothering me for months, despite the way I've been acting at work."

Wait a minute. *Months?* "You mean—"

"I wasn't really trying to get out of my contract, Syd. I love this job. It's the best gig ever. I mean, I get to anchor in New York, and even though I didn't have you I had Madison, and I do like spending time with her a lot. But you hurt me and I wanted to hurt you back. I know that's really immature."

I didn't say anything. His eyes were moist, sincere. Then he totally took the wind out of my sails.

"I felt really bad when I read the paper this morning and they dredged up the story again. I was really hoping it would go away, that maybe over time you'd forgive me. And then some idiot has to file a lawsuit."

Son of a bitch.

Scott's not the leak.

He wiped his eyes, then wrapped one arm around me and pulled me close. "I feel a lot better now that it's off my chest. You wanna go again and let me finish *my* apology the right way?"

Oh, shit.

CHAPTER NINE

"Oh, shit!" said Rica. "You're friggin' kiddin' me!"

I shook my head as the girls looked at me in amazement from my office couch. "It's not him." I rolled my eyes and leaned back in my chair, staring at the ceiling. "Dammit!"

"Are you *absolutely* sure?" asked Jillian.

"I did everything but waterboard the man's genitals. If he can keep a secret after five times—"

Neely interrupted. "I thought you said four?"

"Hell, he wanted to apologize *to me* this morning."

"Boy's got stamina," said Rica. "I'll give him that."

"Oh, shit," said Jillian, her eyes suddenly going wide and telling me she'd just gotten the second part of the equation. "I just realized something. Not only do we not know who the leak is, but now you're back in a relationship with Scott."

"Oh, shit," said Neely.

"By the way," said Jillian, "if this makes you feel any better, you looked gorgeous last night."

I sat up straight in my chair. "Huh?"

Jillian handed me a New York tabloid, open to the gossip page. There I was, in all my sequined glamour, heading for the limo with Scott Harry in tow.

Oh, shit.

"At least the caption is complimentary," said Neely.

I read it aloud. "Red Queen paints the town blue. CGR's va-va-voom exec Sydney Hack doing the hot spots with local anchor Scott Harry."

"So do we call you *va-va* or *voom* from now on?" asked Rica.

"Very funny," I said. (Though deep down I must admit that being called attractive with a 1950s term was kinda cool.)

"By the way, Madison stopped by before you got in," said Jillian.

"Oh, shit," I said, not laughing. *Could this day get any worse?*

"Oh shit nothing," said Jillian. "She's beaming about the overnights. The ratings are great. Put all the crap with Scott and the Monopoly Guy aside, we're a hit."

"People are sampling," I said, shrugging off the news. "That's all."

"People were sampling the *first* day," said Neely. "That always happens for a new show, then the ratings drop by half the second day. In our case the ratings have actually *gone up* each day this week. You should be thrilled. *We're* all thrilled. All this other stuff with Scott and the lawsuit means nothing as long as the ratings are up. Look on the bright side."

"Whatever," I said, still trying to sort things out in my head as I stared at my desk blotter. "Did she say anything about the picture in the paper?"

"She said you looked great and wanted to know where you got the dress," said Neely. I was still looking down at my desk when her finger reached across and lifted my chin. "C'mon, sweetie, the product is a hit, we're getting tons of publicity and we're all getting nailed more than a house on a remodeling show. These are just a few bumps in the road. It's not that bad."

"Not that bad? I've just had more sex than a girl at a frat party for reasons that now make no sense, Scott thinks I'm interested in him again, my ass is splashed all over a tabloid in four colors, and I'm being sued for not sleeping with bald men."

"Do you have any idea how ridiculous you sound?" asked Jillian.

"If you were in my shoes," I said, "you'd see things differently."

"Ah, suck it up," said Rica.

I glared at her.

"Okay," she said, "poor choice of words. Get tough. You can handle this."

(I know, at this point you're saying, "Jeez, the girl has hot and cold running men at her beck and call and she's complaining?") I'm sorry, but I want everything perfect.

And I'm going to have it.

The Red Queen will not be denied.

* * *

The world looks better at the beginning of a new week.

The girls took me out last night and it felt good to let my hair down, though between my copper top and the tabloid picture, my days of being able to hide are over. The parade of older men coming over to our table was getting to be annoying, so Rica decided it was time we all learned how to perfect the death stare. Being Italian, with those dark features, she's got an advantage. (Not that she really needs it with that voice when she says, "Get lawst, buddy.") But it was still interesting to try putting up a force field while three sheets to the wind. Jillian has too much class to pull it off, and let's face it, blue-eyed strawberry blondes aren't terribly scary. Rica said she ends up looking like a hung-over version of the Little Mermaid. Neely, meanwhile, squints too much and ends up with something resembling an angry squirrel. Me? Well, I made the mistake of wearing a tight angora sweater, so no man was looking at my eyes anyway. Rica says I have potential and am a work in progress, though Neely said I reminded her of Patrick Swayze in *Ghost* when he's trying to move the soda can in the subway with his sheer will.

Despite the fact that the death stare is a tactic for evenings, it will be appropriate this morning, since we're having our first meeting with the Monopoly Guy and his team of attorneys in the hope of making this thing go away quickly. Of course, the chances of that happening are the same as me going down the aisle with Scott, or of Neely being celibate for Lent.

Today, of course, my game face is different. Oh, I still have some make-up and my dress is too short for business, but Neutron Syd is in the building.

Death stare or not, I'm here to kick ass. As are the rest of the girls.

Stacy Heller, our attorney, had us all gather an hour early to brief us and told us we had to "draw the curtains on our anger" since it was fifty-fifty that Rica might, at some point, actually take the Monopoly Guy out in the hall and kick the living shit out of him. She'd already told us not to expect a settlement, that this is all part of the game with lawyers marking their territory. We insisted on meeting in our conference room, since Stacy said it is important that we remain on our own turf. The Monopoly Guy's attorney bitched about it but caved. If the guy wants money, he'll have to come over here to get it. I had no idea that so much about law was psychological warfare. Get this, Stacy's got a pot of ice-cold coffee and very stale donuts on a silver tray in the middle of the table, part of that "revenge is a dish served cold" thing. We, of course, have the hot steaming java in our cups and fresh Danish.

I like Stacy immensely. She's a ballsy little thing, and, like Rica, I'd want her in my foxhole because I get the feeling she wouldn't fight fair.

The intercom buzzed with the news that the enemy had arrived. Stacy, Madison, and Amanda took seats at the table, while the girls and I grabbed chairs that lined the wall behind them.

A polite knock on the door preceded the contingent that followed. We all stood up as the Monopoly Guy entered first, followed by the people who he obviously hired to fight fire with fire. Two hot young male attorneys who looked fresh out of law school. (Future anchors?) And… what the hell is this? One statuesque mid-thirties redhead with a briefcase.

Hey, woman, you're wearing my Red Queen outfit.

I stared daggers at her. Jillian leaned over and whispered in my ear. "Down, girl."

Big Red sized me up, threw her shoulders back, and gave me a quick glare. (Redheads don't like other redheads in the same room... we like being the novelty.) I tried to stand taller and fired what I think is the death stare back at her, though I'll have to wait for Rica's review.

"Good morning," said our attorney, extending her hand to her counterpart. "Stacy Heller."

The towering redhead shook it. "Kate O'Hara." She turned toward the rest of the group. "My associates, Stan Karven and James Florell. And the plaintiff, Mister Todd Jones."

Stacy finished the introductions as I sized up the opposition. The two guys were, I decided, just window dressing. I'm guessing the subliminal message they'd be going for in the courtroom was that men could work for women without having to sleep with them. (Though considering Ms. O'Hara's appearance, I'm sure these two wouldn't complain.)

But Big Red was all business, despite the pale green eyes, porcelain skin and killer legs that cried out for a career on a modeling runway, or a street corner. The red hair was brighter than mine, a little more fire engine to my copper, and cut straight, to hit the shoulders, with some bangs that worked well for her. I guessed she was about six feet tall as she stood in a burnt sienna business suit, skirt at the knee and low heels complementing her well-turned ankles. Her jacket accented her broad shoulders, kind of a throwback to the stuff Linda Evans wore on *Dynasty*.

She's the glamazon attorney. She looked as though she could snap Stacy like a twig, but our girl stood toe to toe with her and didn't back down.

Meanwhile, in the shallow end of the genetic pool, the Monopoly Guy was even uglier up close, and his apparent tendency to bathe in cheap musky cologne announced his arrival at our end of the room. If he was forty-five years old, his face didn't get the memo.

Bald as an egg, with indentations on each side of his forehead that looked like he'd been whacked with the pointy end of a steam iron. His handlebar moustache attempted to draw your attention away from deep-set beady brown eyes and puffy jowls which made you wonder if he was storing acorns for the winter. He was eyeing the donuts like a starving man in the desert. (Newspeople cannot resist free food. Remind me to tell you about the laxative brownie episode sometime.)

"This guy was an anchor?" whispered Rica? "On what planet?"

(He is obviously what is known as a "piece of the furniture" anchor, who generally starts in one small market and doesn't have the talent to go anywhere else. The audience grows fond of him, like a favorite old recliner they're too sentimental about to throw out. Doesn't matter if he turns into a mountain troll, they'll still watch him because he's been there forever.)

Monopoly Guy is short, maybe five-six, and built like a fireplug. I look at him and keep thinking that with the right hat and a white beard he's got a future as the real-life version of the Travelocity Roaming Gnome.

Stacy started the meeting as soon as everyone was seated. "Ms. O'Hara, why don't we cut to the chase and you can just tell me what you're looking for, and maybe we can make this unpleasant situation go away with a minimum of animosity."

"Very well," she said, as she pulled some documents and a legal pad from her briefcase. "My client has suffered emotional distress from this ordeal—"

Stacy cut her off. "Excuse me, emotional distress? He applied for a job and didn't get it, like millions of Americans do every day." Well, that didn't last long. She was setting the tone right away. So much for the minimum of animosity.

"In addition," said O'Hara, "we contend that the hiring practices of this network do not comply with federal guidelines, and that you are also in violation of sexual harassment laws—"

"Your client is not an employee so he can't file a harassment charge—"

"My client was not hired simply because of his age and the fact that the female executives of your network do not find him sexually attractive." Her voice was measured, almost staccato in delivery, without emotion.

"I think she's a cyborg," whispered Neely.

Meanwhile, Monopoly Guy was not paying attention to his attorney or what's going on; he was apparently trying to flirt with me. Was this some fishing expedition to see if I'd nail anything in pants? He gave me a quick smile as he sucked in his gut and thrust out his chin, trying to create a jawline that was probably last seen during the Reagan administration. I had planned to give him the death stare, but what the hell, I'd play along. I ran my tongue over my lips just to yank his chain, and his eyes widened.

"It's TV," said Stacy. "In case you hadn't noticed, it's filled with pretty people. Sexually unattractive people are kind of hard to find these days on the tube." Stacy noted that the Monopoly Guy was now staring at the donuts with the same lust he'd been throwing in my direction. "Help yourself, Mister Jones." The guy waited one nanosecond before pouncing on a donut, while he began to fix a cup of coffee.

"But this is a news broadcast," said Big Red. "The rules do not apply—"

Stacy interrupted again. "And where do you see the word *news* anywhere on this network?"

"Fine, so you call it a *report*. It's all semantics. Everyone knows it's a newscast."

Stacy put up her hands. "Look, we can argue all day, but let's get to the bottom line. What does your client want? What figure makes this all go away today?"

At this point it should be noted that Monopoly Guy has prepared his coffee (not noticing the milk is curdled) and is about to take a bite of a jelly donut which is so petrified that if New York were suddenly nuked, we'd all be vaporized but the donuts would survive.

Big Red wrote down a figure on the legal pad, tore off the page, and slid it across the table to Stacy. (Why the hell she couldn't just say it out loud is beyond me. I guess she wanted to read Stacy's reaction.)

Stacy raised one eyebrow. "You gotta be kidding. Two point four million?"

As luck would have it, she said this just as the Monopoly Guy, now back to leering at me, took a big bite of the donut, realized it had an expiration date of 1999, then tried to wash it down with very cold, very old coffee. He gagged just as Stacy finished her sentence.

"You okay, Mister Jones?" she asked. "Or do I take it that you're as flabbergasted over the amount as I am?"

Nice.

He coughed a few times, wiped the powdered sugar from his mouth, and managed to get out the words, "I'm fine," though it sounded like he was underwater. He shook his head as he looked at me. I took a sip of my own coffee and smiled as the steam rose from the cup, then shrugged at him like I had no idea what was wrong with his brew.

Stacy flipped the paper back to her counterpart like a card dealer in a casino. "Offer rejected."

"This will be the only day an offer will be made," said Big Red. "If I don't have a check by the close of business today, we're going to court, and then all the dirty little secrets of this network will be out in public. Surely the damage from that will far exceed the amount we're asking for."

"We don't have any secrets," said Stacy. "In fact, half of them are already in the tabloids, so that ship has sailed already. You want to go to court, take your best shot. And let me save you the trouble of hanging around the office all day. No way in hell we're cutting you a check."

"Very well," said the attorney, gathering up her documents and reloading her briefcase. "We'll be in touch." We all stood as they got up and left the room, the Monopoly Guy coughing the whole way.

Stacy moved to the door and closed it. "Okay, that was round one."

"I thought there was going to be a negotiation," I said.

She shook her head. "I wanted them to *think* there would be, but I had no intention of offering anything. If we settled this case it would open the floodgates for everyone else who applied for a job. Always get their hopes up and then pull the rug out from under them. It demoralizes the client, who thinks he's going to walk away with an easy victory."

"You really think we can win this," I said.

She nodded. "No doubt." She started to pack up her things and then changed the subject. "Before I go I'd like to get all your impressions of the plaintiff."

"Not your typical anchor by any means," I said. "There are a few bald guys on the network, but there aren't many. Where did he work again?"

"He spent eleven years in a small town in West Virginia," said Stacy.

"Not surprising," said Jillian. "He looks like a one-market anchor."

"He looks like an ad for a laxative," said Neely. "The *before* part of the ad."

Rica cracked her knuckles. "I could take him. No problem."

"I meant," said Stacy, "your impressions on his marketability in the broadcast industry. He's been out of the business for a long time."

"Well, I haven't seen his tape," I said, "but strictly based on appearance he'd have a hard time getting hired anywhere for an on-air job."

"Any other thoughts?" asked Stacy.

"That is one big cold redhead," said Neely. "You think I should send Vance over to defrost her?"

Despite the imminent threat of a jury trial that would create more national headlines, we're back to the business at hand of running the network. Week two is going so smoothly it's almost on autopilot, while the buzz about the product continues in the newspapers and entertainment magazines. The action in the loft has slowed down to a more normal level, though I'm still going to have to adjust the budget for the linen service.

And with everything going so well on the air and in the bedroom, we can spend a little time on an exciting new project that Amanda assigned to Neely.

Simply known as *The Manual.*

Well, that's not the official title, and we don't even have one yet, but the concept is simple. We're going to put together a how-to guide for every woman over thirty who wants a younger man, and we're supposed to come up with every possible scenario. Amanda has already got a publishing deal in place and wants to strike while the iron is hot, so we're fast-tracking this thing. She also likes Neely's creativity and thinks her traditional Southern Belle biscuits-and-buns philosophy will add a nice touch.

(I also think Amanda wants to lighten things up a bit for us, as we're much more productive when we're having fun. While the lawsuit and the source of the leak are still in the back of my mind, I'm not letting those things dominate my life.)

So we're at Neely's place tonight, gathered around the gas fireplace in the living room that has nicely taken the chill off the room. Since this is her project she wanted to host a little "launch party" and start collecting ideas. And since we're on our second pitcher of vodka-something-or-other, coming up with stuff should be a breeze. My muse is always more productive minus a few brain cells.

One look at her townhouse tells you she's perfect for the job. While she may spend more time looking at ceilings than Michelangelo, her place has a real homey feel to it. The living room is classic, filled with dark wood antiques and vintage leather furniture. Lace curtains filter out the light, creating interesting shadow patterns on the hardwood maple floors. She's always got fresh flowers in a vase (probably because men send them to her all the time), so the faint scent of roses hangs in the air. But the bedroom wouldn't be found in a decorating magazine, unless you pick up a copy of *This Old Bordello*. It kinda looks like Martha Stewart had been called in to decorate a brothel, with things like little pink ribbons accessorizing the ropes hanging down from the slats of the canopy bed. She's even got one closet filled with "play clothes" which includes, not surprisingly, a Catholic schoolgirl outfit. She claims it is actually the same one she wore to high school and is damn proud that it still fits perfectly. I do question, however, that the hemline was probably not the same back in the day or that the outfit came with patent leather black platforms. Had Neely showed up for Catechism class like that, the priest would have been the one going to confession.

"Chapters," she said, sitting on the floor next to the fireplace. She put a yellow legal pad in her lap as she sipped her drink. "Shout 'em out."

"*On the prowl*," said Rica, who was stretched out on the couch. "It would give women a guide to going out and taking the initiative with younger men. How to approach a man, how to ask him out."

Neely nodded and wrote it down. "Ooooh, I like it. Good start. C'mon, more."

"*Convertible sex*," said Jillian. "How putting your top down for certain men makes for a better ride."

"Very clever terminology," I said, as Neely wrote it down.

"All men like the top down," said Rica.

"*Reference checking*," I said. "For women who are in management and in the position to hire people."

"Wait a minute," said Jillian, putting up one finger. "Let's rephrase that a bit. For women who have… positions to fill."

"Very nice," said Neely.

"By the way," said Rica, "are we gonna have to write this whole thing or just come up with the concepts?"

"I thought we could divide up the chapters," said Neely. "Maybe intersperse some personal experiences along the way. Amanda just wants a rough draft, then she's got some ghostwriter who is going to polish up the manuscript."

"I got another one," said Rica. "*Woman on top.* A guide to taking control in the bedroom."

"Great," I said. "I think we need a chapter on one-night stands, but I don't know what to call it."

"How about *catch of the day*?" said Neely.

The girl is going to be the Martha Stewart of sex.

* * *

"I'm sorry, I couldn't hear your answer through the giant bouquet," said Jillian, craning her neck so she could see me. "Do you think you could move the flower shop?"

Her original question, "So, how are things going with Scott?" was dripping with Rica's brand of sarcasm. I slid the crystal vase filled with two dozen long-stemmed red roses to the side of the desk, and saw all the girls snickering.

"Leave me alone," I said.

"He obviously enjoyed things Friday night," said Neely, getting up to take a closer look at the arrangement. "I just love a man who sends flowers. Hmmm. No card. I guess none is necessary."

"So," said Rica, "would that be one dozen per—"

"Shut! Up!" I said, putting my hands up.

My intercom buzzed. Saved by the bell. Hopefully it was something business related so we could move off the subject of the roses and Scott, who was now known as *The Fly* (as in ointment, not the classic horror movie in which the scientist swaps heads with an insect.) "Yes?"

"*You have a guest here to see you, Ms. Hack.*" There was a

long pause, then the receptionist dropped her voice. "*It's... your mother.*"

My face twisted and my shoulders hunched up as my blood pressure immediately spiked. The sweet smell of the roses instantly took on the aroma of a New York garbage strike.

"And the hits just keep on coming," said Jillian.

Scott is a big enough fly in the ointment, but Mother is a different story. Will someone please put a screen door on my life?

"What the hell is *The Frigidaire* doing here?" asked Rica.

"No friggin' idea," I said, opening my top drawer and pulling out the industrial size bottle of Tums for a pre-emptive strike. The multicolored tablets bounced around like bingo balls as the bottle shook in my hand. I opened it and popped two, chewing them fast as a squirrel and letting the chalky calcium run down my throat in preparation for an onslaught of stomach acid that was already on the march to greet Mother. It's a professional courtesy thing.

"I have a meeting," said Neely, fear spreading across her face as she quickly gathered up her things and headed for the door.

"Me too," said Jillian, whose look matched Neely's as they grabbed the first lifeboats and bailed on the sinking ship.

"Cowards," I said.

"I wanna see this," said Rica.

"Masochist," said Jillian, as she and Neely blew out of the office.

"You think she read the paper?" asked Rica.

I put my palms up and shrugged as I punched the button on the phone and answered the receptionist, who I knew would route all my calls to engineering if I let Mother sit in the outer office for more than two minutes. "Have someone escort her back, please."

Of course she read the damned paper. And if she didn't, the women at the Old Southwich, Connecticut bridge club surely did and proudly presented her with a copy.

Her daughter was a slut, and now the whole world knew it. But what really mattered was that Old Southwich knew it, and the world beyond its borders doesn't really exist.

I guess I haven't told you about Mother. Not *Mom*, but *Mother*. It's an Old Southwich thing. The term *mom* implies warmth. Hence Rica's *Frigidaire* reference. And in Mother's case the defrost feature is permanently broken and can never be repaired. I've been avoiding the subject, but since she's here I guess I'd better brace you for her visit.

Bootsie Hack (maiden name, Phyllis Hartshaw) grew up like Jillian but embraced all that goes with a life of privilege in the tony bedroom communities of Connecticut. You'd think she would have married someone named Farnsworth or Wellington, but instead she went off the trust fund reservation and hooked up with my dad; steady, reliable Bill Hack, a blue-collar guy from Stamford who turned her head at a high school football game. This, apparently, was the Old Southwich version of *Rebel Without a Cause* since Bootsie's family considered the relationship a scandal, as one night in the back of my Dad's Buick resulted in what is commonly referred to as a shotgun wedding, but in New England carries the more genteel term of *compensation marriage*. The result, in case you hadn't figured this out, is me.

The night in the Buick is also why I'm an only child.

After a honeymoon at the Hartshaw's Hamptons getaway, Dad took new bride Bootsie with him to college, which added even more to the scandal, since he attended a school that wasn't in the Ivy League. (The fact that I was conceived in an American car didn't help either. Any man who's knocked up a girl in a car in Old Southwich has at least had the decency to do it in a Volvo.) By the way, Dad is tall, well built, and has a strong anchorman's jaw; thankfully I got his eyes instead of Mother's satanic yellow. He's always turned the heads of women, and back in his younger days I imagine they would have been beating a path to his door, if not for the troll guarding the bridge that led to it. Anyway, Dad soon discovered that he was, indeed, now married to an anorexic refrigeration appliance who promptly announced after my birth that since her first sexual encounter was so unpleasant she never wanted to have sex again. Ever, ever, ever. (Must have been one hell of a honeymoon.) Dad chalked it up to some sort of post-partum thing, but when this dragged on for two years and the poor guy's pipes were about to blow, he pulled the plug on the marriage. Incredibly, Bootsie didn't want custody of *moi*, finding toddlers as repulsive as sex. (I'm told I was hell on wheels with finger paint, and on one occasion added bright red moustaches to all the Roman emperor lawn statues at the Hartshaw estate.) So I grew up under the wing of one of the coolest dads on the planet. He married a terrific woman after he graduated, who I *do* call Mom. Dad, bless him, has always been supportive of everything I do. He even understands the older woman thing, having spent two years with The Frigidaire turned up to her coldest setting.

Bootsie, meanwhile, has spent the time since without so much as a date, clinging to her one bad experience in the Buick for dear life. Though only in her mid-fifties, she looks and dresses like she escaped from an Amish prison. If there were a line of clothes called "dowdy" she'd be the best customer, as I think she watches reruns of *Dallas* and is trying to channel Miss Ellie. Pictures of Mother in her younger days would carry the description of "plain", as she was typical of the no-make-up, non-feminine, straight-cropped haircut of Old Southwich girls. Now, along with her chin-length blonde hair having gone to that horrible mix of what can only be described as *dishwater gray*, she looks like someone blew up a balloon and then let all the air out of it, with so many wrinkles she probably has to screw her gloves on. About five-six in flats (she doesn't own a pair of heels) and rail thin with a hunched over posture, her appearance makes one wonder where she might have parked her broom. Sadly, the traditional Old Southwich nose job removed what surely would have been a permanent Halloween costume. (I once asked Dad, "What the hell were you thinking?" His reply was, "I wasn't. The six pack of beer was making the decisions that night." Then he put his arm around me. "But look what I ended up with." The man is a sweetie.)

I took a deep breath in anticipation of the visit, but the air didn't come out smoothly. "Be strong," said Rica, who probably noticed my hands were already twitching.

A male college intern led her into my office, "Nice to have met you, Mrs. Hack," he said, then shot me a quick look of wide-eyed fear. She nodded at him, not deigning to return his politeness or noticing Rica on the couch.

She had what looked like a New York newsstand under one arm as she turned to me. "Sydneeeey…" she said, as she always did, taking the last syllable up a notch and leaving my name hanging in mid-air like someone else was supposed to finish the sentence. I caught a faint hint of the Chanel she always wore.

"Motherrrrr…" I said, trying my best to match her tone.

"Yo, Missus H," said Rica. "How's it hangin'?" Rica knew her Brooklyn got under Mother's skin, so she always laid it on thicker than usual.

Mother turned and narrowed her gaze. "Ah. *Frederica*. I didn't see you there."

(At this point it should be noted that nothing, with the possible exception of Central Park mimes, pisses off Rica more than someone using her given name.)

Rica's death stare begins to coalesce as Mother continues to look at her. While Rica's gaze is unparalleled, Mother's could be likened to Superman's laser beam ice-melting glare. This could be the clash of the titans. Seconds pass. Nothing is said. Finally Rica gets up from the couch. "I gotta go to a meetin' and I need a cuppa cawfee. We'll tawk laytuh, Syd." She gets up from the couch and moves close to Mother, looking her right in the eye. "Nice ta see ya…. Phyllis."

The name hits ol' Bootsie like a blowdart in the neck, as her head jerks back. Rica smiles as she leaves my office, happy that she's gotten the last shot.

I wish Rica had stayed because now I'm going one on one with the only person on the planet who not only can push my buttons but knows the secret launch codes and can turn both keys simultaneously and send my confidence into outer space where it will be vaporized in a nanosecond.

She unfolds the newspapers with a snap, turns them around and spreads them out on my desk so all the front pages are screaming at me. "Aren't you *so proud* of yourself?" The headlines jab at me, her little ink soldiers in the war she is waging to save her reputation back in Old Southwich.

I shrug my shoulders. "Whatever. It's New York," I say, and hear my voice quiver a little. *Dammit, Syd, be tough.* "They're always making up sensational stories here."

"Well, then they all appear to be making up the same sensational story." She licks her thumb and flips open one newspaper to page three. "And what's this? A nice little lawsuit involving my daughter that reveals her place of business is the second coming of a Roman orgy. You hire people with a casting couch. How am I to ever walk through downtown Old Southwich again when the entire town knows my daughter is nothing more than a common trollop?"

(You should know that Mother cannot say words like "slut" or "tramp" or any other colloquial terms that might refer to my escapades in the bedroom. To me, trollop sounds like something you'd get on Valentine's Day... chocolate covered trollops. Of course, if Harrell wants to cover me in Hershey's syrup on February fourteenth, I won't complain.)

"Mother, what I do in my personal life—"

"Affects *my* personal life. You are dragging the Hartshaw name through the gutter."

"My last name is Hack, and so is yours. In case you had forgotten."

"I'm still a Hartshaw, and Hartshaw blood runs through your veins. This is a scandal from which the family may never recover."

I folded my arms and stood tall. "Maybe if you had sex once every decade you'd understand the rest of the world's point of view."

"The rest of the world doesn't go around jumping from one bed to another like a game of hopscotch."

"Then where the hell did six billion people come from?"

She waved away my comment. "Pffft. I would have thought you'd be over this sex thing by now. I assumed it was just a phase during high school—"

"You mean like you and Dad?" (Damn, I wanted to save my trump card for the end, but it fit so well at this point in the argument that I couldn't keep it from escaping.)

Her eyes narrowed into gunslinger mode as she finished her thought. "But this? You can't go running around like a cheerleader sleeping with every member of the football team anymore. You are, after all, nearing forty."

"Sorry, Mother, I didn't get the memo that middle-aged women stopped having sex."

This went on for ten minutes, back and forth, Mother slowly beating me down and sending my blood past the boiling point.

Then, incredibly, it actually got worse.

The Fly walked into my office.

Just give me the gun and let me put myself out of my misery.

"I heard your mother was visiting," he said to me. He took her hands. "Mrs. Hack, I'm Scott. So very nice to meet you."

Mother ran one wary eye up and down Scott's body. "Likewise," she said, with all the sincerity of a New York State Thruway toll-taker saying thank you.

"I've been wondering when I was finally going to meet Sydney's parents."

Gun! Now!

Just when I was cursing the fact that jumping out the window would have no effect since my office is on the ground floor, a gentle tap on the door announced Jillian's entrance. "Syd, we have that four o'clock meeting upstairs in a few minutes," she said, pointing to her watch. She looked directly into my eyes and I got the message. She then turned to my mother. "Oh, hello Mrs. Hack,

I didn't know you dropped by. Nice to see you again."

Mother loosened her death grip on her facial muscles and managed a smile. (It's actually not a smile in the traditional sense, as I believe Mother had a plastic surgeon do a procedure that prevents the corners of her mouth from tilting up.) Jillian was, after all, a blueblood, even though she's strayed from the fold. In Mother's eyes, there was still hope that she would ditch this silly thing called a job and find a wealthy husband who would bring her *petit fours* and not demand anything in the bedroom. "Very nice to see you, Jillian."

"I'm really sorry to interrupt your visit," said Jillian, who then turned back to me, "but we've really got to get going, Syd."

"This might take a while," I said to my mother, gathering up a pad and some papers to make a show of it. "Scott can fix you a glass of hemlock from the bar."

She picked up her purse and the newspapers, presumably for a new scrapbook she was dedicating to my escapades. She'd probably have some local artist design one with the word "trollop" in needlepoint on the cover. "I'm going shopping anyway," she said.

"I'll be happy to show you the way out," said Scott.

An AK-47 would be nice at this point.

Mother faced the door and stopped. "I assume we'll see you at Thanksgiving?" she asked, without turning to look at me.

"If I don't have to work." I've just put myself on the schedule.

"Your grandmother will be *deeply* disappointed if she doesn't see you." She fired her final volley, knowing how much I loved Gran. (Souls in the Hartshaw family apparently skip a generation, as it is a recessive gene.)

"I'll let you know," I said.

Mother left my office without saying anything else, just pausing at the door and leaving me with an audible sniff that conveyed her disgust. Scott followed, and I heard his voice trail off as they headed for the reception area. "Your daughter is just wonderful to work for..."

The Fly and the Frigidaire. Sounds like a children's story.

One with a really unhappy ending.

I shook my head and rolled my eyes. "Dear God, thank you Jillian," I said, knowing that Jillian found being in the same room with my mother repulsive.

"When I saw Scott come in here I knew you'd be approaching meltdown status. I'm sure you didn't anticipate that wild card in the deck from hell."

"Well, the fake meeting was brilliant." I tossed the pad and papers back on my desk and noticed my hands were actually still shaking a bit. She apparently did as well, and moved forward, giving me a strong hug. I held on for a moment, savoring her sweet floral perfume and the embrace of a true friend.

"You'll be okay. She's gone." She pulled away after a while and brushed my hair aside. "The meeting isn't fake, by the way. You need to get going," she said.

"What do you mean?" I quickly checked my day planner and there was nothing on it. "I don't have anything scheduled."

"It's something *I* scheduled. Just go to the loft. It's all taken care of."

CHAPTER TEN

The "on air" light was already blazing as I reached the top of the stairs. I stopped a moment, still shaking a bit, heart hammering away to an angry beat, wondering if I needed a ton of animalistic sex, a really good cry, a very long hug, an I-V of liquor, or all four. Anger and sadness did battle for my emotions, as was always the case when Mother did a number on my head. I wiped my eyes, not wanting to show the flip side of Neutron Syd to whoever was on the other side of the door. I took a few deep breaths in an effort to exhale the stress, but it had no effect. What the hell. Whoever was inside was going to have to see me in this condition and just accept it. I stood up straight, threw my head back and entered the loft.

The Snack was sitting on the couch, one arm across the back of it. "Jillian said you needed to relax," said Shawn.

"That's an understatement," I said.

He patted the cushion next to him, not saying anything.

But it wasn't a come-on, and, for once, this wasn't about sex. His eyes were filled with sincerity and a kindness that told me it was safe to let down my guard. I closed the door behind me, locked it, moved to the couch and sat down next to him. He leaned over, put both arms around me, and pulled me close.

I lay my head on his shoulder, melted into his embrace and

held on as he began to gently stroke the back of my head. I felt my
eyes well up, so I held on tighter, not wanting him to see Neutron
Syd cry. I closed my eyes as I felt a few tears run down my cheeks,
let his warmth fill my heart, and concentrated on his touch. The
waterworks slowly turned off as he seemed to absorb the stress
in my body. He didn't say anything for a couple of minutes, then
finally pulled back and looked at me. My heart finally downshifted
from its twenty minute marathon through the ninth circle of hell.
"Can I get you anything?" he asked. "Need a drink?"

I wiped my eyes and shook my head, struggling to keep the
flood of emotion in check. "No, I'm okay," I said softly, the words
barely audible. "I didn't ever want anyone to see me like this."

"Turn around," he said, taking my shoulders and guiding me on
the couch so that I faced away from him. His hands then began
to massage the muscles around my shoulders and neck, the firm
pressure from his thumbs serving to melt away the tension. "My
God, you're tight."

I surrendered immediately to his touch. My head went limp as
I let him work out the Gordian knots my mother had tied in my
muscles. "Oh God, Shawn, that's wonderful. Where in the world
did you learn to do this?"

"My sister's a massage therapist. She used to do her homework
on me. I picked up some of her better techniques." His hands
continued to loosen the tight muscles around my neck. "I saw
the woman in your office yelling at you. I figured it was someone
from corporate. I didn't know that was your mother until Jillian
told me."

"My mother is wicked," I said. "Pure evil."

"I thought I recognized her from *The Wizard of Oz*."

I laughed and a little more tension dissipated. He continued his
assault on my back, moving down below my shoulders, pressing
his thumbs into the middle of my back. "Ohhhhh, yeah," I said,
wondering why I hadn't been visiting a massage therapist on a
regular basis. (It was probably the first time those words had

been said in the loft outside the bedroom.) He worked the rest of my back for another ten minutes, then stopped. "That was wonderful," I said, ready for a nap and still with my back to him. "Thank you, Shawn."

"You're not done," he said, and in one move pulled my shoulders back until I found myself with my head resting on a pillow in his lap. He looked down at me with those incredible eyes, giving my soul a badly needed hug. He gently brushed my hair out of the way with both hands. I wanted to just lay there and keep looking at him, keep breathing in his subtle hint of Fendi cologne, keep focusing on the kindness he was radiating and block out what I'd just endured. "Eyes closed, young lady," he said. "And no talking."

"Yes sir," I said, shutting my lids and trusting him completely. In another life I would have expected to find a man's hands running up my blouse at this point. Not that I would have minded a Snack attack, but I knew that wasn't Shawn's intent. He gently began massaging my temples as I sank deep into a state of relaxation. He said nothing for a few minutes, moving from my temples to the sides of my head and then taking it in both hands, running his fingers into my hair and rubbing the back of my head. The sound of my own breathing grew louder in my head, like what you hear when you're underwater. Finally he took his hands away and I felt him lightly kiss my forehead.

"Time to wake up, sleeping beauty," he said. I opened my eyes and saw him smiling at me. "Better?"

"Much," I said softly, feeling like I could get a tooth drilled without novocaine. "You're amazing."

He ran one soft hand across my cheek. "Syd, I want you to listen to me," he said, his voice as gentle as his touch. He suddenly looked at me like a parent, but one who actually cared. "You're one of the smartest people I've ever met. You're running an incredible operation here. People who work for you genuinely like you and respect you. You're a devastatingly beautiful woman… I mean, men walk into walls looking at you."

My confidence started to return and I smiled. He didn't say anything else and just kept looking into my eyes. "Hell, Shawn, don't stop," I said. "You're on a roll."

"You've got the world by the tail. You shouldn't give anyone the power to take that away from you with words. She only has power if you give it to her."

"I know, but she's my disapproving mother. It's kind of hard to just dismiss her opinion, even if I can't stand her. I'm stuck with her."

"Doesn't matter. Her opinion doesn't matter. You have to please yourself, not her. Which I assume is what you have been doing most of your life."

My smile grew as I realized how ridiculous it was that such a woman of power as myself ceded it to a button-pushing crone of a biological parent. "You know, for someone who is twenty-five you're a wise old soul."

"My other sister is a psychiatrist," he said, smiling. "She did her homework on me too."

"Figures." I raised my head a bit. "Shawn, thanks for letting me be a girl today. Just don't let the troops know what's really underneath, okay? You can't be a soft touch if you're in management, and you sure can't ever cry."

"It will be our little secret."

His eyes were such deep pools of warmth I just wanted to jump into them and lose myself. The man could have asked me to do anything to his body right now, and I would have obeyed like a fifties housewife. I reached up and brushed a wisp of hair from his forehead. "I can see why you have Jillian's heart."

His smile grew. "I think it's the other way around. She's pretty special."

"Yeah," I said. "She really is."

* * *

It was nearly six when I left the loft and headed back to my office. The smell from the roses hit me in the face. I grabbed the vase from my desk and headed across the hall to Jillian's office, walked in without knocking, and placed them on her credenza.

"What's this?" she asked.

"I was going to take them home, but you deserve them. Take them back to your place."

"Don't be silly," she said. "They were sent to you."

"By someone I don't care about," I said. "Enjoy them. Pretend they came from Shawn."

Her face lit up as it always does when she gets flowers. "Well, okay. If you're gonna twist my arm."

"Speaking of Shawn, take him home and drain him of all bodily fluids. He deserves a reward."

"On that, you *don't* have to twist my arm. I'll leave nothing but an empty husk."

I leaned one leg on the edge of her desk, looked around to make sure no one was within earshot, and dropped my voice. "Seriously, thanks for what you did today. You're a true friend."

"You don't have to say that, Syd. You know you're like a sister to me."

"I know. By the way, Shawn and I... we didn't—"

"It doesn't matter what happened up there. I just knew the little guy could set things straight for you."

"Jillian," I said, "Shawn may just be the biggest guy I know."

CHAPTER ELEVEN

Random thoughts as we head into week three:

—Shawn's little therapy session is paying wonderful dividends. Mother called the day after her visit to vent at me some more when she put two and two together and figured out Scott was the guy who had originally gone to the tabloids. I put her on hold and left her there, watching the little light blink for twenty minutes while I did some paperwork and then letting out a tiny cheer when the thing flatlined and went dark. Meanwhile, Rica did something to my cell phone she calls the "Frigidaire early warning system" so that if Mother calls that number, instead of the normal ringtone I get the slashing sound effect from the Janet Leigh shower scene in the movie *Psycho*. It cost me a buck ninety-nine, which is appropriate, since Mother thinks of me as a two dollar hooker anyway.

—We need a scheduler for The Loft. Too damn many people want to skip lunch lately, and the stairwell looks like a line for the bathroom at a trendy bar, with people hopping up and down on their toes like they really have to go. Meanwhile, Madison initiated what is known as a "reciprocal trade agreement" with a chain of linen stores because the clean sheet situation was getting out of hand and the maid was tired of trudging up and down three flights of stairs seven times per day. Thanks to this deal, we get bushels of sheets, pillowcases, towels and an industrial sized laundry hamper; they get free advertising. So anytime you see one of their ads, a CGR anchor is taking care of her to-do list on five hundred thread count Egyptian cotton. Not exactly like an angel getting wings when you hear a bell, but you get the idea.

—I bought two tickets to the best Broadway musical in town and gave them to Jillian and The Snack, a thank you for rescuing me last week, with the stipulation that they not "leave early due to bad choreography." And I don't wanna hear, "We got back late from intermission," either. I know we are supposed to be acting like men and playing the field, but I'm really rooting for those two.

—I'm keeping The Fly at bay, which is no small trick these days. We're still letting him go at some point, but I can't have him going off the reservation with the Monopoly Guy's lawsuit coming up because you know damn well that Big Red will call Scott as a witness, and I want to make sure he's on my side when he takes the stand. While Scott is a master in the bedroom, I still cannot get the underlying thread of commitment out of my mind while he's running a feather duster over my ass. Neely suggested I simply pretend I'm *with* someone else, and when that didn't work, Rica said I should imagine that I *am* someone else. So just to have fun I'm imagining that I'm a famous woman whose husband cheated on her and is getting even. This week I pretended I was Hillary Clinton, and it was highly entertaining getting back at Bill. I even wore a cheap blue dress and a beret. Next up, Jennifer Aniston taking it out on Brad Pitt. Take that, Angelina.

* * *

"Jersey?" said Rica, suddenly grabbing her coffee and standing up. "We gotta go to friggin' Jersey for the trial?" She started to pace around our conference room.

Stacy nodded. "That's where the lawsuit was filed, that's where the trial will take place."

"I don't understand," I said. "Why not file here in New York?"

"They obviously wanted cameras in the courtroom," said Stacy. "They're taking their case to the heartland. How it plays in New York is one thing, but the concept will probably send the conservatives in this country off the deep end."

Oh shit. I hadn't even thought of that. I know, I know… you're saying, "Jeez, Syd, you work in television and you can't tell when a lead story hits you in the face? Did you think the other networks would just ignore dirty laundry this good?" And I can hear my mother now after the first day of the trial. "Sydney…that dress you wore on the witness stand made you look like a trollop."

"Anyway," continued Stacy, "cameras are not a problem in the Jersey courts, but in New York it can be a major issue. A judge can allow them, but you never know. Besides, the plaintiff lives in Jersey anyway."

"You know damn well one of those court channels will carry the trial," said Jillian. "This is going to turn into a circus."

"Already a done deal," said Stacy. "Actually, I've been contacted by two channels who are planning wall-to-wall coverage who wanted to sit down with me before the thing gets underway."

"Well, I'd cover it if I ran a court channel," said Rica. "It's a no-brainer from a newsperson's point of view."

When broadcasters smell the blood of other broadcasters in the water, it's a feeding frenzy that would make great white sharks look like a bunch of goldfish. We worship success but root for failure. "The cable operations will be all over this thing like the O.J. Simpson trial," I said.

"All us, all the time," said Neely.

"Jersey!" said Rica, shaking her head and looking out the window as she raised her hands to the heavens.

"What's your problem with New Jersey?" asked Jillian. "There are a lot of beautiful places in that state."

"You come out of the tunnel," said Rica, "and it stinks to high heaven. It's dirty. And there's a state law that you can't pump your own gas. You can't order a damned soft-boiled egg in a restaurant because the legislature thinks you'll die and sue the state. And the friggin' tolls on the Garden State every two minutes drive me nuts."

Neely turned to Stacy. "Can we get a change of venue to Brooklyn?" she asked.

"I got your change of venue *right here*," said Rica, glaring at her.

Stacy clapped her hands a few times. "C'mon, we're getting off topic here. We're all going to have to rehearse for this trial."

My face tightened. "Rehearse?"

Stacy nodded. "Perhaps that was a poor choice of words. I don't want you to rehearse your answers because I want you all to tell the truth."

"Aw shit," said Rica. "If we're gonna tell the truth we're screwed."

"No, you're not," said Stacy. "If you tell the truth in *a certain way*. There's the tone of your voice, body language, the way you phrase your answers, your comfort factor on the witness stand, the way you dress."

"And on that subject, I assume we're going to have to dress down for the trial," said Jillian. "Damn, I gotta go shopping for frumpy clothes."

"No, you don't. Now I wouldn't wear the blue sequins," said Stacy, looking at me. "But I don't want you putting your hair up in buns of steel and wearing those high-necked long dresses like those whack jobs in Texas with all the kids. You are all women in positions of power, and your clothes need to convey that. But in this case you are also very attractive women, so while your outfits should be of a business nature, they should not hide your sexuality. In fact, they should enhance it. You're showing that you have authority in the workplace *and* the bedroom."

"That," said Rica, "will definitely not be a problem with this group."

"Really," said Neely. "We don't even need to go shopping."

I took one look at the gleam in Neely's eyes and knew she was already making a list.

CHAPTER TWELVE

"Anna Nicole is still dead."

Okay, I admit that sentence is horribly tacky, but it's basic code around any newsroom for, "there's no news today." The world never runs out of famous dead people, and you can always come up with something, anything, that will "advance the story", even though the person in question reached room temperature months ago.

Every station has a morning meeting in which story ideas are discussed. Reporters take turns pitching their ideas, then the News Director parcels out the assignments. The morning conversation during the story meeting of a slow news day usually goes like this:

News Director to reporter: "You got any story ideas today?"

Reporter: "Nope. But… Anna Nicole is still dead."

News Director: "Hmmm. You got a new angle?"

Reporter: "I met a woman who thinks she once sat next to Anna Nicole on a plane and saved the plastic cup with her lipstick on it."

News Director: "Great! Do it! Take it to a lab and get some DNA analysis on it. You can make a two-part series! What she was drinking and what kind of lipstick she used."

And that's why America is bombarded with endless stories even after the story is, and forgive my choice of words again, dead and buried. When there's nothing going on, our industry can beat a dead horse until the remains are down to the molecular level and nothing is left but the horseshoes. "Death by sidebar" is another term that describes a story that seems to have no end even though it's been over for months. Stuck for a story? Just find a new twist on a famous person's death, no matter how bizarre or hard to believe. The promotions people can tease it all afternoon. "Anna Nicole's first-class airline confessions….tonight at six!"

Fortunately for us here at CGR, we're never going to run out of stories, as the discussion of sex-related topics never dries up. Anna Nicole's name has not popped up even once during our first few weeks.

But apparently it has at the competition, as they've exhumed the poor woman and every other dead celebrity, thinking this weird kind of counter-programming will put a dent in our quickly growing female audience. And along with the parade of Anna Nicoles, they've got a glut of missing beautiful blonde girls and the people who are tirelessly looking for them. This tactic falls under the heading "people sympathize with pretty things that are broken." (It should be noted that by sheer coincidence, the only missing people in this country are rich, pretty blonde teenage girls. Incredibly, boys, minorities, brunettes, ugly children and poor kids never disappear. Amazing how that happens. It's a story that deserves an investigation, don't you think?)

Here's a newsflash for the competition. The sort of women who watch that stuff are not the women who are watching us. That kind of trashy programming won't have any effect on what we do. We're the only game in town for older women and the men who want them. And the men who are searching for beautiful missing blondes are hoping the search ends in the bedroom.

Incredibly, our ratings are still growing a little each day. The word of mouth is spreading. The buzz continues in the newspapers on a regular basis, and for a cable channel, that's pretty unusual.

The Loft, meanwhile, has done more for "anchor chemistry" than years of work experience. It has given new meaning to the term *working lunch*.

So all is right with the universe, at least in the television end of it. The satellite gods are happy with me.

Still, I'm hitting the Tums bottle more often. That trial is hanging over my head like a swinging guillotine.

CHAPTER THIRTEEN

The last time I was part of a dress rehearsal was in a high school play. For some inexplicable reason, the drama teacher thought we should do "A Chorus Line", which is classic Broadway but contains a song entitled "Tits and Ass." Not exactly appropriate for a senior class production, but we weren't going to complain since we'd get to wear revealing costumes and swear on stage. The students, of course, thought this was very cool, knew it would be quite the scandal, and would probably make the front page of a Big Apple tabloid since the school was situated in the Long Island community of Babylon, New York, and you can't make up stuff that good. (My father had fled there from Connecticut, probably figuring people who lived in a town called Babylon had to be more receptive to having sex. Yet another scandal to have someone with Hartshaw blood living in a place that didn't have the decency to change its suggestive name. Although one would think that Sodom and Gomorrah were still available.) A few days before the production, the principal, who had no knowledge of musicals, walked in on a rehearsal in which a tall redhead in a skimpy outfit sang the virtues of her front and back. (Yes, the tall redhead would be me. I had the requisite T&A by senior year.) The principal's jaw dropped like a stone and he fired the drama teacher on the spot. But since tickets had already been sold, he appointed a substitute director from his church who made discreet changes in the lyrics and costumes. At my high school reunion, my rendition of "smiles and class" while wearing a gingham dress was voted the highlight of senior year. Sadly, a photo of that disaster is forever preserved in the yearbook, and will hopefully not make its way into a tabloid during the trial.

Fortunately we're not wearing gingham for this rehearsal. Stacy has put together our own private fashion show, asking each of us to choose a half dozen of what we would consider appropriate outfits for the courtroom. Her stipulations: no New York black, which makes up about fifty percent of all closet space in Manhattan; no white, no earth tones, no gray pinstripes, no high collars and above all, no pants. She wanted bold and brassy, with bright primary colors that would stand out in a sea of muted courtroom tones. "Your clothes need to reflect business *and* pleasure," she said, which made me think there needs to be a line of fashion with that name. (*Women who work hard and play harder wear B&P. Kinda catchy, huh?*)

We're doing this little runway thing at Neely's place. She argued that she had far more than six "possibles" in her closet and she was not going to wheel her wardrobe across Manhattan on a rack, "like some garment-district worker with a hot pretzel hanging out of his mouth." So Rica, Jillian and I have brought several hanging bags full of stuff to her townhouse. Neely, ever the Southern hostess, greeted each of us at the door with another wonderful vodka concoction, like we were buyers from a department store and were here to see the fall line. Then, just as we were about to start the show, she fired up some upbeat instrumental music from the eighties to add some energy.

Rica went first, for no particular reason. She disappeared into Neely's bedroom for a few minutes, while we all slipped deeper into the couch and a vodka coma at the same time. I noshed on the hot bacon-wrapped shrimp that sat on the coffee table, which, when dipped into an old-fashioned fondue pot filled with warm melted Gouda, created a decadent hors d'oeuvre to die for. (Neely, by the way, is also a fantastic cook, hence the "biscuits in the oven" line to which she often refers.) Stacy, who was on her way to starting a chapter of her own at the law firm, had a legal pad in her lap, a pen in one hand and a drink in the other. We had asked Stacy to bring some of her outfits as well, but she said she'd already chosen her wardrobe. But we badgered her, so she brought some stuff. We want her to feel like part of the group.

Rica emerged, prancing to the music wearing a tight burgundy business suit: a cropped jacket with a skirt about three inches above the knee and a pair of stiletto heels. "Hot damn," said Neely, bringing back memories of the gong show. Rica's black hair made a striking contrast with the burgundy. She took off the jacket which had a beige silk blouse underneath that was tight enough to reveal a pair of party hats.

"Very nice," said Stacy. "Though I'd like to see it with a bra."

Rica shrugged her shoulders. "If I owned one, I'd put it on," she said.

Jillian's turn brought out seven outfits which all had the same strategy. Legs, legs and more legs in shoes that could qualify as stilts. The Snack was right about that; keeping those long stems in flats (or covered up) was ridiculous. We all vetoed the one pair of pants she brought; even though it broke Stacy's rule and the pinstripes made her legs look endless, nothing compared with a short skirt that showed off her perfectly toned calves. Her collection of bright, satiny silk tops in blues and greens worked great with her hair and eyes. Neely described her look as, "A lot of class in the boardroom and a great ass in bed."

Neely was next, and saved the best of her outfits for last. I knew damn well she'd gone shopping, since the first seven outfits she'd modeled for us had never made an appearance at work, and one still had the tags. Then she disappeared into the bedroom and five minutes later cracked the door opened and announced, in a deep dramatic voice, "Ladies and Gentlemen, we have been transported to the future. Please welcome the next President of the United States!" She then power-walked into the living room (just as "Walking on Sunshine" started to play…she must have timed it) in a candy apple red business suit with an incredibly tight skirt that ended about four inches above the knee. The jacket partially covered a blouse that was straining to keep her boobs from exploding out of it. But the best part of the outfit was above the neck. Neely's upswept hair and no-frame rectangular glasses left no doubt she was a doppelganger for a certain politician from a very cold state. If that certain politician had done an ad for Victoria's Secret and worked as a slutty librarian during the day. "*Your books are overdue, young man, but I'm going to take out your fine in trade.*"

"Gives new meaning to the term *swing vote*," I said.

"You betcha," said Jillian, adopting a nasal twang.

"If that top button on that blouse goes, you might put the judge's eye out," said Rica, popping another shrimp.

"Ah, but this is only part one of the outfit," said Neely, smiling and quickly raising both eyebrows.

"What, there's a hockey stick that goes with it?" asked Rica. "A stuffed moose head?"

"No, silly," said Neely. "What's every Republican man's fantasy about her?" Neely slowly removed her glasses, reached behind her head, removed her barrette and shook out her hair, which fell loosely about her shoulders.

If Scott were here, he would have said, "Whoa."

"That's fantastic," said Stacy. "You should do that in court once each day."

"Really?" asked Neely. "I thought you guys would think it was too much. I was just having a little fun."

"No, seriously, it's great," said Stacy. "I mean, here's what you do. You walk into the courtroom every morning like that, with the hair up and the glasses on, looking kind of serious, and maybe right after lunch you drop the hair and the glasses in the courtroom just before the judge comes back. You do it every day and the cable channels will start looking for it while they're doing their commentary during the recess."

"Yeah," I said, "they'll start speculating on the daily hair drop. You'll have your own cult following."

Except in red states, where CGR will be pulled from every cable system and replaced with a shopping network.

"As long as I don't get cited for contempt," said Neely. "Meanwhile, I'm not done."

"You can't strip in the courtroom," said Rica.

It was my turn to hit the dressing room. I knew I wouldn't be able to top Neely's display, but I did manage to get five of my six outfits approved, as one dress wasn't deemed "slinky enough" by Stacy. Apparently she sees me as the seductress of the group. Must be the redhead thing. Since her courtroom opponent is also a copper top, she wants me to be the polar opposite of Ms. O'Hara. We're playing a game of "good redhead, bad redhead", but in this case my being the bad redhead is actually good for the men on the jury.

* * *

There was a little bite in the air. The leaves were changing. Roadside produce stands were ablaze with orange pumpkins and colorful gourds.

That only meant one thing in the television industry.

November sweeps were coming.

Years ago this was an insider thing, but now, thanks to entertainment magazines like *TV Guide* and *Entertainment Weekly*, the public knows about "sweeps" months (February, May and November) during which stations and networks pull out all the stops to entice viewers to watch. Ever notice that all sorts of good stuff is on all at once and then it's a parade of reality and reruns? Well, that's because sweeps months are when the almighty Nielsen

Company calculates ratings, and those ratings determine what you can charge for commercials. Even one rating point can literally mean millions to a network.

Years ago stations and networks would do what are called "sweeps series" which were multi-part stories that carried enough interest to attract new eyeballs. Most of them were legitimate pieces of investigative journalism on things like unscrupulous car mechanics or crooked politicians. Back then the evening news was appointment television in many households, and you could run a five-part series reasonably assured that viewers would watch all five parts if they liked the first one.

But no one has that kind of time anymore, so a "series" might just be two parts. Or you might have a "sweeps piece" that is just one part. And, of late, sweeps have become a game of "can you top this?" as broadcasters are becoming more outlandish than ever. Journalism doesn't even enter into the picture anymore.

There are three sure-fire hits when it comes to sweeps.

Fear, money and sex. And if you can combine two or more of those, you've really got something.

Under the *fear* heading we find the sweeps pieces that are simply designed to scare the living shit out of you while you're sitting on the couch, and the titles often contain the phrase "can kill you" somewhere in the promotional copy, while featuring video of something disgusting. "The bacteria on your dish scrubbie can kill you! Details at eleven!" Viewers must be cowering under the bed when they learn that they can die at the hands of things like sponges, kitty litter boxes, or the latest hot unseen killer on the loose, germs on the handles of shopping carts. Run for your lives! The all-time classic in this category, however, was one on escalator safety that followed the Super Bowl, resulting in a unique promo that managed to combine fear and football. "Stairway to death! After the game!"

Money stories, while not as sexy or scary as fear pieces, subscribe to the theory that people vote their pocketbook on election day and do the same if they have a ratings diary. So if you can save a viewer a buck, you might have a loyal viewer. Some, however, manage to combine money issues with sex, (the two often go together quite well in television, as in real life). In the case of a California station's sweeps series titled, *Make Ends Meet as a Daytime Madam,* the story spotlighted a woman who pretended to be June Cleaver while her husband was around but was actually Heidi Fleiss when he wasn't. (We've come a long way from stories about housewives who clip coupons, huh?) The print ad featured a woman who had basically been sliced right down the middle. On the left side she was dressed in an apron while holding a mop, on her right she wore a black leather bustier, matching boots, and a whip. The caption read "Jekyll and Hide", with the "hide" referring to the leather.

Sex, of course, is a no-brainer to grab some ratings, as anything remotely kinky brings out the voyeur which lurks in every viewer, especially those who don't subscribe to Cinemax. Stories that include transvestites, hookers, women in thigh-high boots (no comments, please... I wore them as part of my managerial duties), male strippers, pole dancing or erectile dysfunction can generally bring out the viewers in droves. If you could ever find a story with a transvestite pole-dancing prostitute who had a bad reaction to little blue pills, you'd have the perfect storm for sweeps. Speaking of those E-D ads, one station created a great deal of water cooler talk last year with a series on men who exceeded that four hour red zone you hear about in those commercials and ended up in the emergency room. The title for the series, *Stuck Up,* was an instant classic.

While we often see two of the big three topics combined in a sweeps piece, it is rare that anyone has come up with a riveting series which incorporates all three. The only one that comes to mind is the piece on condoms that were sold in a close-out store (money) and past their expiration date, which if used for more than five minutes (sex) tended to break (fear, the thought being that knocking up your girlfriend can be as scary as death). The series, titled *Killer Raincoats*, sort of backfired when people tuned in expecting a piece on shopping for bad weather outerwear and instead were treated to an exposé on prophylactics whose lubricant had dried out.

Luckily for us here at CGR, fear is not an option. (I'm talking sweeps here, not the way we run the place. Though I do like the slogan.) We're taking some time off from the trial preps to brainstorm some topics for November, since we're slaves to the ratings like everyone else. Sex, of course, is a given with our product, and we should be able to tie that into money quite easily. Sadly, CGR does not broadcast any sporting events, so the possibility of hearing, "Top ten uses for riding crops! After the game!" will simply remain a pipe dream.

We've asked our anchors to submit sweeps ideas on these little forms that Neely made up. Now every other station has plain old sheets for story submissions, but she's doing the Martha Stewart thing again, and has taken the blank page (mauve paper, no less) to a whole new level:

Name:

Story idea:

Reporter involvement:

Female element to the story:

Please place a checkmark next to the item(s) that will be included in the story:

__**Shirtless men**

__**Stiletto heels**

__**Bedroom toys: whips, handcuffs, costumes, etc.**

__**Edible items**

__**Inflatable accessories**

Oh, I just realized you probably don't know the definition of "reporter involvement" so I'll explain it. You know how you always see a reporter holding a microphone in any story? Well, that's called a "stand-up" and serves as a way to place the reporter at the scene so the viewer knows he or she was actually there. "Reporter involvement" takes the stand-up to the next level, as it not only gets the reporter's face on camera but shows the reporter doing something that relates to the story. For instance, if you were doing a cooking story, you might be stirring a pot or tasting what you've just made, instead of just standing there talking about it. It's basically show-and-tell. In the case of CGR, a woman might be doing a piece on "lowering your blood pressure with chocolate during sex " and could do a stand-up holding a dark chocolate bar; but the piece would be so much more interesting with reporter involvement. For example, if she licked melted dark chocolate off a chiseled chest while talking about the positive effects of flavonoids on your arteries. She runs her tongue over the guy's pecs, turns to the camera and says, "This gets your blood pumping in more ways than one." Now see, isn't that more interesting to you as a viewer?

And, now that I think of it, that would make a very good sweeps series. *"Screw your way to good health! After the game!"*

Neely had collected all the ideas and had well over one hundred. She handed each of us a stack in my office and we began to sort through them.

"Here's one I like," said Neely. *"Grocery shopping for the bedroom: how a trip to the supermarket can spice up your sex life."*

"Sounds decent," I said. "What's on the shopping list?"

"Well," said Neely, "some of the usual, like whipped cream and dipped strawberries, but the basic premise is that if your partner has a flat stomach, you can use it as a plate and eat breakfast off of it. But you can't use any utensils."

"Sounds interesting. Who submitted that?" asked Rica.

Neely's eyebrows went up. "The Snack," she said, and all eyes turned to Jillian.

"What?" she asked, her face pleading ignorance.

"Spill," said Rica.

"Okay," said Jillian, as the freckles started to bloom. "So one morning I thought it would be fun to have pancakes in bed, but the plate slipped off the tray and I spilled syrup all over The Snack. One thing led to another, so I just put the pancakes on his abs and worked my way down."

You just know those two will never run out of ideas.

"Sounds like a keeper," I said. "Next?"

"This one sounds interesting," said Rica. "*Trading down.* For women who are stuck with a balding, overweight, middle-aged man. How to "trade down in age" and turn your life around. Part one is ditching Shamu and part two shows how to find a newer model."

"Love it," I said. The others nodded.

"I've got a winner," said Jillian, waving a piece of paper in the air. "*Age inappropriate.* Lists all the things women over thirty aren't supposed to do or wear. Short skirts is number one on the list."

"Hell," said Rica, "We could shoot that without ever leaving the office."

After an hour we'd agreed on a few dozen sweeps series, of which my favorite is "*Hot bods and cattle prods*", submitted by Denton's co-anchor Kristin. The premise is how to "train" a man with a perfect body to perform in the fashion that pleases you.

Just as we were wrapping up, Amanda stopped by with the news that our lawsuit has been fast-tracked (unheard of in New Jersey, whose legal system moves at a glacial pace) and will begin on Thursday, November first.

The first day of sweeps.

"So," asked Rica. "Are we going to be covering our own trial?"

"That would imply that we're a *news* organization," said Amanda. "We'll leave that to everyone else. Believe me, there won't be any shortage of coverage on this one. What we *can* do, however, is buy some ads on the court channels. I'll bet lots of people who haven't sampled us or even heard of us will want to check out the source if they're watching the trial."

Damn, she's brilliant.

I guess 'tis true that what goes around comes around, or payback, or whatever you want to call it.

We used the gong on job applicants, and now Stacy has a buzzer for us which will be used during the rehearsal. Actually it's a piece of a *Taboo* board game that makes an annoying game show wrong-answer noise, but it's effective for what we're doing.

Welcome to Stacy Heller's mock courtroom, where we're going to legal charm school. We've got Stacy, four other lawyers (two of whom are exponentially cute guys just a few years out of law school… hmmm… another recess, perhaps?), a retired judge, and a video technician so we can play back and watch our performances. So, in a twisted bit of irony, our on-camera work is going to be harshly judged on things that are basically superficial. It's Karma with a gong!

We learned how to sit, how to smile, when to be serious, how to use our eyes, how to walk, make eye contact with the jury, nod our heads during positive answers, shake it during negative ones, use humor when appropriate, flirt with the male jurors who seem receptive, not look to the lawyer for help on a tough question, and, in Jillian's case, how to sit at the end of the table nearest the jury box and cross her legs every fifteen minutes while extending her toe in what might be considered a sensual Pilates move.

Then there's the biggie; what words to choose that will let us sway the jury, while still telling the truth. Personally I think we should bring some politicians in as consultants for that one, as they've mastered the art.

The "courtroom" was part of the law firm's office, and is a scaled-down version of the real thing. And, of course, everything isn't a hundred years old like most courthouses in the Northeast. There's an oak bench for the judge, a jury box, two long cherry tables for the attorneys, with one on each side of the courtroom, a dozen or so nice leather seats behind them for us, three stationary video cameras, and a small video set-up off to the left where the lawyers can see how all of it plays out on camera. The only thing missing was a jury, but otherwise this is a full dress rehearsal. The judge, a portly man in his early sixties with snow white hair and wire-rimmed glasses, even had a robe and a gavel. Two attractive middle-aged female lawyers were seated at one table, while Stacy was at the one directly in front of the jury box. The other lawyers will "represent" the plaintiff, while Stacy will "defend" us. The two male lawyers were seated behind the young video guy and were keeping an eye on the monitors. We were dressed in the outfits approved by Stacy, Neely had her Sarah Palin thing going, and Rica had switched to decaf in an effort to "draw the curtain on her anger" which is, as she puts it, "A nice way of telling me to keep my Brooklyn temper in check and shut the hell up."

The bad thing was that the thermostat had been turned down to sixty-five degrees to keep us "alert" during all this. Great for bringing out the party hats, but I'm not sure I saw the point. It won't be that cold in the real courtroom, and I'm certainly not going to nod off during rehearsal. But I'm sure there's a method to the madness.

I hate having to go first, but rank apparently has its privileges. I must admit my pulse was a little quick as I walked to the jury box, and I was hoping to dial that down when we got to the real thing. Like many television people who have always worked behind the scenes, being on camera makes me uncomfortable. It always feels unnatural to me, which can perhaps be traced back to the "Chorus Line" debacle in high school. (That may also account for the fact that whenever I see a gingham dress, I break out in hives. Thankfully, the T&A song is never played on the radio.) At least we won't have to rehearse dealing with the media, as Stacy has asked us not to speak to anyone about the lawsuit, as she will do all the talking on our behalf. I sure don't want to be on the other side of all the reporter's tricks we've used over the years, so the gag order is welcome.

The judge swore me in and I took a seat as my heartbeat kicked up a notch. I folded my arms in front of my waist.

"Body language," shouted one of the cute male lawyers before Stacy even said a word.

"Yes," said Stacy, as she approached me and pointed at my hands. "Don't fold your arms. That says you're closed, you're hiding something. Arms apart, on your knees or the arms of the chair. Be open, inviting. Sit up straight. You're happy to tell your story. You have nothing to hide."

"Okay," I said, and put my hands on the arms of the chair and held on for dear life.

"White knuckles," shouted the other male lawyer.

Geez! I can't even get out of the gate.

"You've got a death grip on the chair, Syd," said Stacy. "For now, just put your hands on your knees."

"Sorry," I said, and moved my hands.

"You're not used to this, that's all," she said. "Okay, we're going to start the questioning phase now and we're going to skip the preliminaries like your background and your official title and get to the good stuff. You ready?"

I wasn't, but I wanted to get it over with and hit a liquor cabinet. "Sure. Let's do it."

"Ms. Hack, would you please take us through the hiring process at your network?"

"Well, it all starts when we place ads in all the trade magazines and job-hunting sites that list openings in the news business—"

Buzz! Stacy fired the little green box at me.

"What'd I do?" I asked.

"You said the word *news*. That word, for our sake, doesn't exist in this trial. It is… taboo." She held up the box and hit the buzzer again. "Use words like television, program, broadcasting, entertainment, information… anything but news."

"Got it," I said.

"Continue…"

"After we run ads in the… television trades, job applicants send us what are known as résumé tapes, which contain samples of their best on-camera work. We review the tapes—"

Buzz!

"You first review the *applications*, then move on to the tapes of those qualified to meet the job description," said Stacy.

"But the job description is looking hot."

"We'll deal with that later," she said. "Remember, you didn't look at all the tapes. Never volunteer anything more than they need to know."

"Got it." I paused a moment, formed the thought in my head, and started again. "After we run advertisements, we look at the applications and choose the ones we think will best fit the criteria for the job. Then we review the tapes that have made the first cut…" I stopped, looking for approval.

"You're doing fine," said Stacy, nodding. "Keep going."

I felt like I was choosing my words while walking on eggshells with a few landmines sprinkled in, ready to explode. I spoke slowly. "After we've reviewed the tapes we narrow it down to those we feel are the right fit for the jobs. We then bring those people in for interviews, and eventually hire the ones we think are best suited for the positions."

"Is that how you filled all the anchoring slots for CGR?"

"Yes."

"What would you say are some of the most important factors?"

"Well, it being television, the anchors have to be attractive. But sometimes even the most attractive people don't communicate well on camera. So it's a combination of appearance and the ability to communicate well in a conversational manner that makes the viewer feel comfortable."

"What would happen if you put unattractive people on your network, even if they communicated well?"

"The same thing that would happen if we put attractive people on who couldn't communicate. No one would watch. It's all about ratings. Anchors have to have those two qualities if you're going to attract viewers. They need the right personality to go along with the looks. If they didn't we could just put a bunch of robots on the set."

"And if you don't attract those viewers?"

"You're either out of business or out of a job. The higher your ratings, the more you can charge for advertising. If you don't have strong ratings, sponsors won't want to advertise with your station."

"Thank you, Ms. Hack. Nothing further. Pass the witness." Stacy moved back to her desk and took a seat. I was beginning to relax a bit when one of the female attorneys got up from the other table and moved toward me. She was perhaps forty, very tall, and though she was a brunette, was a pretty good stand-in for Big Red, though not nearly as attractive. Horn-rimmed glasses perched on her pointed nose and no make-up, while her stern look conveyed a lack of personality. I wasn't sure if she was playing the part or if that was her true demeanor as she looked at me with small dark eyes.

"Ms. Hack, my name is Jocelyn Dix. I represent the plaintiff. Now let's get back to this… hiring process you talked about. I'd like to skip the part about running ads and go right to the selection process. After you've reviewed all the applications, looked at the tapes and interviewed the people, what happens next?"

"We present offers to those we want to hire."

"Hmmm. Nothing between that interview process and the offer?"

I looked to Stacy for a lifeline. How the hell was I supposed to answer?

"Don't ever look at me for help," she said. "It has to be your own answer."

"Okay," I said, then turned back to the other attorney. "The answer is no."

"Let me rephrase," said the attorney. "What happens during the interview process?"

Well, we talk a bit, but just like men we really don't listen and give them the bobblehead. Then we drag the guys up to a hotel room by their Johnson, tie them to the bedposts and screw their brains out. The ones who make us scream and leave claw marks on the headboard get hired. The others get thrown back into the pool like little fish.

"Well, we do a standard interview—"

She cut me off with a wave. "No, Ms. Hack, I want to know what happens *after* you're done *talking*." She moved closer and leaned on the witness box. "Isn't there part of this job application that takes place in a horizontal position away from the office? Something physical?"

I looked at Stacy again as I could feel beads of sweat running down my sides. She pointed me back to the other attorney. I didn't turn back to the attorney, instead looking at the floor. "We… uh… sleep with the applicants."

"I'm sorry, Ms. Hack. I didn't hear you. Could you repeat your answer?"

"We sleep with the applicants," I said, a little louder, still with my head down.

"Sleep… or have sex?"

"We… have sex with them."

"And the ones who give you the most pleasure get hired, is that about right?"

"Uh… basically."

"Way too apologetic," yelled one of the male lawyers.

Stacy got up and moved to the jury box as the other attorney stepped aside. "Syd, if you sound like you're apologizing for your actions you're admitting guilt. Don't look down, either. In your mind you did nothing wrong and you must convey that in court. And stop looking at me for an answer. When a jury sees that they'll think you're looking for a legal way to get around the question. When you even give a hint that you're trying to avoid the truth, everything they hear will be a lie in their minds."

"How the hell do I answer questions like that without looking like a total sleaze?" I asked.

"Answer truthfully. Hide nothing. As a manager, you've been acting like a man," she said. "Remember, they've been doing this for years. You're just following their playbook. Keep that in the back of your mind at all times."

"Okay," I said. "I think I'm getting it."

Well, as they say, the truth needs no rehearsal.

The other attorney continued her questioning as Stacy returned to her seat. "So, once again, take me through the interview process, from the questions and answers till the time you get a goodnight kiss from these… job applicants."

I sat up straight and looked at Rica, suddenly getting an infusion of confidence. I needed her *screw it* attitude.

"Well," I said, leaning on one arm of the chair and looking straight at the lawyer. "We've pretty much made up our minds by looking at the tapes. The actual interview is just a chance to get acquainted and to make sure they look the same as they do on the video. We have a suite at the Plaza and we take the job applicants there and have sex with them. If we enjoy it, if they know how to treat a woman, and we want more, we hire them."

"If not?" asked the attorney.

"We don't."

"Is this consensual?"

"Of course. What young single man is going to turn down sex, especially with a woman who takes the initiative? Every man's fantasy, right?"

"So that's it?" asked the attorney. "*That's* your criteria for hiring an anchor?"

"We can't sell a product if we haven't sampled it ourselves, can we?"

"Excellent!" shouted the male attorney. "Much more confident."

"You really want it that way?" I asked. "That sounded awfully arrogant."

"It's the only way we can win," said Stacy.

I exhaled and began to relax as the other attorneys peppered me with more questions for about thirty minutes. The waterworks under my arms turned off. I was beginning to see the justice system was not at all about right and wrong, but winning and losing.

Only in America. *Yes, your honor. We're a bunch of sexually aggressive women and we chase younger men around desks at work. So sue me!*

Jillian picked up the ball after me and did very well. Once again, tough to find any anger for a blue-eyed strawberry blonde even when she talks about an employee being asked to lick whipped cream from her body after removing her Wonder Woman costume. I did note the male attorneys turned away from the monitors when Jillian walked to and from the jury box, their eyes following her legs. I also noted that at the mention of said Wonder Woman costume, they both looked at each other with raised eyebrows. You could tell they wanted to be wrapped up in her magic lariat.

Rica, on the other hand, might need more practice with her answers and have to tone down the Brooklyn, even though her confidence in the jury box is unrivaled. She took Stacy's call for honesty a little too literally. Here's a typical exchange:

Attorney: "Would you explain the term *checking references*?"

Rica: "Yeah, I jump their bones until they beg for mercy. If the gum falls out of my mouth, they're hired."

Neely, meanwhile, had no trouble with anything. Her on-camera background came in handy as she knew how to play to both the camera and the audience while turning on the Southern belle thing.

Attorney: "Would you explain the term *checking references*?"

Neely: "Well, you know, y'all don't buy a brand of baking powder if another woman tells you it won't make your biscuits rise. So we're just making sure the recipe works before we tell other people out there in TV land to try it."

Then, as she left the jury box, she debuted what is now known as "the drop" as she removed the glasses and let her hair down. This was followed by an audible "whoa" in stereo from the two male attorneys as she (and there's really no other word to describe it) *sashayed* back to her seat while her hair bounced gently off her shoulders. I swear to God the woman has mastered the art of moving in slow motion and that there are unseen electric fans scattered around the universe that blow wisps of her hair back.

"That…uh…works," said one of the men, voice cracking. Neely shot him the cat that ate the canary look as all the women in the room laughed.

"We'll do this a few more times," said Stacy. "But I think we're off to a good start."

I thanked everyone as we left, noting that the two men were playing back the hair drop over and over.

YouTube, here we come.

CHAPTER FOURTEEN

I was really glad when Stacy put the gag order on us regarding the trial.

Now, with just a few weeks to go, I'm wondering if she should put one on herself.

Because tonight she's a guest, along with Big Red, on cable's most popular evening news talk show, *Up Close*. Honestly, I don't see how anything good can come out of this, but I'm not a lawyer. The host of the show, Vince Gallo, is a solid, tough, pit bull journalist in the Mike Wallace mode. He also goes for the kill when he has someone backed into a corner. Gallo, incredibly in this day and age, doesn't skew left or right politically. He may be the last truly objective guy in the news business.

I'm just worried about which way he skews sexually. I don't mean if he's gay, because he isn't, but where his morals lie regarding what we're doing here at CGR. I mean, if he's a guy who has sex the same way with his wife in the same position every Friday night and the raciest magazine in his home is Redbook, we're in trouble. If, since he's in his late fifties, he's one of those guys who chased women around the news ticker and nailed a cute intern or two in an editing booth while tying her up with videotape, we might be okay.

Stacy contends that since the story has taken on a life of its own in the papers lately, television coverage couldn't hurt. After all, we're gonna have cameras in our faces for God knows how long in just a few days.

So we're at my place tonight, sitting down with wine and some killer Brie around the television, like we're getting ready for the Super Bowl.

"I wish they'd let *us* go on," said Rica. "I'm not wild about this gag order."

"Problem is, you'd tell him what you really think," said Neely.

"Your point being?" asked Rica, as she popped a cracker loaded with cheese.

Jillian turned up the sound as the commercial ended and the craggy face of Vince Gallo filled the screen. "Here we go."

Gallo was one of those guys who looked like he'd closed down a few bars in his day. The bulbous red nose with the tiny visible veins is always a dead giveaway. Despite the extensive wrinkles around the deep-set olive green eyes and across his forehead, he still maintained a strong jaw and looked fit. Thirty years ago he might have even qualified for the doable category, but it was hard to imagine now, since he had so many miles on his face. His thick black hair didn't have a hint of gray, though he could be doing the Grecian Formula thing and could really be on his way to the gold chains, white chest hair and black socks club of Boca Raton.

"Welcome back," said Gallo, as the camera did a slow zoom.

"Check out the graphic," said Neely, as she pointed to the screen. Sitting brightly over Gallo's shoulder was a still-frame of a woman perching on the edge of the desk, taken from the CGR promo we'd run at the Upfront.

"One of the hot legal stories these days is sex discrimination," said Gallo, "though it's not the kind of sex discrimination you're used to hearing about. This case isn't about hiring men or women, but whether a person is good looking enough to have sex with a boss. And the bosses in this case, are women. Incredible? Well, that sounded pretty strange to us, so we invited the two lawyers involved in this bizarre lawsuit to our show." The shot went to a split screen, with Stacy on the right and Big Red on the left.

"Stacy looks good in red," said Neely.

Gallo continued. "With me tonight are Stacy Heller, the attorney representing the CGR network, and Kate O'Hara, the lawyer for the plaintiff who is suing CGR for discrimination. I'm going to start with you, Ms. O'Hara. So let me get this straight. Your guy contends he wasn't hired as an anchor because he's too unattractive to have sex with the women who run this network? I mean, I know this trial is in New Jersey, but is this for real?"

"Absolutely, Vince," said Big Red. "My client is forty-five, bald and stocky. And apparently not sexually desirable by the women who run the new CGR network. Those are the reasons he wasn't hired."

The screen cut to video of the Monopoly Guy at the anchor desk. The tape was a bit grainy and obviously old, since he was much thinner.

"Yeah, we would've hired him," said Jillian.

"Maybe after a gallon of vodka," said Rica.

Big Red was still on her soapbox. "All the male anchors on CGR are under thirty and look like models, and some don't even have any television experience at all. The women who run CGR hired them for two reasons. They look good, and they were willing to have sex to get the job. My client wasn't even considered for a job, despite the fact that he has extensive television news experience."

The shot went back to a full screen of the host, who was trying to suppress a grin.

"Gallo wouldn't have hired him either," I said.

"Ms. Heller," said Gallo, "these are pretty strong charges. How do you respond?"

Stacy filled the screen. "Well, Vince, first of all Ms. O'Hara is wrong about one thing. CGR is not a news network, so any news experience had no bearing on the people who were hired. Some did have news experience, but many did not. Some had television experience that had nothing to do with news. CGR was looking for attractive people who communicate well, much the way your network does, Vince. I don't see any ugly people running around your network, and I dare say, if blonde hair dye were taken off the market you guys would be out of business."

"Okay," said the host, "I understand that point, but let's get to the stuff that is making headlines here and makes this lawsuit so unusual. That little thing about the female managers having sex on job interviews. That kind of jumps out—"

Big Red interrupted. "If the women doing the hiring didn't want to sleep with the job applicants, they weren't considered. I don't know how to say it any plainer than that. CGR has a casting couch mentality and my client didn't warrant a space on the couch."

"If that is true," said Stacy, "how is that any different than the way men have been running television stations for years? Or any other business for that matter? You've been around a while, Vince. I'm sure in your younger days, back before political correctness and sexual harassment, that you might have come on to a female co-worker, or you might have known of a woman who was inter- viewed in a hotel room." A sheepish grin grew across the host's face. "And I can tell from that look on your face that you know what I'm talking about. Are you not married to a woman who works for you in the news department? I'm sure you might have stolen a kiss or two in the station hallway when you first met. And did she get promoted because of her relationship with you? Talk about sleeping with the boss."

"Damn, she's good," said Jillian.

"Girl does her homework," I said.

Vince Gallo's eyebrows went up, and I knew Stacy had him. "Well," he said, "we've been married a long time and how we met is ancient history—"

"No, it really isn't," said Stacy. "You know damn well this stuff still goes on in America, but because CGR is run by women this is somehow different. I'm sure plenty of female anchors have earned their broadcasting kneepads in the boardroom or the hotel room."

"Whoa," we all said in unison.

"And she wants *me* to draw the curtain on anger," said Rica.

"It's still sexual harassment," said Big Red. "As well as discrimination."

Stacy ignored the comment. "And as for people being hired because of their appearance, Vince, I don't suspect you'd have this show if you looked like Frankenstein. I did a little checking on your network's website… turns out four of your anchors have actually won beauty pageants and one has gotten married to a corporate executive who works for this network. She wasn't anchoring when she was hired, but since she got married she's one of the faces of this network. I'm sure if your conference room could talk it could fill a romance novel. So let's not pretend this doesn't go on in news organizations… and once again, let me remind you that CGR is not a news organization."

"Then, Ms. Heller, how would you define CGR's product?" asked the host. "I checked it out for a few hours, and I'll admit the network does have a lot of lifestyle pieces and features, but it does broadcast stories of current events."

Stacy shook her head. "CGR doesn't run death and destruction stories, stories about war or politics. CGR is a theater of information—"

"Oh, please," said Big Red. "Here we go with the semantics again. If there's news in it, then it's a newscast."

"Ladies, we're coming up on a break," said Gallo. "So we need—"

"One more thing," said Stacy. "I'd like to point out that some of the female anchors on CGR are over forty, so you can't say we discriminate based on age. Are there any women over forty on your network, Vince?"

"Couldn't tell you, Ms. Heller," said the host, suddenly growing a sly grin. "You should know a gentleman never discusses a woman's age."

"Then we shouldn't be discussing a man's age in this lawsuit," said Stacy. "It's all about talent and ratings, giving the viewers what they want. If your ratings went down to zero, Vince, what would happen?"

"I'd be out of a job, but luckily that isn't the case," he said. The music that led to a commercial faded up as Gallo shared the screen with the two lawyers. "The trial begins with jury selection on November first in New Jersey, and will be covered in its entirety by our sister network, The Justice Channel," he said. "Ms. O'Hara, Ms. Keller, thank you for being with us, and I'm sure we'll be hearing more from you both in the future."

Jillian muted the sound. "Jeez, if she can stand up to Vince Gallo, imagine how she'll do in court. She really controlled the interview."

"She left the other attorney in the dust," said Rica. "I don't think the woman really made her case at all."

"I originally thought this was a bad idea," I said. "But now I'm seeing the method to her madness. Stacy actually made what we're doing in the bedroom seem like it makes sense."

"Yep, we can hire whoever we want and screw their brains out," said Neely. "Isn't America great?"

* * *

"Good morning," said Catwoman, "and thank you for joining us."

"It's Wednesday, October thirty-first," said Superman. "Happy Halloween."

And that's how we began our October 31st morning show on CGR. In costume.

It was Amanda's idea, and I think it's absolutely brilliant. She called Stacy on Monday with the concept, Stacy loved it and sent us all running down to a costume shop. (Some people didn't need to rent costumes, having a, ahem, decent supply of their own, but that's beside the point.)

Here's the theory with the trial starting tomorrow: we're going to have all our people anchor in costume all friggin' day. Then, when we hit the courtroom and Big Red tries to paint us as a legitimate news organization, we can simply point to our Halloween airchecks and contend that no newscast in America would let its anchors do entire shows dressed as superheroes or varying degrees of trollops for the whole day. I should point out that we had to buy the costumes instead of renting them, because we then took them to a tailor for, shall we say, alterations. While some outfits, like Catwoman, are naturally seductive, other classics were rated *G* and needed to be hemmed up to an *R*. I'm sure when American men saw one female anchor dressed as Dorothy from *The Wizard of Oz* in a low-cut minidress and ruby platforms many considered moving to Kansas, tornadoes be damned.

So all that Big Red will be left with is Monopoly Guy, who doesn't need a costume to go trick or treating.

I can see it now. One of our anchors on the stand, dressed to the nines in a revealing outfit, being hammered by opposing counsel.

Big Red: "Is this the type of attire you usually wear around the office? A short skirt and four inch stacked heels?"

Anchor: "No, sometimes I dress up in leather like Xena, Warrior Princess."

Of course, this means we're having a big Halloween party tonight. Amanda rented our favorite hotel ballroom (while booking several rooms, natch) and dropped a dime on the local tabloid photographers, so we're hoping our news reputation will be torpedoed and sink like a stone in the morning papers. We've finally figured out how to use the tabloids to our advantage. They want sexy gossip, we're gonna give it to them. Let Big Red wake up to something lousy for a change.

I know, I know, you want to know what the girls and I will be wearing tonight.

We had a ball at the costume shop. Rica got a wild idea when she found an antebellum dress in the back and came out of the dressing room wearing it while twirling a matching pink parasol, looked Neely in the eye, and before she could say anything Neely put up her hand and said, "Don't even think about it, or I'm getting that Rizzo costume from *Grease*." Rica, of course, probably intrigued at the prospect of Neely smacking gum in a pink satin jacket, remained in character and attempted to do the famous line from *Gone With the Wind*. Though it came out, "As Gawd is my witness, I'll nevuh go hungry again. Eh, fuhgeddaboudit." Rica decided against the costume, realizing that a hoop skirt required a good deal of clearance just to get around (and a great deal of trouble to remove in a hurry), and instead settled on a gypsy fortune teller costume, which, she said, would enable her to "predict" any man's immediate future in her bedroom. I got your crystal ball *right here*.

Neely, seeing that Rica had ditched the My-Cousin-Vinny-meets-Scarlett-O'Hara idea, did the same with the Grease costume and chose a nun's outfit. But she altered tradition a bit, and didn't remotely resemble Sister Mary Hatchetface. While keeping the habit, she added a miniskirt, thigh-high boots, and a whip, saying she was going as "Mother Superior" and that she would be doling out "penance" during the evening. That girl is gonna be in confession forever, and if her picture makes the paper, the Cardinal himself will ban her from Saint Pat's. She's just begging the man upstairs to hit her with a lightning bolt. Rica, who also grew up Catholic (though Neely obviously missed the classes on guilt) took one look and said, "I'd better go light a candle for her."

Jillian probably has The Snack on her radar for the evening, as she went right for the cave girl costume, complete with club. No one will ever be able to look at Wilma Flintstone the same again after seeing Jillian in that short bearskin outfit.

I was originally drawn to the genie costume, but since I'm not taking orders from men it didn't make much sense to walk around granting wishes like Barbara Eden. I decided to forego anything revealing for once and go for something classy, and will be dressed as Aphrodite, the Greek goddess of love. I just thought it was appropriate given the circumstances.

The tabloids took the bait.

The prospect of seeing the defendants in the hottest trial since O.J. partying the night away in costumes, the day before the opening day of jury selection, was too much to resist.

Vegas had nothing on the fantasies that must have been flying around the room. Men dressed as superheroes, sultans and exotic dancers (The Snack came as a Chippendale. Wonder who gave him that idea?) and women flitting about as everything from a slutty hospital candystriper (injection, anyone?) to Disney characters who had gone off the wholesome reservation. The sight of Cinderella asking men to help her try on heels with straps that snaked all the way up around her calf is not something you're ever gonna see in Orlando.

I was snacking on the wonderful hors d'oeuvres when Amanda (dressed as a pirate wench) escorted a woman toward me who was wearing digital cameras like bandoleros and had a giant duffle bag slung over her shoulder. This is why photographers are sometimes known as lens mules. Though they are artists, they still have to haul a ton of gear.

"Syd, I'd like you to meet Dina Herschel," she said. "She's with the Daily Tattler."

I swallowed my spinach quiche, wiped my hand with a napkin and extended it. "Thank you so much for coming on short notice," I said. "Make yourself at home."

"This is incredible," she said, as she gazed around the room with large emerald eyes like a starving woman. She dropped her voice. "I've never seen so many gorgeous men in one place." She was my age, medium height and slender, and despite the frazzled shoulder-length brown hair you could tell there was a swan underneath all the weight of the gear and deadlines. Her eyes locked on Denton, who was wearing a genie's costume. She grabbed her camera and quickly snapped a few pictures. She then took out a small pad and pen. "That large man over there who came out of a bottle? His name would be?"

"Denton Hale," I said. "One of our anchors."

"Man, if only I had three wishes…" She wrote down his name as she continued to stare. It was obvious that she was intoxicated by him.

"Why don't I introduce you?" I asked.

"Well, sure." Big smile. "I mean, if you insist."

I waved Denton over and the photographer stood up straight and hurriedly smoothed her hair. He arrived in puffy harem pants, a turban and a vest that didn't cover much of his chiseled torso. "Denton, this is Dina, she's a newspaper photographer. Would you please do me a favor, escort her around and take care of introductions? She needs help putting names to faces."

He bowed to her, staying in character. "Your wish is my command, Miss. May I carry that bag for you?"

"Thank you," she said, gazing up at the man who towered over her as he took the heavy bag from her shoulder and put it over his own as if it was weightless.

"Have you had dinner yet, Dina?" I asked.

"No, I was going to grab something on the way back to the paper."

"Make sure she gets something to eat," I said to Denton. "And take care of any… other needs… she might have."

Denton nodded as he got the message and escorted the beaming photographer through the crowd.

Thirty minutes later I saw her sitting at a table, eating dinner with Denton.

Ten minutes after that they were headed for the elevator.

An hour later the photography Sherpa was back, beaming, with Denton on her arm. He looked happier than I'd ever seen him.

"I have to get back to the paper now," she said. "Just wanted to thank you for the, uh… hospitality. I must say this beats covering perp walks and stalking Hollywood drunks."

"Thanks for coming by," I said. "Oh, if you could do me a favor and not publish a picture of the woman dressed as the nun, I'd appreciate it. We don't need to lose the Catholic vote."

"Not a problem," said Dina, who took one last look around the room. "Looks like this is a great place to work."

"It's also a fun place to work," I said.

"I don't suppose you'd have much use for a still photographer at a television network?"

"Not really," I said. "But we're always looking for good video people, and you've already got a photographer's eye. If you'd like to learn the business I guess you could be sort of an intern. Maybe come by after work or on your day off?"

"I'd like that," she said. Denton's smile grew. "I work weekends, so Monday and Tuesday are my days off."

Oh, this is too easy.

It's a hanging curveball over the middle of the plate, Syd. Swing, batter!

"Tell you what," I said. "Why don't you come by Mondays and you can work with Denton."

She looked up at him. "That okay with you?"

"If that is your third wish, Miss," he said, bowing again as the genie.

"So, you already blew two wishes, huh?" I asked.

Dina leaned toward me and whispered. "Among other things."

CHAPTER FIFTEEN

"Yabba dabba *do me*?" said Jillian, incredulous that her picture in the tabloid had such a suggestive headline.

"You're the one who picked the cave girl costume," said Rica. "Wilma Flintstone wasn't drawn with legs up to her neck, you know." Neely and I laughed as the driver headed toward the courthouse. I could hear him chuckling as well.

"I didn't deserve *that*," said Jillian, snapping the newspaper closed and slapping it on the seat.

"Hey, we made all the gossip pages, that's what counts," I said. "You just took one for the team. And may I remind you that it was your dress that got me the va-va-voom caption."

"You betcha," said Neely, getting into her own character as she checked her pinned-up hair in a compact mirror.

"You look good, governor," said Rica. "Going hunting?"

"Just for some male jurors," said Neely. "They're in season." She put on the glasses she didn't need and began to touch up her lipstick.

Our driver turned a corner and the courthouse came into view. And just like that, my edge was back in a flash.

I now knew what it felt like to *be* the lead story.

A half dozen satellite trucks were lined up outside the building, their white dishes pointing toward the sky like giant electronic petunias. Long, thick black camera cables snaked their way through various doors and windows. Some reporters were doing live shots, while other crews circled like sharks waiting for our arrival.

They smelled the blood in the water and moved toward the car as it rolled up to the curb.

"Here we go," I said, my heart suddenly jumping into overdrive. "Remember, say nothing and stay close together." They nodded as the car came to a halt.

The crisp November air and low angle of the morning sunshine hit me in the face as I exited the car with the girls. The familiar smell of the north Jersey swamps filled my lungs and instantly left a stale taste in my mouth. Amanda, Madison, Stacy and her legal team emerged from the car directly in front and moved toward us.

And then the media horde descended on us like children at an Easter egg hunt.

The shoe was on the other foot.

Bodies began to press closer, while camera lights added to the glare from the sun. We got bumped and shoved like we were being packed into a subway car at rush hour; manners went out the window when it came to big stories. Reporters jockeyed for position, while questions and microphones jabbed us like daggers.

"Is it true a man has to sleep with you to get a job?"

"How many members of your staff have you slept with?"

"Are all the female anchors having sex with their co-anchors?"

And one that actually caused me to smile.

"Hey Sydney, am I good looking enough for your bedroom?"

(The answer, by the way, would have been no, as the man asking the question made the Monopoly Guy seem like George Clooney in comparison.)

Stacy led her group to ours and started herding us up the steps of the courthouse toward the front door.

A young male reporter and burly photographer stood their ground right in front of our path and obviously had no intention of moving. The reporter shoved his microphone within inches of

Stacy's face as she reached his position. "Miss Heller, how can you possibly put up a defense for these charges?"

That one got Stacy to stop and answer a question.

"You'll see our defense inside," she said. "I'm confident that once the jury has the full story, they'll see the charges are without merit. And considering the amount of news coverage here this morning, the rest of the country will see it as well. My clients have done absolutely nothing wrong. This is simply sour grapes from a man who didn't get the job he wanted."

"What exactly is that *full story*?" shouted another reporter.

"As they say in television, stay tuned," said Stacy, who then turned and led us up the stairs.

"Nice tease," I whispered in her ear.

We made our way through the doors, with the media horde trailing us like the wake of a ship. A few guards cleared a path for us and kept the outdoor reporters at bay while we headed down the hall to the courtroom.

But the courtroom was no bargain either, as just about every seat was taken by a member of the media. Three cameras were stationed in the room, with a photographer manning each one. At least the place was warm compared to our rehearsal courtroom, between the sunlight pouring through the long windows and the body heat from the packed house.

Stacy led us to our table, an ancient oak number covered with nicks and cigarette burns, which, I was happy to see, was the one closest to the jury. They'd get an up close and personal look at Jillian's skirt and Neely's falling hair. Amanda, Madison, and the other two lawyers took seats directly behind us in the first row. Still photographers jumped in front of our table, snapping pictures as fast as their digital auto-winders would allow.

This was going to be a lot more than fifteen minutes of fame.

Oh, shit, indeed.

* * *

If anyone is smart, they'll edit the jury selection process into a reality show. Just pick any courtroom in any city and you've got built-in entertainment five days a week. And you'd only have to pay your "stars" a few bucks a day.

Here I thought courtrooms were these stately symbols of decorum, and this one didn't disappoint, with marble floors that echoed when you walked, ornate wood railings and antique ceiling fans right out of *Inherit the Wind*. Despite the trappings, they're a haven for the sophistication challenged. Stacy had told us that juries are made up of people too stupid to get out of jury duty, and from the looks of things she's right.

Half the people in the jury pool looked like they rolled out of bed, didn't bother to comb their hair and had set their clothes dryer on the "add wrinkles" setting. The rest were a mixture of casually dressed people, with a few business types mixed in who acted like they wanted to be anywhere but here. But for many, the prospect of being on national television trumped any inconvenience. You could tell a lot of prospects saw this as a chance for their shot at reality fame, while being paid the whopping sum of, get this, five dollars per day by the Garden State. If the trial goes longer than three days (and this one should), they get a raise to forty bucks. Then they can afford a hot dog from the cart outside.

An elderly female clerk who looked like she didn't even have enough personality to work at the Department of Motor Vehicles (either that, or she died in 1989) called the name of the first prospective juror, Robert Jenks, in a lifeless monotone. Rica leaned over toward me as the man, who had come to court with a sleeveless shirt despite the chilly weather, made his way toward the jury box. The burly guy in his forties smiled for the camera, revealing stained brown teeth, while his bare tattooed shoulders the size of canned hams had so much fur you wondered if he was the New Jersey cousin of Bigfoot.

Rica leaned over toward me. "Syd, do you hear that?" she whispered.

"What?"

"Theme song from *Deliverance*."

Sadly, this wasn't the gong show, as each lawyer only had three strikes by which a prospective juror could be dismissed without cause. In our case, this meant any woman dressed like a prude, or my mother.

Big Red approached the man. "Mister Jenks, how would you feel if part of your job description required you to sleep with your boss on a regular basis?"

"I'd quit," said the sasquatch, a grin slowly growing across his face. "Harry's not my type."

The courtroom roared as Big Red's face started to match her hair. She shook her head, obviously mad at herself for setting the guy up for such an easy punch line. I was beginning to see Stacy's point about how important it was to phrase things correctly.

"Let me rephrase," said Big Red, trying to shout over the laughter, as the judge, a man with a salt and pepper crew cut and a taut face in his mid-fifties, swung his gavel and called for order. "How would you feel if your boss was a woman?"

The guy turned toward us and nodded at Jillian. "Well, if my boss looked like Strawberry Shortcake over there, hell, I'd work for free."

Steeee—rike one!

Big Red quickly used her first peremptory challenge. The New Jersey sasquatch trudged off, disappointed that he'd have to go back to the forest, while Jillian's freckles went ablaze.

"At least your new nickname goes well with The Snack," whispered Neely.

"Dear God, this is not my day," muttered Jillian, as the cameraman next to the jury box zoomed in on her. She tried her best to keep her chin up and look straight ahead.

Other highlights of the morning bound to make the recap segments of other networks:

—The seventy-year-old woman with a beehive hairdo, long

skirt, and blouse buttoned up to her neck whose tightened catcher's mitt face told you she hadn't had sex in decades. (*They're selling costumes of my mother? Who knew?*) The line that made Stacy use one of her strikes was, "Of course men want to work there. These women paraded into this courtroom like a bunch of wanton harlots." Well, at least it's a step up from *trollop*.

—The lone businessman in a suit who said, "Hell, I've been getting screwed by my company for years. What's the difference? At least with them I'd enjoy it."

—The young flight attendant who admitted watching our network. "I'm not gonna look this good forever. They've got a lot of good information for women over thirty. Now I know I don't have to rush out and get married. That I can still get a younger man when I'm older."

—The fortyish woman who said CGR had already turned her life around. "That channel gave me the courage to ask a thirty-year-old man out on a date. And when he accepted, I felt young again." When Big Red asked if she had slept with the man, she rolled her eyes and said, with an accent like Rica's, "No, we held hands and played Parcheesi while listening to Perry Como records."

—The hardbodied bike messenger who couldn't stop staring at Rica. "I wouldn't mind having her on my delivery route."

By the lunch recess eight jurors had been seated, four men and four women. Stacy was down to her last strike, and Big Red had already burned all of hers.

So in that respect, we were winning.

* * *

"Remember," said Neely, as we walked back into the courtroom after lunch, "just like we rehearsed."

"I know," said Rica. "We all sit down first after the judge comes back."

The cameras followed us as we walked down the center aisle,

176

over to our table, and sat down.

The bailiff stood up and bellowed, "All rise!"

Everyone in the courtroom stood up as the honorable James Courtney made his way to the bench. "You may be seated," he said.

And then, what happened next may go down in the annals of the American court system as the day Justice dropped her blindfold.

Neely stood in front of her seat as the entire room sat down. Then (here's that slow motion thing again) she calmly removed her glasses with one hand and with the other pulled her hairclip out. She closed her eyes, leaned her head back like she was in a shower, and shook out her long brunette locks. The loose curls gently cascaded to her shoulders (there's really no other way to describe it) and bounced perfectly into place.

An audible gasp from the men filled the room. The judge's jaw dropped as Neely opened her eyes, took her seat and smiled at him.

The judge tried to compose himself as he started to shuffle some papers on the bench. "Uh… Ms. O'Hara, call your first witness," he said.

"We haven't finished jury selection, your honor," said Big Red, obviously annoyed.

"Right," he said, wiping his brow. "I knew that." Stacy bit her lip to keep from joining in the snickers that floated through the courtroom.

At least we know the judge is human.

* * *

Luckily, jury selection finished quickly after lunch and the judge sent everyone home at two-thirty, which gave us some time to get back to the office and do some actual work. Although we hired plenty of good producers who can keep the ship afloat while we're away.

Tomorrow the trial starts for real, and we get to do the run through the media gauntlet all over again. Final total on the jury:

six men, six women. I suspect two of the middle-aged women wouldn't mind dating our anchors, while three of the men kept checking us out. But one guy has an obvious crush on Big Red. *Hey, buddy, there's a copper top over here who's not a robot!*

Speaking of potential in the bedroom, Stacy decided to have our trophy bucks rotate through the courtroom when they were off the clock, and sit directly behind us. Gotta let the women on the jury understand two things, a: what they're missing; and b: why we do what we do.

And of course, let the people watching the court channels see what they need to watch when the court is not in session.

Judge Courtney, meanwhile, kept stealing occasional glances at Neely, while she of course kept smiling at him and batting her eyes. There may be a bit of snow on the judge's roof but there's still fire in that furnace.

Oh, I almost forgot. I got a very interesting call around five this afternoon from a well-known publisher of a well-known men's magazine in which clothing for women is not an option. His slick FM-overnight voice practically oozed through the phone, every word sliding into the next as if it were covered with oil.

Publisher: "I'd like to strike while the iron is hot, Ms. Hack. I'm thinking of a pictorial called *The Babes of CGR*. If you agree, we'd have just enough time to get you into our Christmas issue. This would be great publicity for your new network. And I'm willing to pay each woman who participates one hundred thousand dollars."

Me: (Playing along.) "A pictorial? Well, that sounds interesting. What sort of pictures do you have in mind?"

Publisher: "Well, they would of course be very tasteful. Perhaps some of your anchors could lie across the set, or do some fun things with television equipment."

Me: (Really playing along.) "What sort of outfits would they be wearing?"

Publisher: "Uh, Ms. Hack, I assumed you knew that we publish nude pictures. But they are very artistic."

He explained some of the "settings" he had in mind. I was almost tempted to do it just to send Mother headfirst into her own vomit, but only if the pictorial carried the title "Trollops of Cable Television." But then the thought of sitting naked on top of a studio camera straddling a teleprompter while giving an oral exam to a microphone seemed too damned uncomfortable.

By seven o'clock we'd caught up on stuff at work, and, exhausted, headed over to my place, had Chinese delivered, and sat down to watch the coverage that had just about filled up my DVR.

Jillian, obviously wanting to see the fallout from the Strawberry Shortcake comment, practically dove for the couch and grabbed the remote just before Neely got it. We had taped three different channels and Jillian cued up one of those giving us wall-to-wall coverage. I downed some kung pao chicken which set my mouth on fire, but it was a good kind of hot, and something I needed after sitting down all day. Smells of garlic and soy sauce filled the air while takeout boxes covered the coffee table. Four fortune cookies taunted me, but I wasn't about to tempt fate.

"Roll it," said Rica, as she settled down on the floor with her plate and speared a wonton with her fork.

Jillian fired the remote and we saw ourselves getting out of the car. "And there are the defendants in the case," said the male commentator. "Those are the executives who run CGR and are accused of discrimination."

"They look like a bunch of fashion models," said the female anchor. "I'm not sure I've seen outfits like that in any trial of this nature before."

"Honey, it's what *all* the defendants are wearing these days," said Neely. "Would you rather see us in orange jumpsuits and shackles?"

"Really," said Jillian, sipping some egg drop soup. "Do they expect us to dress like the jury?"

Jillian hit the fast forward button until the sasquatch came into view. She hit the play button just as he hung the new nickname on her and the screen offered a high-def view of her blushing face. The audio from the courtroom faded down just as the man was dismissed.

"The woman he referred to as *Strawberry Shortcake*," said the male commentator, "is Jillian Charles, one of the executive producers at CGR. Before joining the network she was a News Director in Chicago for the network's affiliate there."

"Don't let the innocent face fool you," said the female anchor. "She presided over one of the biggest staff purges the Windy City has ever seen. She's known in broadcasting as one tough cookie."

"So which do you prefer, cookie or shortcake?" I asked. "You're just collecting all sorts of baked goods for your aliases."

"Cupcake is still available," said Neely.

"At least they said I can be tough," said Jillian. "Still doesn't make up for *yabba dabba do me*, though."

Rica washed down her food and turned to her. "You know, I, for one, would like to see what your game face looks like when you fire someone. It's not like you had a lotta success with the death stare."

Jillian smiled. "Ah, but that's the advantage of looking so innocent. I just seem so sad when I let someone go, they can't possibly get mad at me."

"But you *love* canning people," said Neely.

"Yeah. Killing them with kindness as I lop off their heads," said Jillian. "All right, enough of this dessert talk, I wanna see the hair drop." She hit the remote and fast forwarded to the point where we re-entered the courtroom. "I hope there's a reaction shot."

"The defendants are coming back," said the female commentator, "just in time, I might say. And Judge Courtney is a stickler for punctuality. You don't want to get on his bad side on the first day of the trial."

"There are just a few more jurors to seat, so jury selection should be wrapped up this afternoon," said her male counterpart. "And here comes the judge now."

We heard the bailiff bark his orders as the judge entered the courtroom. We saw everyone sit down except for Neely. Then we got lucky as the coverage cut to a tight shot of her.

"One of the defendants is not taking her seat," said the male commentator, just as Neely started her routine. "Maybe she is going to address the court—" We heard an audible exhale from the anchor, who didn't say anything else as the hair came to rest. Neely then sat down and the view cut to a wide shot of the room, with every man in it staring at her.

"That's Neely Collins," said the female anchor, picking up the ball. "She's a former reporter from New Orleans who made her way into management and ran the affiliate in Dallas before coming to the new network. She's got a few Emmys under her belt for her work in the field. And apparently a few tricks up her sleeve. If she's looking for attention, she just got it."

The screen then filled with an instant replay of the hair drop. "Some people commented this morning that she looked like a younger version of the former Governor of Alaska," said the male anchor.

"I can't picture Sarah Palin doing *that*," said his co-anchor. "Well, at least not in court."

"Sonofabitch," said Rica. "It actually worked."

"Aren't you glad I don't have a pixie cut," said Neely.

"You know they'll be waiting for that tomorrow," I said.

"Happy to oblige," said Neely, running her fingers back through her hair.

Eeeeee! Eeeeee! Eeeeee!

That's my cell phone and Rica's early warning system! It works!

Rica lunged across the table and grabbed my phone. "It's your mother! Don't answer that!"

"You think I'm nuts?" I said. "I'd rather talk to a telemarketer about life insurance."

"The voicemail ought to be good," said Jillian, pointing to the phone as she dipped an egg roll in hot mustard. "Play it back on speaker."

"She can't figure that part out," I said, "so she'll call the house phone next. The cell stopped ringing. "In five, four, three, two, one…" I pointed at the answering machine.

Annnnnnnd…. Cue the landline!

"Will she leave a message there?" asked Neely as the phone continued to ring.

"She will when she hears the new recording. I had Harrell do it for me." (Harrell has the sexiest voice on the staff. If he ever gets tired of anchoring, he could make a fortune with a 900 number asking lonely women, "So… what are you wearing?")

"This oughta be good," said Jillian, who muted the television. We all turned and stared in the direction of the answering machine.

The phone rang four times before the machine picked up and Harrell's satin voice filled the room. "You've reached the residence of Sydney Hack. Sydney is… tied up at the moment. Please leave a message and she'll return your call when she's… free."

The girls roared as the machine beeped. "Quiet!" I yelled. "Here it comes."

"Sydney… this is your mother calling. Well…(heavy sigh) I take it from your message that you are now… living in sin."

(At this point Neely jumps up from the couch and makes the sign of the cross over me like the Pope giving a blessing.)

"The women from the club have been calling me all day regarding your attire in the courtroom. I sincerely hope you and the rest of your… girls… will button up tomorrow. I'm really surprised at Jillian, she came from a good home. Don't call me back, I'm taking a pill and going to bed."

"Do your daughter a favor and take the whole friggin' bottle," said Rica.

"Jillian, will y'all tell us about what it was like growin' up in a real home," said Neely, laying on the accent. "The rest of us were raised by wolves out in a turnip patch."

With Mother banished thanks to technology (God bless whoever came up with the concept of personalized ringtones), we returned to the DVR.

Other highlights from the coverage on various networks:

—The anchor bimbette (we later discovered she was a twenty-four-year-old pageant queen) who commented that, "A verdict for the defendant would be seen by many as something which could seriously damage the credibility of journalists everywhere." She followed this up with a tease that said, "Coming up, we'll show you how a plane covered with icing crashed in the Rockies." It was probably chocolate frosting, but pilots have told me that buttercream is a real bitch to deal with when it gets in the engines.

—The man anchoring solo who didn't know his mike was on when a commercial dumped out early and said, "Did you check out the rack on—and we're back." The girls argued as to whose boobs he was referring to, but since the anchor would not have even fallen into the "doable" pile the point was moot. (It was probably Rica, in case you're wondering. She gets less eye contact from men than any of us, and she's the shortest one of the bunch, so guys really have to look down and it becomes blatantly obvious.)

—The legal analyst who stated that if all defendants looked like us, death row would be empty and the prison overcrowding problem would be solved.

—A talk show host who said, with a twinkle in his eye, "It's a good thing the judge was wearing a robe when that brunette let her hair down." His female co-host replied, while looking at his lap, "And a good thing that you're behind a desk."

Tomorrow though, it might not be all laughs, as some of us will be taking the stand.

And just for you, Mother, I'm going to wear something scandalous.

As Rica would say, I got your *living in sin* right here.

CHAPTER SIXTEEN

The horde was waiting for us again the next morning.

Yesterday we were just anonymous faces getting out of a car. Now, thanks to the wall-to-wall coverage, we are all household names.

While reporters peppered us with questions as we emerged from the car, the voice of a telephone worker in a bucket truck cut through the chatter.

"Hey, how 'bout a little whipped cream with that shortcake?"

Jillian snapped her head in the direction of the voice and saw a rugged middle-aged man in a hard hat twenty feet off the ground smiling at her. He blew her a kiss. "Ah, what the hell," she said. She waved at him and he pretended like he was hit with Cupid's arrow, as he put both hands over his heart. Of course, all of this was captured for the cameras.

"You've got a fan club there, Shortcake," said Neely.

"Like you don't," said Jillian. "You just don't have your own nickname yet."

* * *

"Call your first witness, Ms. O'Hara," said the judge.

I would have guessed that Big Red would start with Amanda

or Madison, and then work her way down the corporate ladder.

But it turns out she was going the other way.

"We call Frederica Carbone to the stand," said Big Red.

Rica's eyes narrowed and shot laser darts at the attorney. I could see it in her eyes. *This is war.*

My face tightened in puzzlement. "What's the deal?" I whispered to Stacy. "Why are they calling Rica first?"

"They're going for a big hit on day one," she said. "She'll try to take advantage of Rica's temper and get her to say something stupid. She wants to set the tone."

Rica stood up, still seething after hearing her proper name for the second time in a month, straightened her outfit and power-walked to the jury box, head held high. She raised her hand and took the oath. When asked if she swore to tell the truth, instead of saying yes, she said, "Absolutely." (I'm sure she wanted to say fuhgeddaboudit, but it might have played havoc with the court stenographer.)

Sure, she's got a temper and won't mince words, but she's really street-smart. That usually trumps book-smart around this part of the country.

I'm just hoping she's smarter than the Monopoly Guy's attorney, who has already pushed one big button.

"Ms. Carbone," said Big Red, clicking her heels on the marble floor as she slowly walked toward Rica. "What is your current position at CGR?"

"I'm one of the Executive Producers."

"And in that position, you have direct input into the people who are hired?"

"That's correct."

"What else does an Executive Producer do?"

"We have a hand in everything you see on the network, from the color of the set to the stories we produce to the interviews we book."

"Can you give us a brief recap of your career and tell us how you rose to that position?"

"Sure. I started as a newspaper reporter right out of college, and after two years I got hired by a television station as a writer. I worked my way up to field producer—"

The attorney put up her hand and stopped Rica. "For the benefit of the jury, what exactly is a field producer?"

"Well, you go out on the shoots, sometimes with a reporter, but a lot of times it's just you and the photographer. You gather all the information and even do the interviews. Then you might bring everything back to the reporter and help them put the piece together."

"So you basically did everything but appear on the air?"

"Yeah. All the work, none of the glory. Still, a great job if you don't have an ego problem."

"Well, I guess the obvious question for you is, why didn't you work on-camera? I mean, if this is a medium that values attractive people, you're certainly pretty enough."

It was at this point that Rica's accent came in real handy, and she laid it on thick.

"Well, thank you for the compliment, but this voice ain't exactly smooth like Sinatra. In fact, I can hear the mute buttons bein' pressed by people watchin' the channels coverin' this trial." Then she turned and faced the jury. "Any viewer outside of the New York area just switched ovuh to closed-captionin'."

Scattered laughs floated across the room. The jury, all residents of New Jersey, many of whom probably didn't think she had an accent, smiled and nodded.

She was one of them.

"Okay," said Big Red. "Let's get back to your career. After field producer..."

"Various management positions until I became News Director in Los Angeles for our affiliate there. A News Director oversees the news department of any station."

"And that was at the time when your network adopted what

we shall call its... *philosophy*."

Here we go.

"Call it whatever you want, but if you're referring to pairing a younger man with an older woman, yeah."

"What was the reason for that change?"

"The ratings weren't moving with the traditional distinguished older man and a young twinkie as anchor teams."

"Twinkie?"

"Bimbo, airhead, pretty face with nuthin' upstairs. A woman with the IQ of a Hostess Twinkie. Though some of 'em act more like Ho-Hos if you know what I mean."

"Okay," said Big Red. "So why did you reverse the roles?"

"Sydney Hack had success with it at the New York affiliate. The theory being that women over thirty still like to look at younger men. And that women over thirty are still attractive. We're just older, we're not dead."

Big Red walked back to her desk and picked up some papers. "And while running the news department in Los Angeles you hired a man in his mid-twenties named Dirk Anderson to be one of your main anchors, correct?"

"Yes."

"And would you tell the court what Mr. Anderson was doing for a living at the time you hired him?"

Rica looked at the attorney and answered very casually. "He was an underwear model."

More snickers from the crowd.

"Well, I'm curious as to how someone who poses in boxers is qualified to deliver the news?"

"Actually they were bikini briefs," said Rica, with a raised eyebrow. More laughs from the room. A gavel from the judge.

"So why did you hire him, Ms. Carbone? Nobody else out there in the entire country who fit the qualifications and actually had news experience?"

"I was looking for an attractive young man who communicated

well and had some name recognition in the market. Dirk is well known in Los Angeles, as he'd been on just about every billboard in town, and I'd seen him on a few talk shows. He had a great personality and a quick wit, so I invited him in for an interview. I found out during the interview that he's very smart, has two college degrees, and he's a nice guy who was looking for a career change."

"But there's more to the *interview* than just talk, isn't there, Ms. Carbone? You women at CGR have a code..." Big Red walked back to her table, picked up a legal pad and looked at it. "Something called *checking references*? What exactly does that mean?"

(Now Stacy had coached us on this and told us to answer very matter-of-factly, without using any of the following terms: jump their bones, injections of Y-chromosomes, or screw their brains out.)

Rica crossed her legs and leaned on one arm of her chair. "Checking references means having sex with the job applicant."

"So you had sex with Mr. Anderson."

"Yes," said Rica, smiling. Then she turned to the jury. "And his references checked out very well." Enough laughter this time for Judge Courtney to swing his gavel several times and call for order, though he was suppressing a grin when he did it. Big Red and the Monopoly Guy were the only people in the room not laughing.

"Suppose his… references… hadn't checked out?"

"Well, I wouldn't have hired him."

"That sounds a little harsh. So if a man doesn't meet your personal preferences—"

Rica waved her hands and interrupted. "You're not getting it. It's not about *my* preferences, but what our viewers want. It's more than just great sex. I needed a guy who understands what women want, as much as a guy can. As a gender we *are* pretty hard to figure out. I needed a guy who knew how to talk to a woman, how to make her feel special, how to ask what she wants and not just take. How to give when *she* asks. How to look at her as an equal in the bedroom and out of it. How to be comfortable when a woman wants to be the aggressor in bed and not be threatened by a woman supervisor at work. It's that total package that has to come across on television, and all those qualities translate to communicating in the way we wanted. Dirk may be a pretty face, but he had all the qualities I needed in an anchor. And considering the ratings have tripled since he came on board… at the station I mean… (more laughs) I'd say he's been a very successful hire."

"I assume the hiring process is the same at CGR as it relates to the male employees?"

"Yes."

"And what do you say to people like my client who didn't get hired at CGR under the same parameters?"

Rica looked at Monopoly Guy, put her palms up and shook her head. "I don't know. Hit the gym and join the Hair Club for Men?"

That brought the house down. By this point Big Red knew enough to put the shovel away, as our girl had put her in a trench. Rica owned the room and there was no point in trying to paint her into a corner.

* * *

"You really kicked her ass," said Stacy, shoving a forkful of salad into her mouth. We had a corner table in a dimly lit part of the restaurant, but we were still getting lots of looks from the men. The flat-screen above the bar was tuned to The Justice Channel, which didn't help.

"Fish in a barrel," said Rica, after swallowing a bloody bite of her rare hamburger. "You know, I was really hoping she would ask me to get into specifics about things in the bedroom."

"Yeah, that trapeze would have made a good headline in *The Post*," said Jillian.

A harried waitress came by and topped off our water glasses. I waited for her to leave before I turned to Stacy. "So if you were representing Monopoly Guy, what would your strategy be *now*? I mean, if you'd gotten off to such a bad start."

"Well," said Stacy, "if I totally bombed out on my first witness as badly as she did, I'd move directly to my next best bet and try to turn things around quickly."

Jillian sipped a glass of mineral water. "And that would be?"

"Scott Harry," said Stacy. "He's the only possible victim out of anyone who works for you guys. His story has been in the paper and at the time he did ask to be released from his contract. You guys still convinced he's not the leak?"

"No way," I said. "I've got him by the short hairs, among other things."

"How did he do in rehearsal?" asked Neely.

Stacy bit her lower lip and exhaled. "Well, as you guys told me, he's not exactly the poster child for Mensa."

"But he's definitely a team player, thanks to you, Syd," said Rica.

"Don't remind me," I said.

Stacy put down her fork and looked directly at me. "By the way, if he should… profess his love for you in open court—"

"Dear God," said Rica. "You can't be serious."

"It wouldn't surprise me, considering what I heard in the rehearsal," said Stacy. "In any event, it is important that you not, well, laugh. Try to look serious about the relationship, that you actually might be interested in him long term."

"I'll imagine Harrell is on the stand without a shirt," I said.

"Speaking of the men who work for you," said Stacy, "I've decided I want to put one of them up as a witness at the end of the trial. Of all the guys who work at CGR, who would you say is the smartest? I'm talking street-smart."

"Shawn," I said, without hesitating.

"Absolutely," said Rica. Neely nodded and Jillian smiled proudly.

"And who would be the most cool under pressure?" asked Stacy.

"That would be Shawn again," I said. "The guy was a commodities trader on Wall Street. Nothing flusters that guy and he's extremely mature for his age. Court would be a walk in the park for him." The girls nodded in agreement.

"Okay," said Stacy. "I'll set up a session with him tonight or tomorrow night and I'll let you know how it goes. Meanwhile, if she doesn't call Scott after lunch, she'll probably try her luck with one of you."

"I can't wait to see what you're gonna do to Monopoly Guy on the stand," said Rica.

Stacy washed down a bite and grinned. "He'll never pass *Go* again."

CHAPTER SEVENTEEN

"All rise!" said the bailiff.

The photographer behind the jury box swung his camera toward Neely. "Here it comes," he said, whispering into his headset.

"Be seated," said the judge, as he headed for the bench, staring at Neely the whole way.

Same as yesterday, everyone sat down except her.

I saw the camera locked in on her, the zoom lens tightening up.

Same as yesterday, she whipped off the glasses and dropped the hair in one motion.

And the judge tripped over the step on the way to the bench and went sprawling, disappearing behind the furniture and apparently hitting the flag stand that held Old Glory. The bailiff quickly ran behind the bench and we heard the judge say, "I'm okay" as the flag wobbled to a halt, making a noise like a spinning hubcap.

Neely sat down, trying to stifle a laugh. The judge popped up like a jack-in-the box, smoothed his robe, and took his seat. "Gotta get that loose step fixed, bailiff," he muttered, as he looked down at the papers in front of him. The crowd laughed, he jerked his head up and the room went silent.

Rica returned to the stand for Stacy's questioning, which took about forty-five minutes. I assumed Big Red would call Scott next, but Judge Courtney put the gavel to that idea.

"This looks like a good place to stop for the weekend," he said. "We'll résumé at ten on Monday morning."

It was just a little after two o'clock. As a newsperson I knew it was often impossible to find a public official on Friday afternoon, but seeing it first-hand made it even more ridiculous.

"This normal?" I asked Stacy.

She nodded. "The clerk told me he has a standing tee time at two-thirty. Any later and he'll be playing the eighteenth hole in the dark."

"Nice that he has his priorities."

"Well, you guys have sex in the loft in the middle of the day. What's the difference?"

I guess when you put it that way, it makes sense. Having fun on company time is an American tradition.

And our new tradition is a hell of a lot more fun than anything you can do on a golf course.

* * *

Rica's testimony, was, of course, lead story for just about every channel in America Friday night and the topic was already being promoted for some of the Sunday morning talk shows that were usually reserved for politics.

The Sunday papers, the most read issue of any day of the week, were chock-full of stories about older women, sexual harassment, age discrimination, sex in the workplace, and just about every other sidebar you could think of. But in this case they weren't beating a dead horse, because this story was out of the gate at full gallop and hadn't even hit the first turn. Even Anna Nicole disappeared from the tube. (Don't worry, the poor thing will be back, still dead as ever.)

While the headlines ran the usual gamut from "CGR: Up Close and *Really* Personal" to "Evening Nudes" to "Undercover Journalism", the stories and columns had an undercurrent of fun

193

running through them.

Undressing for Success

By Jenna Cantrell

I've decided to apply at the new CGR network for a job. I don't want to be an anchor, a producer, or a photographer. Or even a writer.

I want the position in which the only duty is "reference checking."

We've known for years that television can be a superficial business, but I had no idea the casting couch folded out so often into a sleeper sofa.

So let me get this straight; a television News Director needs a male anchor, decides to interview an underwear model for the job, then "checks his references" by discovering first-hand how quickly he can remove his briefs.

We've sure come a long way from the typing test.

I know my mother told me to change my underwear every day, that I might be in an accident and end up in a hospital and then what would the doctor think?

Turns out she was just giving me a hint about a career in broadcasting.

And now I know what "references under separate cover" means.

"Reference checking" by the way, has become a national catchphrase overnight. Last night I took the girls out for a few drinks and I overheard one woman ask another if she'd checked her new boyfriend's references yet.

Meanwhile, Neely's escapades were burning up the Internet water coolers. "Neely Collins" was one of the top searches of the weekend, while one newspaper posted before and after pictures under the heading "Hair Affair" and asked readers to vote online as to which they preferred. Hair up, hair down, or in motion. So far "in motion" has about eighty percent of the vote.

As expected, a montage of Neely's hair drops had been edited to some music (okay, it wasn't just *some* music, but the instrumental known as "The Stripper") in slow motion and has made its way to YouTube. As of Sunday morning, the video had already garnered more than one hundred thousand hits, and the comments posted below the video told me that about ninety-nine thousand of those were men.

"If Palin had done that, McCain would be President right now."

"She can check my references any day."

"Please let this trial go on as long as possible."

"How can I be her cellmate?"

* * *

On Monday, Stacy assembled us for breakfast at one of our favorite Belgian waffle haunts, wanting to go over things after the weekend just to keep us sharp. She was still pretty convinced that Scott Harry would be the first witness called today. With that in mind I was shoveling in my syrup-soaked confection, trying to get the sugar into my veins as fast as possible. (However, I must say that seeing the whipped cream on the waffle while discussing Scott created a mental image that was extremely distracting.)

Stacy was like a cheerleader, getting us up before the big game, as waiters raced around delivering plates of food. The energy of the place, the pure empty sugar calories of the breakfast, had its desired effect.

We were ready.

Then Amanda took off on a tangent. "Before we head back to the courtroom, I wanted to tell you that a Hollywood movie company contacted me this weekend, wanting to buy the rights to your stories," she said.

Rica nearly choked on her orange juice. "Good God, already?"

Amanda nodded. "Trust me, it won't be the only call I get on the subject. I just wanted to run things by you guys before I cut a deal. I'm probably going to get an agent to put it up for auction."

"This is all too fast," I said. "And I'm not sure I want my story up on a giant screen—"

"Then they'll just make it without you," said Amanda.

"They can do that?" I asked.

Amanda dipped her head and gave me a look that said *Are you that naïve?* "Syd, haven't you ever heard the term *unauthorized biography*? Hollywood has absolutely no scruples, so when they offer money you take the check and run like hell to the bank. They have accountants out there that will get up on that witness stand, put their hand on a bible and swear that all the Star Wars movies lost a ton of money. Do you really think anything is going to stop them from doing what they want? Let me cut a deal and I can put some cash in all your pockets."

"I hate to be the mercenary in all this," said Jillian, "but, uh, how much cash are we talking here?"

"Probably, oh, at least fifty grand apiece."

"Sold!" came the answer that sounded like it was in old-fashioned quadraphonic sound.

"Do we get to pick out who is going to play us in the movie?" asked Neely.

"Nope," said Amanda. "But trust me, they'll have to cast some hot actresses for the roles. And, we might be able to get you a job as consultants for the production, which could wring a few more bucks out of them."

I can see it now, sitting on a Hollywood set watching some actress writhe around on the sheets playing me while I tell the director what's wrong with the scene. "The chaps and cowboy hat are fine, but I never would have stood for the spurs." Cut!

If I had to choose, though, I like the tall redhead who does the car commercials.

At least she'd have experience with cruise control.

* * *

Sure enough, all the coverage from the weekend took the trial to another level. The media horde looked like it had doubled when we pulled up, and police had put up barricades to keep the onlookers at bay. Old-fashioned wolf whistles permeated the questions from reporters as we headed up the stairs. Jillian's bucket truck phone guy was gone, but she had a few fans holding signs on her behalf in the crowd, one of which was held by a man with a fake milk moustache. It read, "Got shortcake?" Another man yelled at Neely, "You gonna let the hair down today?" To which she replied, "You betcha!" The guy stood there, biting his knuckles as he stared at her.

Stacy turned out to be right about Big Red, as she called Scott to be her first witness. He made his way to the witness stand, taking a quick look at me as he walked. But his walk wasn't the confident one I'd seen that first night in the bar; his head was down, like he had been called to the principal's office. When he sat down I saw the lovesick wounded doe, not the anchor who seemed so credible delivering the news to the biggest city in the country.

I leaned over toward Stacy. "We're in trouble," I whispered.

"Why?" she asked.

"Just the look on his face," I said. "Get ready to object."

Scott's voice quivered as he took the oath, his shoulders hunched up like he was freezing as he sat down. Big Red must have noticed this, as she moved close to the witness stand so that she towered over him like an authority figure and looked at him over the top of her glasses. She led him through his background in the news business, then moved on to her attack.

"Mister Harry, give me your first impression of Sydney Hack when you came to New York for your interview."

"Well," he said, pausing to look directly at me, "I got a lump in my throat. She's incredibly beautiful with that long red hair and those turquoise eyes—"

Oh, no.

"I meant in the professional sense. What did you think of her as a newsperson?"

"Oh," said Scott. "Well, I thought she was very smart, knew a lot about the broadcasting business. Seemed like a nice person to work for. The people in the newsroom looked like they were having a good time."

"I'm sure they did. So you had a standard interview in her office, and then what happened?"

"She asked me to meet her at a restaurant so we could negotiate a deal on a contract over dinner."

"And when you got to the restaurant, what happened next?"

"We talked for a few minutes at the bar, then she said it would be a while before we could get a table for dinner, and that we could go to a hotel and order room service."

"Room service," said Big Red, as she started to walk toward the jury. "Kind of an unusual thing to hear on a job interview. Mister Harry, what did you think about that suggestion?"

"I didn't understand at first why she would want to do that, but then she told me if I wanted the job I should go to her hotel room so that she could… check my references." (Polite laughter from the crowd.)

"So what did you do?"

"Well, I wanted the job, so I followed her to the room."

"Did you understand that she wanted to have sex with you?"

"I did when we got there."

"What did she do?"

I was about to bury my head in my hands but Stacy caught me. "Head up," she whispered, as she grabbed my arm. "You've done nothing wrong."

"Well," said Scott, "she pretty much ripped my clothes off, shoved me onto the bed, got on top of me and we had sex. Twice."

Big Red looked at the jury to gauge their reaction. They were, not surprisingly, riveted. "Then what did she say, exactly? After she raped you."

Stacy jumped up. "Objection!"

"Sustained," said the judge. "Ms. O'Hara, you know better than that."

"Sorry, your honor," she said. "Mister Harry, what did she say after you consummated the act?"

"Well, after we were done she said that my references had checked out very well, and that I could have the job under one condition."

"And what was that condition? What did she say, exactly?"

(At this point I actually felt the hot breath of my own words on my skin, poised inches from the back of my chair, fangs apart, ready to bite me in the ass.)

Scott pulled out a handkerchief and wiped his forehead. "Well, if I remember correctly, she said, 'You can have the job, but I want to ride you like Secretariat.'"

(I just heard a dull thud from the direction of Old Southwich as Mother keeled over.)

The courtroom erupted in a combination of shock and laughter. Judge Courtney hammered his gavel a few times and restored order, though he had to bite his own lip to keep from joining in.

Big Red shot a quick smile in our direction, then turned back to Scott. "And, Mister Harry, after Sydney Hack told you she wanted to *ride you like Secretariat*, what did you say?"

Scott paused a moment and then delivered a headline writer's dream.

"Giddy-up."

* * *

The judge had ordered a recess for the day after four and a half hours of Scott Harry's testimony, as he had to preside over the sentencing of another case. Of course he brought us back after lunch for thirty minutes, as you know damn well he wanted to see Neely's hair drop. He did, by the way, stop on his way to the bench to watch the show, thus avoiding the "loose step" the bailiff had to fix. It was just as well that we finished early, as I'd taken more torpedo hits than the entire US Navy during World War Two.

All launched by Scott's unwavering honesty and incredible attention to detail. Who knew ol' Secretariat would have such a good memory on the backstretch?

I'd spent the rest of the day holed up in my office, then headed straight home, where I cooked dinner, drank a bottle of wine and went to bed. The girls wanted to take me out but I had no desire to be anywhere in public. Mother sent my cell phone into "Psycho" mode at least six times during the afternoon. But she never called the house phone, so I knew she was out there lurking, waiting to strike.

The next morning, as you can imagine, the Sydney Hack headline festival was in full swing.

All because of one word used to encourage a horse.

The headline writers pulled out every double entendre that could even be related to horse racing and my current situation with Scott Harry.

One newspaper simply printed "**Giddy-up!**" in two-inch letters across the top of the front page. They had then dug up an actual picture of Secretariat coming down the stretch, put Scott's face over the head of the horse, then pasted my face over that of the jockey's. They were kind enough to give me a little green helmet, but left off the goggles, while my arm was cocked back toward the backside of the horse while holding a whip.

Other publications eschewed the Photoshop tactic, simply going the clever headline route.

Whipped!

Boss to anchor: "I want to ride you like Secretariat."

Another went with this, which, depending on your situation, might be one you'd want to keep away from the children:

Stuffed and Mounted

Another played with the lyrics from "Mustang Sally" and slapped the words **"Mustang Harry"** over Scott's face while my picture carried the caption **"Ride, Sydney, Ride."**

The tabloid which had run the picture of me in Jillian's blue dress ran it again, only they changed the caption:

CGR exec Sydney Hack leads her mount back to the stables

At least Scott took one shot on his own, as his picture sat under the headline:

"Not the Dallyin' Stallion"

Despite all this, one column actually made me laugh. It was in the sports section of all places, done by a columnist who covers horse racing.

Anchorman in the Winner's Circle Every Week

By Will Jenkins

I never thought the day would come when I would write the words "Secretariat" and "Zorro costume" in the same sentence.

But after watching coverage of the CGR discrimination trial yesterday, I'll never be able to look at the sport again without thinking of sex.

Who knew that so many horse racing terms were double entendre codes for acts in the bedroom?

Next time I hear a track announcer say a jockey "goes to the whip", the image of the thoroughbreds racing down the stretch will be replaced by that of Sydney Hack and Scott Harry heading for their own photo finish on satin sheets. Next time I see a horse with blinders on, I'll think of an anchorman with a mask, a cape and a sword slashing the letter "Z" wherever he goes.

Hack, in case you've been living under a rock the past few days, is the tall, stunning redhead who runs the CGR channel, and if you can read the Daily Racing Form, you can figure out the meaning of the acronym. Harry is the local anchor who felt his oats (there's another term I can't use anymore) when he was forced to spend the night with Ms. Hack as part of his job interview.

Oh yeah, according to the lawsuit, all the men at CGR have sex with their co-anchors. This may be the first case in history of fillies being put out to stud.

And apparently the term "daily double" doesn't even apply to these two, as Harry admitted to five hook-ups with Ms. Hack in one twenty-four hour period. That kind of stamina you only see on the stretch at Belmont. (Thankfully Hack and Harry didn't stop at three or that would have given new meaning to the term "Triple Crown.") After a night like that, you have to wonder if Harry sends Hack a horseshoe of roses.

Then again, I would assume that in a race like those two are running, the best thing to do is end up in a dead heat.

And finally, when my clock radio went off this morning, the deejay decided to dedicate a song to me.

Gene Autry's "Back in the Saddle Again."

CHAPTER EIGHTEEN

"She's got momentum," said Stacy, sipping her freshly squeezed orange juice as she turned to me. "I'd bet the mortgage she's going to put you up next."

Aw, crap. "Why wouldn't she call Neely or Jillian fist?" I asked.

"Because those two have already become media favorites and they're basically Teflon. I'll put them up when it's my turn, but she would have nothing to gain. After what she did to Scott yesterday she's gonna go for the kill shot with you."

Just what I needed to hear. "Ah, the kill shot. How nice." I sipped my chocolate hazelnut coffee, letting the rich mocha warm my insides. It also gave me a shot of caffeine I didn't need.

Neely reached across the table and patted my hand. "You'll be fine, Syd."

"Really," said Jillian. "You did great in rehearsal."

"This is the real thing," I said.

"Screw 'em," said Rica.

"Really," said Stacy. "Just take that attitude up to the stand."

I played with the scrambled eggs on my plate. "I was really hoping for a break after all the headlines this morning."

"Well, you had to know that was coming after the *giddy-up* thing yesterday," said Stacy. "But the articles weren't bad at all. They may have had fun with the headlines, but no one painted you as a criminal."

I know, so why do I feel like one?

*   *   *

My heart was still trying to escape my chest as I headed down the hall to the courtroom.

Then, before I even stepped on the witness stand, I was hit smack in the face with something more demoralizing than any headline.

Now I know why Mother didn't leave a message on my house phone last night.

Because she came to deliver the message, a big box of maternal kryptonite, in person.

I stopped dead in my tracks as I walked through the door into the courtroom.

"Well," she said, standing there just inside the door with arms folded like a classic disapproving parent. "Before you sink what is left of the good Hartshaw name, I wanted to tell you something face-to-face. Since you obviously aren't taking my calls or returning them."

I put up my hand as I felt my pulse kick into overdrive. "I don't want to hear it, Mother. This is not the time nor the place. I don't need this right now." I glanced around, hoping the media didn't pick up on the fact that ol' Bootsie was the woman who had birthed the redheaded trollop on trial.

"Well, you may want to avoid me on the phone, but you're going to hear what I have to say. This *cannot* wait."

I lowered my voice and did my best interpretation of the death stare. "Whatever it is you want to get off your chest, and I can pretty much imagine what it is, it will *have* to wait. In case you haven't noticed, I'm on trial here."

She moved closer, backing me up a step. "Oh, the whole world has noticed, young lady. Especially the town of Old Southwich, from which I will no doubt have to move." My temples began to

204

throb as she tilted her head down and looked up at me like she was possessed by a demon. "You are still my daughter and I'm going to give you a piece of my mind right here whether you like it or not—"

"No, you're not," said a strong, familiar male voice from behind. "Your daughter needs support right now, not a lecture."

I turned just as Shawn stepped between me and Mother and folded his own arms.

"Who *is* this man?" asked Mother with an indignant tone.

"I'm one of Sydney's attorneys, and she certainly doesn't need any more stress in her life right now. So why don't you get on your broom and fly back to Connecticut?" he said.

Damn.

Mother's jaw dropped and her beady eyes widened as much as possible. "How *dare* you—"

"Get out right now or I'll have one of these officers remove you."

Mother's eyes narrowed as she locked in on Shawn's. "You *wouldn't.*"

"Unless you'd care to use your wings and fly out through a window. Oh, I forgot. You're not supposed to go out in direct sunlight or you'll burst into flames."

Whoa.

The Snack has a set of brass ones the size of grapefruits.

Mother reached back and sent her right hand flying toward Shawn's face, but he caught her wrist a few inches from his chin and held it there. The police officer at the door noticed.

Then I saw the gunslinger that Shawn had obviously been on Wall Street. He waved at the policeman who was standing just a few feet away while still holding firm to Mother's wrist. "Officer," Shawn said, just as the cop arrived, "this woman is harassing my client and just tried to assault me. She is not a member of the media and is not on the witness list. Would you please escort her out of the courtroom?"

He said it so convincingly, like a prosecutor from hell, that the police officer gently took my mother's other arm and led her toward the door. "Let's go, ma'am."

Mother yanked her arm away. "Take your hands off of me!"

"Ma'am, don't resist and make a scene or I *will* place you under arrest. You're lucky this guy's not pressing charges, and he'd win because I saw the whole thing." He grabbed her arm again, more forcefully this time.

"And if you return to this courtroom I'll get a restraining order," said Shawn.

Mother turned back one last time and glared at me as the officer led her out of the room.

I shot her a smile that I'd been saving up for years. All the hurt, all the pain she'd put me through, suddenly gave me the energy to give it back.

Then Shawn looked at me, still in faux lawyer mode. "You okay, Syd?" he asked.

"How the *hell* did you do that?"

"My sister's a psychiatrist, remember? Everyone's buttons can be pushed, even if they're the ones who always do the pushing," he said, with a little twinkle in his eye, as one corner of his mouth curled up.

I wanted to give him a huge hug but there were too many cameras. I leaned down and whispered in his ear. "I owe you big time, Mister."

"You don't owe me a thing," he said. "Just get up there and kick ass like we all know you can."

Confidence flooded into my veins like never before, as the life-long anvil on my shoulders magically disappeared. Suddenly the air in the musty old courtroom was pure oxygen. My headache disappeared and my heart downshifted as I turned and walked confidently down the center aisle, head high and wearing a smile that told anyone who noticed that I hadn't done anything wrong and was probably going to hit the loft during the lunch recess. All the tension of the past twenty-four hours was gone. In less than sixty seconds Shawn had turned me from a terrified defendant back into Neutron Syd.

I slid into my chair as Shawn took a seat in the first row. I leaned over to Jillian and whispered in her ear. "You know that really cute guy sitting behind me, the one you like a whole lot?"

She turned, spotted Shawn, smiled at him, then turned back to me. "Yeah. What about him?"

"If you don't ask him to marry you one of these days, I'll do it for you."

* * *

Neely's vodka something-or-other ran down my throat and started a badly needed internal massage of my body. It had been a fifteen round fight, a six-hour courtroom battle that didn't leave an external mark, thanks to Shawn. Anytime I felt any sort of anxiety coming on, I simply looked at him for an infusion of confidence.

But inside, I was seared like a piece of frozen chicken thrown into a deep fryer. All the emotions, stress and feelings toward my mother poured out of my body as I dumped the Russian alcohol in. I needed Harrell Karr tonight, but not now.

Not until I came down from the tightrope I'd been walking.

Rica turned on the DVR as we all settled down to watch the coverage. "I'd pay good money for some video of Shawn getting your mother tossed," she said.

"I would have loved to have been a fly on the wall of the train she took home," said Jillian. "I'll bet the conductor disconnected the car she was riding in around Mamaroneck and it's still sitting on the tracks."

I downed the rest of my drink and Neely was on me faster than a cruise ship waiter, pouring me a refill. "Take your medicine," she said, like a doting nurse. I stretched out on the loveseat, propping my feet up on one arm while my head rested on the other. "You were great today, Syd."

"Well, let's see how it looked on camera first," I said. "That's the true test. Fire it up."

Rica hit the button on the remote and the DVR rolled into action. "This looks like the clash of the redheads," said the male commentator as I was sworn in with Big Red hovering nearby.

"It will be interesting to see how Sydney Hack responds after yesterday's eye-opening testimony from Scott Harry," said the female anchor. "And the newspapers weren't too kind to her this morning. Well, here we go."

Rica zipped through the preliminary questions about my career and cued things up to the good stuff.

"You heard testimony from Scott Harry yesterday regarding the manner in which he was hired," said Big Red. "Do you recall his testimony?"

"Of course," I said. "And the morning papers certainly refreshed my memory."

I'd smiled a little, looking casual on the stand. The worry I'd had about how I appeared began to dissipate, washed away by the vodka. Hopefully it was performing a surgical strike and killing the brain cells connected to my feelings about my mother.

"What is your response to Mister Harry's testimony?"

"It's all true," I said, not showing the slightest bit of remorse. "Every word of it."

"You really told Scott Harry that you wanted to ride him—"

"Like Secretariat," I said. Then I shrugged and put my palms up. "It was the only horse I could think of at the time."

"Great line," said Neely, as the crowd snickered.

Big Red moved closer. "Would you explain to the jury why you feel it is necessary to conduct business this way?"

"Well, we hadn't had any ratings success with the standard anchor teams. I knew there was one demographic out there that was not represented, namely, women over thirty who were interested in younger men. And I knew they would appreciate seeing a woman who hadn't just stepped off a pageant runway sitting on the set next to a younger guy."

"It's nice that you're hiring older women," said Big Red, "but I'm more interested in the men who work at CGR."

"Well, maybe this is a revelation to much of the country, but older women are still attracted to younger men. But you never see that combination on any kind of television program. I thought that pairing an attractive older woman with a good-looking younger man would have an audience. And judging from the ratings, which are growing every day, we do."

"That doesn't explain why you feel the need to have sex with job applicants. Couldn't you just hire them without dragging them to your bedroom?"

"You heard Ms. Carbone the other day. We need to know if the man is the total package, not just a pretty face with a great body. Lots of good-looking people have zero in the personality department."

"Let's move on to your… apology… to Mister Harry," said Big Red. She raised her eyebrows. "Five times in one night?"

I watched a smile slowly grow on my face. "Actually it was four times at night and once at breakfast," I said. The courtroom filled with laughter and the judge swung the gavel.

"So you basically ordered Mister Harry to… service you… five times in a twenty-four hour period?"

"Well, Scott's like the Energizer Bunny in the sack. And he wasn't exactly complaining. Besides, *I* was apologizing to *him*."

"Why did you feel the need to have sex five times?" asked Big Red.

"Because I was still horny after four."

The courtroom exploded in laughter. Rica hit the pause button as the girls joined in. "You sure had a two-hundred IQ ass in court today," she said.

I smiled, licked one finger, put it on my backside and made a hissing noise.

"Imagine if you'd thrown your mother out of your life years ago," said Jillian.

"If she'd been in the courtroom during that line she would have keeled over like a redwood," said Rica.

"You think she'll be back?" asked Neely.

"You kidding?" said Rica. "She's like friggin' Rasputin. She'll never die."

"Yeah, but I haven't heard the theme from *Psycho* all day," I said. "Both phones have been quiet."

"She's home licking her wounds," said Rica.

"Hey, even if it's temporary, I'll take it," I said.

Neely stood up and raised her glass. "A toast. Ding dong, the witch is dead."

* * *

Random thoughts as we head into the defense part of the trial:

—Looking back, I should have fired Scott before the lawsuit made it into court. He could have been tagged as a hostile witness and perhaps some of what he said could have been discounted. Too late now. Now every time I step onto the street I hear "giddy-up" from men. Which I suppose is better than the usual come-on from New York guys, which entails banging on the side of the car door while driving by and yelling, "Hey, baby, you wanna (insert sex act here.)"

—I cannot stop replaying the scene between Mother and The Snack in my head. Every time I do, I get this euphoric feeling that's pretty close to… well, you get the idea. Just for the hell of it, I took an old picture of Mother in which her arms were apart and brought it down to the graphics department. They scanned it into a computer, and Photoshopped a broom into her hands. (It's actually an accessory that, I must say, fits her quite well.) After they printed it out, I framed it, and put it on my nightstand. *Pleasant dreams, my pretty. And your little dog too.*

—Rica, despite her tough exterior and the "screw 'em" attitude, is still a little nervous about the trial even though her testimony is out of the way. When she's on edge she starts cooking these giant vats of spaghetti sauce, then invites men over for pasta and sex. She claims the garlic in her sauce gives guys more staying power. When she's in this state and uses the term *al dente*, she's not talkin' about the linguine.

—I forgot to mention that some of our new prime-time shows are doing quite well in the ratings, much better than the redneck programming we had in the past. In an inspired bit of casting, Amanda found an actress who is a dead ringer for Stacy to star in "Legal Briefs", that show about the former underwear model who runs a law firm. Then Amanda bought commercials on the court channels to promote the show, figuring that anyone turned on by Stacy in the courtroom would love to see someone who looks exactly like her in a thong. Hell, half the country probably thinks it really *is* Stacy. So far it's the highest rated prime-time show. You gotta love the American justice system.

—That men's magazine publisher called again, only this time he wanted Neely for what he termed a "hairstyle pictorial" in which she would pose in Alaska with her hair up and on a beach with her hair down. Neely politely declined, telling the man that salmon fishing in the nude is a bit risky because of all the hooks involved. However, a well-known high-end shampoo company also called about Neely, and that deal is worth considering.

—If Jillian weren't such a close friend, I'd make a serious play for The Snack. Right now he's the most attractive man I've ever met.

* * *

By the way, Big Red didn't even bother to call Amanda or Madison to the stand. Stacy said her thinking was that she'd done enough damage to our defense with Scott and there was nothing either of them could have added to what I said yesterday. Stacy is going to call Neely, then Jillian, then Monopoly Guy, then wrap things up with The Snack.

Neely led off the morning with a slow, seductive stroll to the witness stand. Hair pinned up, glasses on. Stacy had told her to really go over the top with the Southern belle act, the theory being that Northerners found women with Southern accents charming while men with the same twang came off as backwoods hicks. Stacy figures that anything Neely says, no matter how outlandish, will be lapped up by the jury as long as she remains in character.

(Oh, I forgot to mention that Neely's YouTube montage has surpassed two million hits. Someone started a video website called www.IwannaletNeelyshairdown.com in which you push a button and her hair drops. You can even select the speed at which it falls, from real time to super slow motion. Stacy went ahead and leaked the fact that Neely would be called this morning, so you know the ratings for today's coverage will be off the charts.)

Stacy moved quickly to establish Neely's background in the business, asked some basic questions, let her charm the crowd with that baking-powder-rising-biscuits sex analogy, then turned her over to Big Red.

The tall attorney slowly walked to the witness stand. "Tell me, Ms. Collins, looking at my client, is there any way you would have considered him for an anchor job."

Neely turned toward the Monopoly guy, looked at him over her glasses, shook her head and said, "I'm sorry. No."

"Can you tell me why?"

"Well, I don't want to hurt the little fella's feelings."

"Trust me, Ms. Collins, he can take it. Tell me why you wouldn't hire him."

"Well," said Neely, "if y'all insist." She turned to face the jury. "Though as a Southern girl it goes against my principals to be rude." (Most of the jury nodded.) Then she turned back to look at the plaintiff. "I wouldn't consider him because he's bald, he's fat, and he's unattractive. Bless his little heart." (Rica had to bite her lip to keep from laughing.)

"But he might be a solid anchor," said Big Red.

"Maybe if you dropped him off the side of a boat," said Neely. Even the judge snorted and had to stifle a laugh at that one. Big Red glared at him.

"Your female viewers might appreciate someone credible."

"Our female viewers want to look at attractive men." She nodded toward the plaintiff. "They've already got *that* at home. That's why CGR's ratings are doing so well with women over thirty, because they're tired of looking at their husbands who have let themselves go and turned into slugs that sit in a recliner."

"So you'd never even think to… check his references?"

"Not unless I had some fantasy about being squashed by Mister Clean."

More laughs, more gavels.

"You don't see anything wrong with having sex with job applicants, especially given the fact that they'll be your subordinates?"

"No. I'm an affectionate person and I love cute men." Neely's face turned into that of a little girl who'd been bad. "I'm sorry. I can't help myself."

The attorney shook her head and walked back to the witness stand, leaned on it, and faced Neely. "I have to ask you, what's the deal with your hair?"

"I'm sorry, I don't understand y'all's question," said Neely.

"Well, much has been made of the fact that every morning you arrive in court with your hair up while wearing your glasses, and then, after lunch, you remove the glasses and let your hair down just as the judge comes back. Why do you do that?"

Neely smiled as she gently patted her upswept hair with one hand. "Well, it's all about business and pleasure."

Big Red folded her arms. "Now *I'm* the one who doesn't understand."

"Well, I thought it was important for the jury and the rest of y'all to see both sides of me. Now this…" she gestured toward her hair with both hands, "is business. And…"

But this time Neely didn't use her now patented move of quickly changing her look. She slowly removed her glasses, folded them, and put them in her pocket. "…This…" Then she reached back, turned her head toward the camera that was directly behind the jury, closed her eyes, removed the hairclip, and tilted her head back as her hair fell to her shoulders, then shook it out. She dipped her head, opened her eyes, batted her lashes and finished her thought in her lower whiskey voice that slithered its way through the room. "…is pleasure." The coverage cut to a shot of the jury, featuring the six men with their jaws hanging open, glazed eyes staring at her. Then it went back to a tight shot of Neely, who wore a seductive smile. "Any questions?"

CHAPTER NINETEEN

Stacy's strategy is simple. After loosening up the jury with Neely, she'd let Jillian take care of the business side, then go for the kill with Monopoly Guy, and leave things warm and fuzzy with The Snack.

Big Red, sensing she was fighting a losing battle with Neely, cut things short after the hair drop, since the men on the jury wouldn't have heard a damn thing she'd said anyway. The judge, red in the face at that point, had called for a short recess to presumably, ahem, adjust his robe. The jury looked like they were awfully sorry to see Neely go.

But Jillian perked them back up, walking to the witness stand in her shortest skirt and highest heels. I glanced at the men in the jury; they were all zeroed in on her legs. In fact, the women were as well. You just don't see gams that perfect very often.

Stacy took her through some background, then moved on to our philosophy. She was going to take the questions out of Big Red's hands. "Your network has an agenda, doesn't it?" she asked.

Jillian nodded. "As do all networks these days. Some skew liberal, others go conservative. If you're programming politically, it's not about information, but affirmation. Make the other side look stupid and your viewers will feel better about themselves. Channels that run science fiction are targeting young men, those who run what we call romance novel movies are going after women. It's called *narrowcasting*. You pick a niche audience and broadcast things of interest to that demographic."

"And your demographic would be?"

"Well, let's be honest here. We're going after women over thirty who dream about relationships with younger men and need to know that kind of lifestyle is possible. We were kind of surprised, though, that we're getting a lot of younger male viewers. Apparently men find our female anchors very desirable. Perhaps, after watching our channel, they're considering a relationship with an older woman."

"What are some of the components of that… lifestyle?"

"Well, bottom line, that if you're a woman over thirty your sex life isn't over. You can still date men in their twenties, you can still dress young. You don't have to stop dressing sexy or doing your hair because you assume men aren't looking at you anymore. This *age appropriate* thing we've been taught is a bunch of bull. If a forty-year-old woman wants to go out in a hot outfit and chase men fifteen years younger, she needs to know that it's okay, and she should go for it. And she should have the same attitude in the business world as well. Men have been doing this for years, and it's accepted. It's our turn now."

"So you've had sex with job applicants?"

"That's correct." Jillian smiled.

"Any reason for that?"

"Well, we wanted to sample the product. We can't promote the lifestyle if we don't live it ourselves. The women who watch CGR need to know what we're broadcasting isn't fiction, that the women who run the network are in charge, whether it's business or pleasure."

Stacy then turned Jillian over to Big Red.

The attorney moved toward the witness stand.

"Ms. Charles, you were in charge of screening the applications when they first came in, is that correct?"

"Yes."

"And how did you narrow things down?"

"We sat down one evening and literally looked at hundreds of tapes. The ones we didn't like were eliminated, the others were divided into three piles."

"Why three piles?"

"Well, the applicants were at different levels."

"So, was there a pile for men with more experience, those with none—"

"No, we divided them up according to their on-camera appearance and personality. One group was called *hot damn*, another *exponentially cute*, and the third was *doable*."

Big Red's eyebrows went up and the jury leaned forward as if on cue. This was going to be good. "Would you explain those terms for the jury?"

"Well, a *hot damn* is a guy who is just incredibly good looking, someone who will stop all the conversation when he walks into a room. A chiseled face and a body like a Greek god."

"How could you tell about their bodies by watching tapes of newscasts?"

"That's why we have reference checking." Snickers from the crowd. "Sometimes a guy has a great face but the body of the Pillsbury doughboy."

"What about those other two terms?"

"Well, *exponentially cute* is the boy next door taken to a new level. He has one of those faces that is both sexy and kind, just warm and inviting. And, of course, he has a body that's warm and inviting as well. Again, references must be checked."

"I see a pattern here," said Big Red. "I'm almost afraid to ask what *doable* means."

"It means exactly what it says. A man is doable if there are no *hot damns* or *exponentially cutes* laying around. If you desperately wanted to have sex and needed a vehicle that would serve the purpose."

"So doable would describe my client."

"No," said Jillian, her face tightening. "He wouldn't make any of those three categories."

"What category *would* you put him in?"

"I don't know. Maybe *last call for Duracell*."

"Excuse me?"

"As in *if that's all that's left when the bar shuts down, I'd better buy a pack of batteries for my vibrator, cause I'm sure not sleeping with this guy.*"

(That sound you heard was the headline writers running for their keyboards.)

"Is there any way at all you would have considered him for an anchor position?"

"I hate to be harsh, but you said your client could take it. Television is a visual medium and we're trying to attract female viewers, not scare them away."

"Do you think your hiring practices were fair toward my client?"

"Hey, *life* isn't fair. Lots of guys with more talent than him didn't get hired either."

"Probably because you didn't want to have sex with them."

"If we didn't find them attractive, chances are the viewers wouldn't want to watch them. We are, in a way, selling a fantasy that is actually attainable. The women who watch need to know there are guys out there who look like our anchors and are interested in older women. And believe me, they're out there."

"Okay, let's move on. You mentioned you don't care for the *age appropriate* concept," said the attorney. "Does that account for your outfit today?"

Jillian crossed her legs, left over right, so that the jury saw her skirt ride up her thigh. "It accounts for my *entire* wardrobe."

"You don't think your skirt is too short for the business world?"

"I don't hear any men complaining. Hey, I was blessed with nice legs and I like showing them off. It may not be considered appropriate in a traditional business sense, but I can tell you it gives me an advantage when dealing with men. Both in business and after hours. Every woman has something special, and she should not be shy about accentuating her best features." Jillian looked Big Red up and down. "You know, as tall and slender as you are, you'd probably look great in a short skirt. Lose the stern look and smile once in a while. You oughta give it a try. You'd make a great cougar."

Big Red never saw it coming. She was left absolutely speechless.

* * *

Finally, after all the testimony about nothing but sex, we were going to hear from the guy who started this whole mess.

Monopoly Guy, a/k/a Todd Jones, waddled his way toward the witness stand as Stacy stood next to the jury box. Dressed in an ill-fitting light gray suit, white shirt with collars badly in need of starch, and a red tie with a too-big knot, he didn't exactly project the image of a network anchorman.

What the hell is Big Red thinking? She couldn't have sent him to a tailor?

"Nice outfit," whispered Rica. "He looks like two pounds of shit in a one pound bag."

I kicked her under the table and tried not to laugh as the guy took the oath and sat down, having to unbutton his jacket as it bunched up around his shoulders.

"So, Mister Jones," said Stacy, casually leaning against the jury box, "you wanna be a network anchor."

"That's right," he said.

"Why don't you tell us your qualifications and why you think they should hire you at CGR."

"Well, I've worked in television news for eleven years. I got a job right out of college as a reporter, then was promoted to Monday through Friday anchor."

"Where were you employed?"

219

"I was working in West Virginia."

"Small town?"

"Very."

"Work anywhere else, Mister Jones?"

"No, I spent my entire career at the same station."

"Pretty unusual for a television person. I mean, you people generally move around a lot. So how come you stayed in one place for so long?"

"I just liked it there."

"How long did it take them to promote you to the anchor desk?"

"Ten years. I spent one year as an anchor."

Stacy stood up and slowly moved toward him. "And yet, they fired you after eleven years of service."

He shook his head. "No, they didn't renew my contract. Big difference."

"Okay, but bottom line, they didn't want you working there. Do you recall the reason they didn't renew your contract?"

"It was twelve years ago, I don't really remember—"

Then Stacy moved closer to the witness stand. "You're let go one time in your life and you don't remember? If you like, Mister Jones, I can have your old news director flown in and he can tell us why he let you go. He can be here by tomorrow. Think, now, what did he say when he told you he wasn't renewing your contract?"

Monopoly Guy bit his lip, looked at the floor, and said, "Because of my ratings."

"Be more specific, Mister Jones. What did he say about your ratings?"

He looked away from the jury. "That the ratings for my newscast were lower than whale shit."

Stacy waited for the laughter to die down, then moved in for the kill. "So after you were let go, what did you do?"

"I sent out résumé tapes looking for another job."

"Did you find one?"

"No."

"Any interviews?"

"No."

"Phone calls? Nibbles of any kind?"

"I didn't get any response."

"So what have you been doing the past twelve years?"

"Selling real estate, among other things."

"So let me get this straight. You spent eleven years in the middle of nowhere in West Virginia, couldn't find a job anywhere in television for the next twelve years, applied for a job with CGR, and you're suing because they didn't hire you. Doesn't that seem a little ridiculous?"

"They didn't consider me because the women who run that place didn't want to sleep with me."

"Sounds like a lot of other television station managers didn't want to sleep with you either."

Big Red jumped up. "Objection!"

"Sustained," said the judge, who glared at Stacy.

"I apologize, your honor," said Stacy. "Mister Jones, if you're not qualified to work at any other station in the *entire United States*, what makes you think you could do the job at CGR?"

"I'm a good writer, I'm smart..."

"Then maybe you should work behind the scenes."

"I wanted to be an anchor."

"Mister Jones, I hate to be blunt, but do you really think you have the looks for television?"

"It shouldn't matter. They should be hiring on merit and cred-ibility, not on who they want to have sex with. They hired a bunch of guys who had never even *been* on television."

"And their ratings are going up every day. How do you explain that, Mister Jones, when after eleven years your own ratings were lower than—"

"It's just not fair, that's all."

"Guess what, Mister Jones. Here's a newsflash for you. Life isn't fair."

* * *

He walked with a purpose toward the witness stand, a hint of his now familiar cologne wafting by our table. His thousand dollar dark gray ventless windowpane suit hung perfectly, his burgundy wingtips shone like mirrors. The bold, red-striped necktie was perfectly knotted with a little dimple. The round, black and silver harlequin cufflinks peeked out of his cuffs, adding a little sparkle to a man who didn't really need any. The face was a perfect combination of authority, sex appeal, and warmth.

The Snack took the stand, sitting up straight and head held high with all the assurance of a CEO or head of state.

I got a lump in my throat. *Damn, he's so attractive I need a seat belt on my chair.*

The Snack was sworn in, upon which he became Shawn Carlyle. The man we hoped would save us all, or at least give the trial the send off it needed before closing arguments.

Stacy moved toward the witness stand. "Mister Carlyle, before you became an anchor for CGR, what did you do for a living?"

"I was working as a commodities trader on Wall Street for three years."

"Not exactly the traditional training ground for a career in broadcasting, is it?"

"Well, no, but both jobs come with a lot of pressure and require you to think on your feet. They're more alike than you might think."

"Why don't you tell us how you got the job?"

"Well, I was out one night and my boss had given me two tickets to a Broadway show he couldn't attend. I didn't have a steady girlfriend at the time and I didn't want to go alone. I spotted Ms. Charles, approached her and asked her if she'd like to accompany me to the theater."

"What happened then?"

"We went to the play, and on the way she told me about her job and the opportunities at CGR. They were looking for attractive men who communicated well, and they didn't need to have any television experience since it wasn't a real newscast. Anyway, the play wasn't very good, so we left at intermission and went to a restaurant for coffee and dessert. Then she invited me back to her townhouse. One thing led to another, and I ended up spending the night."

"You had sex with her?"

"Yes."

"And then she hired you?"

"Yes. It was the best sex I'd ever had."

Annnnnd…. cue Jillian's freckles!

"Does it bother you that you are under the direction of a woman both at work and after hours?"

"Not at all. These are a terrific bunch of women."

"They're all much older than you, Mister Carlyle. What exactly do you have in common with them?"

"It's more of what I don't have in common with the women my own age, which is twenty-five. The women I used to date were very superficial. All they seemed to care about was shopping and going to the hottest clubs and getting falling-down drunk. The women at CGR are all past that. They've experienced life, they know what they want, and they go for it. They're past playing games. For society to say they've reached their sexual expiration date is ridiculous when they have so much to offer."

I like that expiration date thing. Wonder where the stamp is?

Stacy moved toward our table and gestured toward us. "These four woman are all your superiors, but when we entered the courtroom this morning, I noticed that you held the door for them. Why did you do that?"

A boy-next-door grin grew across Shawn's face. "Well, I mean, a gentleman always holds a door for a woman."

"But doesn't that fly in the face of all this role reversal stuff? They're your bosses, right. In that role they aren't men *or* women."

"You don't understand. These women may be tough when it comes to business, but at the end of the day they're still women. And underneath all the corporate dealings and high-powered network meetings, there are four women who still appreciate the little things that make them different from men."

"Can you be more specific?"

"Well, Neely loves flowers, particularly tulips. Send her a vase filled with red ones and she melts like any woman in love. Rica is a fantastic cook; she can lose herself in the kitchen and taught me how to make fettuccine alfredo. Sydney is a chocoholic; give her a box of imported stuff and she just lights up... then she'll sit in her office like a kid on Christmas morning trying to pick out the ones with nuts. And Jillian is just an old-fashioned girl at heart; leave a Hallmark card on her pillow and she'll put it in her scrapbook. They may be my bosses, but underneath they're still women who want the same thing every woman in America does."

The jury, had they been permitted to speak, would have all uttered a group "awwww" at this point. I turned around to look at the crowd.

The women all looked as though they were in a trance, heads cocked to the side while wearing thoughtful smiles. Kind of the same look Jillian had the night she spotted The Snack for the first time.

"And what would that be, Mister Carlyle? What *does* every woman in America want?"

"To be loved and respected for who they are, not for the date on their birth certificate. To be treated as an equal, and not be frowned upon if they take charge in the office or the bedroom. Or if they want to spend time with younger men."

"Thank you, Mister Carlyle."

Big Red got up and moved quickly to the witness stand. "Best sex you've ever had, Mister Carlyle?"

He nodded. "Well, I am under oath." The crowd chuckled. "And, amazingly, it keeps getting better."

"But yet you have sex with your co-anchor, Jennifer Darlen, on a weekly basis under the terms of your employment, isn't that right?"

"No. Jennifer and I are just friends."

"So let me get this straight. You spend one night per week with Ms. Charles."

"Well, not exactly," he said.

Okay.... Where is he going with this?

"What part did I get wrong?"

"I spend one night each week having dinner with my co-anchor… you know, to develop anchor chemistry... and the other six nights with Ms. Charles."

Rica, Neely and I all slowly turned our heads in unison to look at Jillian, who was biting her lower lip for all it was worth as she tried to avoid a smile.

"Six nights a week? Sounds like Ms. Charles has you working overtime."

"Believe me, it's not work," said The Snack.

"Well, if she's forcing you to have sex six nights a week—"

"She's not *forcing* me to do anything. We've developed a relationship and we enjoy spending time together. Sometimes we just sit and talk, sometimes we watch movies."

"I can only imagine what kinds of movies—"

"Objection!" said Stacy.

"Sustained," said the judge.

Then Big Red hit him with one out of the blue.

"So, Mister Carlyle… one more question. Are you just sleeping with the boss a few extra nights to get ahead in the business, or are you in love with Jillian Charles?"

Oh. My.

He turned to Jillian and gave her a look that left no doubt as to the answer. "Well, you can find me in contempt for not answering a direct question if you want, but if I'm going to say that for the first time to her, it's not going to be in open court. It will be on a beach under a full moon, or over a candlelight dinner, or riding in

a hansom cab through Central Park while we're snuggling under
a blanket. But I will tell you that I care for her a great deal, that
we respect each other, and that she's taught me so much."

"Taught you about sex?"

"About life, Ms. O'Hara. About life."

And right then it hit me. What we're doing isn't about sex at all.
It's about relationships.

CHAPTER TWENTY

"Bring the girls to the conference room right away," said Madison, with urgency in her voice.

"What's up?" I asked.

"Don't know. But Amanda said she needed to see all of us right away."

Oh, shit. I knew that tone and it didn't sound good. "Okay, be right there."

I rounded up the girls and we headed down the hall as my pulse went up.

We found Madison already seated at the head of the table and Stacy next to her, while Amanda stood by the door. "Have a seat," she said. Her face offered no clue as to whether this was good news or bad.

Amanda closed the door as soon as we grabbed a chair. "I have big news about the trial," she said, a smile suddenly growing across her face. "The lawsuit has been dropped."

Stacy sat up straight with a puzzled look. "I wasn't made aware of this."

"That's because it hasn't happened yet. Officially. But it will before the end of the day."

"You settled this without my being present?" asked Stacy, eyes filled with concern. "That's not a good idea—"

"No," said Amanda, shaking her head while still smiling. "We didn't have to settle. The plaintiff is dropping the suit."

"I'm sorry," I said, "but I'm confused. How do you know the suit will be dropped?"

"It's easier if I just show you," said Amanda. She opened the door, looked outside, and said, "Come on in."

And then the Monopoly Guy walked into the conference room. Our jaws all dropped as Amanda quickly shut the door behind him.

"Are you friggin' kiddin' me?" asked Rica. "What the hell is *he* doing here?"

"Ladies," said Amanda, trying to hold back a smile. "I'd like you to officially introduce you to Bryan Carswell."

What the hell?

"Now I'm really confused," said Jillian. "I thought his name was Todd Jones?"

"That's my legal name," said the Monopoly Guy. "And that was the name I used as an anchor. My *stage name* is Bryan Carswell."

Stage name?

"Bryan is an actor," said Amanda, as the Monopoly Guy's smile joined her own.

The words hung in the air as we all put the pieces of the puzzle together.

Oh, you've gotta be kidding...

I looked at the man, then back to Amanda. "You mean to tell me—"

She nodded as she folded her arms and leaned against the door. "This whole thing was a publicity stunt."

Stacy tossed her pen on the table and stood up. It was clear she was not amused by this turn of events. "Do you realize you could go to jail for this? This is a flagrant abuse of the justice system. I could be disbarred."

"The only people who know about it are in this room," said Amanda. "Attorney client privilege prevents you from doing anything. You were operating in good faith and had no knowledge of what we were doing. He gets a large amount of money in an annuity three years after the statute of limitations runs out, provided he keeps his mouth shut, and for what I'm paying him I know he will. If he ever says anything, he automatically forfeits the annuity. As for the rest of you, I didn't want you to feel as though I put you through all of this for nothing, so you are being compensated for your roles." She reached into her purse, pulled out several envelopes, and handed one to each of us.

"Why didn't you tell us?" I asked, as I took an envelope.

"You guys are all very smart, but you had to be kept in the dark on this," said Amanda. "And as you can tell, Stacy wouldn't have gone for it."

"*No* lawyer would have gone for it," said Stacy, still seething.

"That's why you couldn't know. Meanwhile, the rest of you aren't actors and never would have been able to pull it off. Though Neely came close to getting an Academy Award for her Scarlett O'Hara thing. You all had to actually believe the lawsuit was real to sell it. If you knew it was a publicity scam it would have shown through; somebody would have slipped up. And Stacy, you had to think you were actually defending clients against a serious charge. I hope this token of appreciation will make up for the stress I've put you all through."

I opened my envelope and peeked inside. My eyes grew wide as I saw a cashier's check made out for fifty thousand dollars.

"What the hell, stress is overrated," said Neely, after looking at her check.

"Where the hell did you get this money?" asked Madison.

"It just goes under *legal expense* for the entertainment division. Don't worry about it. Trust me, guys, every possible loose end has been taken care of."

Rica got up and walked toward the man, still ticked off despite the money. "You're a friggin' actor?" she said, hands on hips.

Monopoly Guy nodded. "Ever since I left television news."

"So you really were an anchor in a previous life?" asked Jillian.

"Yeah, a bad one," he said. "That stuff about West Virginia was all true, even the line about my ratings. I knew I couldn't get another job in news, but I was comfortable on camera, so I started auditioning for commercials and bit parts. Being bald and funny-looking might not work in broadcast journalism, but it is an asset in Hollywood and New York."

"I put him in several roles during the years I was working as a casting director," said Amanda. "I knew he'd be perfect for this part. He knew enough about the news business and is a terrific character actor. And he still had actual résumé tapes from his anchor job, which we needed to make the whole thing seem legit."

Rica's eyes narrowed as she looked at the man and folded her arms. "I'd still like to kick your ass," she said.

"And I'd like to grab yours," he said, smiling.

"Dream on," said Rica.

"Look," said Amanda. "Our ratings are going through the roof. CGR is seriously on the map. And the bonus to all this is that you've opened the doors for all sorts of women over thirty to get back into the news business."

"You put us through hell," said Stacy, obviously not feeling the check in the envelope was worth the trouble.

"Sometimes you gotta go through hell to get to heaven," said Amanda.

* * *

Actually, hell would have been a walk in the park compared to Thanksgiving.

I'd decided I wasn't going to let Mother stand in the way of my feelings for Gran, nor let my dear grandmother suffer the fallout of our little courtroom altercation, so I hopped on the mostly empty train early that morning and took the Metro North local out to Old Southwich. Besides, The Snack had given me a pep talk, so I was ready for battle, with my game face on.

I half expected to see torch-bearing townspeople who would drag me to the stake as the train rolled into the station, since I had, after all, given Old Southwich a reputation that would resemble the *real* Babylon. Some Connecticut television reporter had dug up a little family history and traced me back to Bootsie (those damned leaks never stop!), which resulted in a cavalcade of matrons doing spit-takes with their vichyssoise when the story broke at the annual Hartshaw charity auction. But, there was no angry mob to greet me. I simply found the lone taxi I'd summoned spitting steamy exhaust into the chilly air. (I did, however, see some graffiti decorating a Broadway show poster on the train platform that read, "For an absolutely lovely evening, do call Sydney Hack." Only in Old Southwich would a trollop get such a genteel notation in perfect penmanship.)

The memories flooded back as the taxi navigated the old streets of Old Southwich, past the overpriced boutiques and restaurants that served fru-fru watercress sandwiches that left you hungry an hour later. We headed out into the country, such as it is in Connecticut. As we turned past the gate into the Hartshaw estate I felt my pulse quicken. Half excitement to see Gran, the other half bracing for what surely would be an onslaught of Mother's barbs flying from one side of the table over the turkey carcass to the other.

Most of the leaves were down from the maples that lined the brick basket-weave driveway, but the reds and oranges on the ground framed the picture of the one place I'd found solace in this entire town. The cab pulled up to the stone mansion, and the crisp fall air greeted me as I paid the driver and got out of the back seat. The door opened before I had a chance to knock.

Oh yeah, I'm Gran's favorite, in case you hadn't guessed by now. (Much to Mother's dismay.) She was waiting by the door with a big hug. "Sydney, so good to see you," she said.

I kissed her on the cheek, taking in her warmth while casting a wary eye for Mother lurking in the shadows. "You too, Gran," I said.

She took me by the hand, the same way she did when I was a little girl. Her skin was a bit rough and wrinkled now, but the touch was still warm. "Come. I'll make you some hot chocolate and then you can help with the turkey."

My steps on the beige marble floor echoed through the foyer as we headed toward the back of the house. Gran, though eighty years old, still walked with a spring in her step, and it could be argued that she looked better than my mother. The hair had gone totally gray, but she had maintained her tall, slender figure, while her knowing green eyes still sparkled out of a relatively smooth face that belied her years. "Anyone else here yet?" I asked.

"No," she said. "Just you and me till about noon."

I exhaled and my blood pressure dropped like a stone. "Good," I said, as we entered the kitchen.

I closed my eyes for a moment as the smells of Gran's kitchen took me back. The fresh herbs, her favorites being cilantro and rosemary, sat on the black and white tiled island, and sent a wonderful, fresh aroma into the room as they waited to become important ingredients in her Thanksgiving dinner. The hanging array of copper pots provided the only color to the room. The kitchen had so much stainless steel I'd imagined it as a funhouse when I was little, enjoying the distorted reflections while learning how to cook. (Mother, it should be noted, could burn a salad. Hence, it was imperative that I be able to fend for myself on my infrequent visits to her home, lest I overdose on ramen noodles.) Gran poured some milk into a saucepan as I looked into the side of the refrigerator and smiled at the funny face that looked back. She placed the pan on the stove and turned on the gas while I hopped on one of the old pine stools that lined one side of the island.

"How is your dear father?" she asked, as she pulled a coffee mug from a shelf and dropped a few marshmallows and her own homemade hot chocolate mix into it.

"You know Dad, always traveling with his job. But he and Caroline are happy as ever, still living in San Francisco." (I didn't call Caroline "mom" in front of Gran, but she knew we had a close relationship.)

"He's such a good man," said Gran. "He's taught me a lot over the years."

"He has?"

"Yes, about first impressions. They're usually wrong, don't you know." She stirred the milk as the steam began to rise from the saucepan, then poured it into the mug, dropped in a spoon and handed it to me.

I wrapped both hands around the warm china and took a sip. The rich mocha with a hint of marshmallow warmed my body, while the flashback brought by the taste did the same for my soul.

"By the way," said Gran, "I have a surprise for you."

I sat up straight. "Oooh. What is it?"

"Not till your mother gets here."

*　*　*

The seating arrangements at Gran's Thanksgiving dinners haven't changed since I was a child. She sits at the head of the table (my grandfather passed away at a young age) while her children line one side of the table and their children (all boys, except for me) line the other. Though I am seated directly across from Mother, I do take comfort in being surrounded by my two favorite cousins, Patrick and Roger. Both, though they maintain the blueblood attitude along with residences in the proper Connecticut zip code, have a warped view of life which always makes me laugh. Patrick, an attorney in his early forties, is known as the "king of the pre-nup" in this state, his reputation solidified since he's now on wife number four and has yet to pay a dime of alimony to the previous three. (He's also on mistress number fifteen, but that's beside the point.) Roger, just turned fifty, rode the Hartshaw name to a Congressional seat and has already survived two sex scandals in Washington, one of which received national attention when he was caught by an elevator camera being serviced by a female staffer. While that doesn't sound like anything unusual for a Congressman, the story took on a life of its own when the woman, after being unceremoniously let go from her job, revealed to the world that she had been born a man before taking a long trip to Sweden. The "ewwww" factor of this lovely piece of news, along with the fact that the woman had changed her name to Jennifer from, of all things, Dick, was a headline writer's dream. But, the Hartshaw name having the lifetime warranty Teflon coating that it does, he was re-elected after outspending his opponent ten to one.

Back to the dinner. Mother had not even spoken to me yet and we were almost completely through the bird, which was acting as a buffer between us. She was wearing her "constipated since 1988" face, while I was laughing it up with my cousins. The topic of CGR had not even come up, since, and let's be honest here, the making of money trumps any indiscretion in this family.

Except, of course, if you're a girl.

Every time Gran looked at me she winked. She was up to something.

And I was still waiting for that surprise.

"Bootsie, dear," said Gran, putting down her fork and folding her hands. "You must be so proud of Sydney. Running her own network and all. Very few women rise to that position."

Oh, shit. What the hell is this?

If this is Gran's surprise, well...

Patrick leaned over and whispered in my ear. "From what I've read, you have more than one position."

I nearly choked on an olive as I stifled a laugh, then elbowed him in the ribs. "You should talk," I said.

Otherwise, the conversation had stopped. Everyone at the table knew the throwdown was about to happen, and no one wanted to have a mouth full of candied yams when the first volley flew on a weird parabola across the turkey. Roger wiped his mouth, dropped the napkin in his lap, then leaned forward toward Mother.

"Yes, Boots, she's really going *all the way* in that industry, don't you think?" He shot me a smile, then leaned back for the show.

Instigator.

"I have remained silent thus far," said Mother, nose in the air, looking slightly to the side.

"Oh, shit, here it comes," I said. My cousins snickered. Patrick did that whistle thing from the Clint Eastwood movie *The Good, The Bad, and The Ugly*. I looked at Gran, who for some reason was smiling. She usually puts a stop to this stuff.

"My *daughter*," said Mother, "and her carrying on like a common—"

"Trollop?" I asked.

Her eyes narrowed.

Re-jected! I channeled Rica and shot the death stare back.

"It's all over the newspapers," said Mother. "I cannot even go out in public anymore. And the fact that she's having sex with much younger men—"

"She's an attractive single woman," said Gran. "People do have pre-marital sex… *you know*."

"Wow," said Roger. (Everyone knows the story of the Buick.) Patrick then pulled out his cell phone and began recording the proceedings.

Mother's head snapped back as she took the surprise shot from Gran. She glared at Gran.

My sweet old Gran debuted a death stare of her own. Who knew?

Mother looked at me, then at Gran, then back to me.

The room was deathly silent. It had become a blueblood spaghetti western showdown at the Old Southwich corral.

"Those men are almost young enough to be your children," said Mother.

"Yeah, maybe in Arkansas," said Patrick, under his breath.

"You know," said Gran. "When I was young I dated a much younger man."

"I find that hard to believe," said Mother. "You're just taking her side. As you always do."

"No, no, 'tis true," said Gran. "I was twenty-five and he was only eighteen."

Mother shook her head. "Women didn't do such things back in the day. You're making this up. "

"No, I'm not," said Gran. Then she reached in her lap, pulled out a yellowed piece of paper and unfolded it. "And back then I couldn't tell anyone that I was seven years older..." She looked directly at Mother. "...when I married your father."

Had Mother's jaw dropped another inch I could have shoved an entire drumstick into her mouth.

Gran passed the paper across the table to Mother. I saw the words "Certificate of Marriage" across the top. Mother's eyes bugged out as they raced across the old document. Then Gran turned to me.

"You see, Sydney, you may think you started this whole trend of older women dating younger men, but in reality, it's in your genes. *I* was the first cougar in this family."

I grinned from ear to ear, as Mother continued to stare at the document. Her eyes glazed over and it looked as though she were in imminent danger of falling head first into the gravy boat.

"Now," said Gran, "who wants pie?"

* * *

Not that this group needs mistletoe to hook up, but any excuse to give a tonsillectomy to a co-worker is welcome at CGR.

Welcome to the network Christmas party, which, along with the usual flashy cocktail dresses and free-flowing booze (I know, really, how is this different from any other day around here?), has a kick-ass band and a few rooms just off the ballroom for anyone who needs to freshen up. And since our reputation is all about sex, I had the decorating committee hang mistletoe all over the damn place. One little sprig just won't do it for this group. I'd decided, for the time being, to grab a drink and park myself under one bunch, and I must say I'd really been enjoying the assorted holiday greetings from the male members of the staff, many of whom have come back for seconds.

Sure as hell beats getting a fruitcake.

I was torn about one thing, however.

I really, really, *really* wanted to plant one on The Snack one time before Jillian takes him off the market for good. Actually, I'd like to do more than just kiss him, but we won't go there. We do have scruples, you know.

Of course, I had a nice little Christmas surprise for the two of them, which I would deliver shortly. (No, I'm not going to tell you. It's a surprise, so you'll just have to wait.)

Okay, you twisted my arm, so I'll give you a hint. Ever since The Snack's testimony when Big Red asked him *the* question, we all figured he'd run right out that night and say the "L" word to Jillian. But what we didn't consider was that fact that they're both too smart to race headlong into anything, so each has been holding back waiting for the other to say it first. It's almost gotten to be a running joke. We'll all be at dinner, and Jillian will look deeply into his eyes, and say, "You know what I'm thinking?" And he'll look back at her, thinking she's going to crack, and say, "What, Shortcake?" (She loves the nickname coming from him, but God forbid anyone else uses it or you get the hung-over Little Mermaid glare.) Then she'll break the trance and say, "I think I'll order dessert. You wanna split some chocolate mousse?"

Anyway, the gift was in my purse and I'd give it to them at the proper time.

* * *

I'd been waiting for ten o'clock, and thankfully the weather report was right on the money; it was cold outside and the skies were crystal clear. You'll see my reasons presently. I walked over to Jillian and the Snack who were standing near the Christmas tree, holding hands while sipping drinks. "I have something for you," I said to Jillian.

"I thought we weren't exchanging gifts till Christmas Eve?"

"We aren't, but this is actually something extra for both of you." I handed Jillian a bright red envelope. "You've both been so special to me this year, and I couldn't have made it without either of you."

She opened it and pulled out the card. "Gift certificate for a hansom cab ride." She showed it to Shawn and he smiled. "Thanks, Syd. That's really nice. I've always wanted to see New York from a horse-drawn carriage."

"That's very sweet of you," said Shawn. "Thank you. It's a wonderful gift."

"You didn't read the fine print," I said.

They both looked closer. "Oh, it expires tonight," said Jillian, the sparkle fading from her eyes.

"Not a problem," I said. "The driver is waiting downstairs right now. He's going to take you through Central Park for an hour." I reached into my purse and pulled out a little vial filled with sand and handed it to her. "It's a little cold for the beach, but this is Coney Island's finest." I cocked my head toward the window. "And it's a full moon tonight. A shame to waste it, don't you think?"

Jillian's eyes grew misty and she gave me the most soulful look I'd ever seen. I finally knew what it must feel like to have a sibling. She then wrapped her arms around my shoulders and gave me a strong hug. "Thank you, sweetie."

She pulled back and Shawn took both my hands, then glanced up over my head. "Wow, look at that," he said, turning toward Jillian and pointing at me. "Beautiful woman standing under mistletoe."

"A shame to waste it," said Jillian. "Don't you think?"

Then Shawn got up on his toes, took my face gently in his hands, and, even though it only lasted a second, he gave me the softest, most sensual kiss I'd ever had.

The place was clearing out, as the band was packing up.

Jillian and the Snack were back from their ride, standing in front of the tree again, its flashing lights providing backlight and giving them a heavenly ethereal look, like a pair of angels.

I stopped a moment to look at them.

Jillian, radiant in a red, off-one-shoulder cocktail dress, hair put up on one side, long dangly rhinestone earrings reflecting the light. Looking at him and totally oblivious to what was going on around her, like they were the only two people on the planet.

Shawn with his hands on her waist, looking up to his dream girl. Literally and figuratively.

And when you think about it, isn't that all any woman can ask for?

Funny, we started out looking for ratings and instead found the meaning of love.

He'd said it first, by the way, in case you were wondering.

EPILOGUE

I know, I know, I have a lot of loose ends to tie up here, but let me take my time. The piña colada I'm sipping is made with fresh pineapple and coconut, and the natural taste is just exploding in my mouth while the island rum that accompanies it is helping me float along with the ship. So I'm on very low power and operating on autopilot.

Oh, yeah, I'm on a week-long Caribbean cruise. We all needed a break after the launch and the trial, so Amanda sprang for some first-class vacations. Too bad we can't all be together at once, but someone's gotta stay behind and mind the store. So it's just me, the clear azure waters off the coast of Grand Cayman, the pristine salt air that fills my lungs, and my poolside bartender friend who calls me "rum runner" since everything I order contains that wonderful sugary alcohol. There's something to be said about having a little pink umbrella in your drink on a floating hotel in which the outside world doesn't exist. The country blew up? Eh, so what. I've got an ice sculpting demonstration in ten minutes and that chocolate buffet is at two this afternoon and then there's ballroom dancing at four with a really cute instructor who had his hand on my ass yesterday afternoon and elsewhere last night. When you're at sea, you have to keep your priorities straight.

But anyway, there's a gentle ocean breeze blowing through

my hair right now, so I guess revisiting the real world for a few minutes won't kill me.

Final random thoughts:

—Just before I left we actually shot a shampoo commercial. Originally the ad agency guy just wanted Neely, but then realized the four of us represented the entire hair color spectrum of blonde, brunette, redhead, and raven. So while Neely is the spokesperson in the spot, we all got to have those invisible electric fans blow our hair around one afternoon in a studio. Neely's line at the end of the commercial is just dripping with lust. She pulls off the glasses and drops the hair, then turns to the camera and says, in that sultry voice of hers, "A woman should never be afraid to let her hair down." Then she deftly slides the straps of her dress off her shoulders and says, "Or anything else."

The network also taped Neely dropping her hair for New Year's Eve, and ran it in super slow motion, one frame at a time, complete with a countdown clock. Ratings for the fifteen minutes before midnight were off the charts.

—Speaking of Neely's alter ego, we never got blown off the cable systems in Alaska. As it turned out, some of our highest ratings came from the last frontier. The Republicans may have lost the election, but I'm sure Democrats don't have the same fantasy about Joe Biden that the GOP guys have about Sarah Palin.

—Rica got a commercial off her little "Hair Club for Men" comment during the trial. A New York City hair replacement clinic that only advertised locally wanted a hot woman over thirty with an accent, so she fit the bill. In the spot, she's sitting in a bar, having just blown off a bald guy who'd hit on her. "You think this girl's goin' out with some cueball? Fuhgeddaboudit!" The commercial then extols the virtue of hair transplants and finished up with Rica walking out of the bar on the arm of a buck with thick, wavy dark hair. (And yes, she checked his references when they were done shooting.)

—Speaking of loose ends, I realized I mentioned the laxative brownie story but never told it to you. So here goes. There was a food thief at Rica's station in Los Angeles, as lunches would routinely disappear from the break room fridge. Everyone had a pretty good idea who the culprit was; a male reporter who hated Rica. So she whips up a batch of brownies and instead of chocolate chips adds a powerful laxative. She put them in a bag, marked it "Rica's brownies: do not touch!" and placed it in the break room. Naturally, the bag disappeared shortly thereafter. That afternoon the reporter in question was seen doubled over in pain at his desk, then making a mad dash for the news department men's room. The toilet paper had already been removed, and as soon as the guy bolted inside Rica actually wedged the door shut. Since she had put enough laxatives in the brownies to uncork a platoon, moans of agony were heard while the staff stood on the other side of the door laughing their asses off. Rica left him in there for an hour, and only sent in a roll of Charmin after the guy had slid a hundred bucks under the door. She took the money and bought lunch for those who'd had theirs stolen. I'm telling you, you don't want to get on that woman's bad side.

—On the subject of practical jokes, I actually got up the nerve to pull one on Mother for the first time ever. I called Dad and asked him to describe the legendary Buick in which he had sent her over the edge. Then I tracked down a blue, 1967 two door Skylark on eBay for a hundred bucks and had the rusted bucket of bolts towed from a Queens junkyard, in the middle of the night, and left in Mother's driveway. I decided to make this a special event, so I rented a limo and took the girls along for the ride as we followed the tow truck. We put two blow-up dolls in the back seat. (At first we had them just sitting there, but then Rica and Neely arranged them in compromising positions, so that the female doll had her feet sticking up in the air. Jillian then took a bar of soap and wrote *Just Hitched* on the back window. The limo driver shook his head in amazement at all this.) Then we parked down the street, sipped champagne and ate chocolate dipped strawberries all night while waiting for Mother to come out for the morning paper. The resulting scream could be heard all over Old Southwich, after which she passed out and did a header into the koi pond.

—We'll be transferring Scott to the new affiliate we just launched in San Francisco. I just didn't have the heart to let him go, and besides, the guy is a ratings magnet. I made a big show about how much I'd miss riding Secretariat and even treated him to a night being attacked by a woman in blue sequins, though we skipped the stop at the billiard hall. Sadly, this means I'll have to find someone to take his place. So many references to check, so little time.

—And I know you're dying to find out what's up with Jillian and The Snack. Though they're together just about every night they maintain separate residences, as some nights The Snack hosts poker nights for the guys while Jillian is out with us doing girl stuff. They're both far too sensible to rush down the aisle, and are just enjoying each other right now, taking their time as their relationship grows stronger. It should be noted that the ratings during The Snack's time slot (three till six in the afternoon) are higher than those of any other, and when I get back I'm going to move him to prime time for February sweeps. And to think I was ready to dismiss the guy for being too short. Jillian has something really special in him.

Jillian also got her picture taken for a magazine ad… for pantyhose, naturally.

—Amanda actually sold the movie rights to our story and gave us another nice check on New Year's Eve. Some guy supposedly working on a screenplay called me and wants to get together with me and the girls when I get back. I got an email from him the other day and the subject line read *Untitled Cougar Project.*

—Neely's manual, "The Cat's Meow: The Over-Thirty Woman's Guide to Men" will be out the day before Valentine's Day. My chapter on checking references is bound to send every human resources manager in America into a meltdown. And, just for fun,

I'm having the publisher deliver a copy to everyone on Mother's street. (The thing with the Buick was so much fun, I just can't stop.)

Oh, hold on a minute. An exponentially cute guy just got out of the pool, was toweling off, and heading this way. Medium height, slender but nicely muscled, dark hair, mid-twenties. He weaved his way around the white deckchairs and black bikinis, getting several looks from the latter, tossed the towel in a giant drum and walked to the bar as the ever-present calypso music fills the background.

He stopped two chairs down and waited for the bartender to finish up with the customer at the other end of the bar. I'd gotten a close up of spectacular olive green eyes and a perfect set of shoulders that were hunched up just a bit.

He nodded at me and smiled, bringing tiny dimples into play. I could tell he was a little shy. I slid my drink across the bar toward him. "You can share mine if you can't stand the wait," I said. "You ought to try one of these. I'm Sydney."

He loosened up, the first move having been taken off those perfect shoulders. "Will Caplin," he said. He pointed toward the glass, which was three quarters empty. "You sure?"

"Go ahead, I don't have cooties."

"I didn't think you did." He grabbed the glass and took a sip, which brought an instant smile to his face. "Oh, that's fantastic."

The bartender moved down to our end. "Two more," I said.

"Very good, rum runner," he said, and started to cut up a pineapple.

"You don't have to do that," said Will.

"I do if I want you to sit next to me," I said, spinning the next chair so that it faced him. "I won't bite." He moved toward it and sat down.

"Actually I've been kind of wondering who the mysterious redhead was who sits by the pool every afternoon."

"I'm not all that mysterious."

"Well, you've got the hat and sunglasses and never go in the pool."

I removed my sunglasses and put them on the bar. "The sun down here is too strong for redheads," I said. "We're very fair-skinned. If I went out there with SPF one thousand I'd still look like the lobster they served last night."

"I didn't know that," he said, as the blender whirred into action. "About redheads." The bartender finished whipping up the blend and poured out the two coladas, stuck the appropriate garnish and umbrellas in the drinks, and slid them toward us. "Thank you," he said to the bartender. "And thank you," he said, turning to me, holding his glass up in a toast. "To perfect strangers who buy men drinks."

"Thank you, kind sir, but I'm not perfect."

"You look pretty close to it from here."

"By the way, I do go swimming. But at night, after dinner," I said, grabbing my drink. "Very refreshing and no one's here. Really neat under the moonlight."

"So if I wanted to see what the mysterious redhead looked like in a bikini, that would be the time."

"It would be a lot easier if you just had dinner with the mysterious redhead, then you could follow her to the pool. And back to her cabin."

"So… you're not cruising with anyone?"

"Nope. Just depressurizing from some long days at the office. How about you?"

"Flying solo," he said. "I did some PR work for the cruise line and they threw me a free cabin."

"No one you wanted to bring?"

He shook his head.

I nodded toward the pool. "I'm sure those bikinis are keeping you busy."

He smiled and shook his head. "Nah. They're looking for Mister Perfect."

"You look pretty close to it from here," I said.

He started to blush like Jillian. "You're very kind. But they're in search of tall and rich. When you're five-eight and clipping coupons, that kind of takes you out of the equation with girls my age."

"Height's overrated," I said, an image of The Snack and Jillian popping into my head. "So is money."

"Nice to hear a woman say that. I'm just not sure if I believe you."

"Why don't I take you to dinner and prove it to you? It's formal night. I have some blue sequins I'm dying to wear. I don't want them to go to waste and you look like the kind of guy who would appreciate them." I took a long sip of my drink as I dipped my head and looked at him. "That is, if you think you can handle me."

"I'd love to escort you to dinner," he said.

"*I'll* be taking *you*," I said. "My rules are different than most women's."

* * *

The light Caribbean breeze seemed to caress my wet skin as I sat on the edge of the pool. The crystal clear sky offered a spectacular view of the stars, a high-def version away from the light pollution of New York City.

Ah, the afterglow of reference checking.

"You're right," said Will, swimming up to me and pushing himself out of the water so that he sat next to me. "This *is* a better time to go swimming." I handed him a towel and he ran it through his hair. "I've really enjoyed the evening," he said.

"You say that like it's goodbye," I said. "We still have three nights left on the cruise."

"I wasn't sure if you were interested."

"You made me scream so loud the cabin steward came to the door and you're actually wondering if I'm interested?"

"I guess when you put it that way it's a stupid question. I haven't had much luck with women."

"Well, your luck just changed. And I'm certainly not going to spend the rest of this trip learning to fold napkins into swans if I've got you around."

He leaned forward and lowered his voice. "I just figured maybe you're one of those women who, you know, likes one-night stands with younger men—"

"Ah, I know the term to which you are referring. That a problem?"

"No way," he said. "I've just become a cat person."

Loved Boss Girl? Then don't miss the next book in this fabulous series,

It Girl

It Girl

CHAPTER ONE

"My network's twenty–million-dollar-a-year morning anchor just got arrested for soliciting a prostitute."

While I've made a habit of getting major exclusives as a television reporter, this latest juicy scoop brought the conversation at our dinner table to a screeching halt.

And the next words you hear should tell you that you need to get out of your conventional mode of thinking.

"She hired a prostitute?"

That's right. *She.*

See what I mean? You naturally assumed said morning anchor was a man looking for a hookup with some silicone babe on a Manhattan street corner. But nooooo, in this case we're talking about television's reigning "It Girl" who heretofore was assumed to be pure as the driven snow by the network executives who hired her.

At least they got the *driven* part right.

Snow White in handcuffs.

Film at eleven.

This simple text message from my contact at the cop shop meant the bigwigs who ran my network would be looking for a replacement. Immediately. You can't exactly get the kids ready for school while watching an anchor who thinks *half 'n' half* is something other than what you put in your coffee. Anyway, it wouldn't take long for the vultures who wanted the job to start circling.

I would not be one of them. But even the chance that the network might pluck me from the local affiliate for this job from hell sent a chill up my spine.

Yeah, you heard me. Twenty million dollar job from hell. It was a gig this intrepid television reporter didn't want.

And in the back of my mind I knew, thanks to Murphy's Law, they'd want me for it.

Sonofabitch. I hate it when people offer me huge contracts.

My best friend Layla raised one perfectly plucked dark eyebrow like a question mark. "Veronica, you gonna throw your hat in the ring?"

"Hell, no!" I said, as I grabbed my wine glass and took a bigger sip than normal. A pre-emptive strike in case said hat ended up in said ring.

Since you're probably wondering why a local TV reporter wouldn't want a network anchor slot that pays a fortune, I should probably tell you a little about my method of deductive reasoning. I'm Veronica Summer, the top hard news reporter for the network's New York City flagship affiliate. The local version of an "It Girl." And at the age of thirty-two, this tall, green-eyed redhead has her career just where she wants it. I get the lead story almost every night, take no prisoners, and am generally considered to be the best old-school journalist in town. So the last thing I need is a job that forces me to talk about purses, hair color and breast feeding at the crack of dawn. There's a network job I want, a dream job, and that aint it.

Even if it pays about a hundred times more than my current salary.

"Why the hell don't y'all apply?" asked Savannah, the sultry Southern brunette who is the most logical in our group.

"Because the morning show is a bunch of soft bullshit," I said. "That's not me."

"I watch that show while I'm on the treadmill," said Layla,

who probably saw the dollar signs that came with the job before anything else. "They do *some* serious interviews. You could still do your Brenda Starr thing."

"Yeah, and that's about ten percent of the show," I said. "The operative word being *show,* not *newscast.* The other two hours are a flying Mongolian cluster of fluff consisting of musical guests, dieting tips and how to avoid picking up killer germs from shopping cart handles." I threw up my hands and shook them. "Run for your lives!"

Layla sat up straight and smiled as a cute guy walked by our table, then twirled a few strands of her jet black hair as she made eye contact. "You're gonna get a call."

"Pffft," I said, waving my hand like I was shooing a fly even though I knew she was right. "They've got a deep bench at the network. I'm not even a blip on their radar."

The discussion was thankfully interrupted as dinner arrived. Our regular waiter, a cute thirtysomething guy named Frank, slid a huge plate of fettuccine Alfredo with shrimp in from of me. I licked my lips. "Lotta cheese, as usual?" he asked.

"You know what I like," I said. His cheese grater hovered over my plate as he carpet-bombed my dinner with parmesan. I was thinking that even with twenty mil per year I'd still eat at this place. Loud and brassy, always busy with hardly any space between the tables, it had great food and portions large enough to end up with a to-go box for a midnight snack. The waiter finished serving and moved on to another table, while I turned my attention to one of the many flat screens that hung around the perimeter in the hopes of changing the topic. "Hey, the Mets are actually winning." I twirled some pasta with a shrimp into a neat ball and popped it in my mouth. Nothing like butter, cream, cheese, pasta and crustaceans to take your mind off things.

"Don't change the subject," said Layla. "You need to apply."

"They don't have someone like y'all," said Savannah. "You're pretty, smart, have the quickest wit of anyone I know. I'm sure men wouldn't mind waking up to you."

"The jury's out on that," said Layla, "because she throws them out the night before."

"I meant *on television*," said Savannah.

"And it pays twenty... million... dollars," said Layla. "Cha-ching."

I shook my head as I dabbed my mouth with a napkin. "The outgoing anchor has been there ten years. They're not going to pay that much for someone new."

"So you wouldn't do it for ten million?" asked Layla. She lowered her voice and said, "Cha-ching," again.

"It's a moot point," I said. "I'd take the evening anchor job in a heartbeat, but I'm not the kind of person they want for mornings. The 'P' word is a necessary skill set for that show."

"'P' word?" asked Savannah.

"Perky!" I said. I playfully batted my lashes as I widened my eyes and turned my voice into that of a high-pitched brainless bimbo. "It's what all morning shows want! Someone upbeat and cheerful before the sun comes up! Good morning! It's a beautiful day! Let's all be happy while you get your precious little snowflakes ready for school!" I went back to my normal sarcastic tone. "Can you picture me on a morning show? Hey guys, I'm Veronica Summer. What the hell are you guys doing up? Fuhgeddaboudit! Go back to bed and let the little bastards make their own damn school lunches!"

"Yeah, you're not exactly little miss sunshine in the morning. But you could fake it," said Layla. "You're good at faking things."

"Funny," I said, sneering at her. "Trust me, they're not going to call."

I really wanted to believe that as the discussion finally ended. But dammit, they called the next day.

***

The network morning show is called, quite simply, The Morning Show. How much they paid someone to come up with that incredibly clever title is a closely guarded secret. Rumor has it that ten years ago network executives went off on a three day retreat to revamp the morning offering and come up with a new name for the thing. After a long weekend running up a huge bill at some exotic getaway in the Bahamas and countless hours of brainstorming someone came up with the ground-breaking idea to add capital letters to the concept.

The people in Congress have nothing on network executives, who have raised lack of productivity to an art form.

Anyway, The Morning Show's executive producer Gavin Karlson was already seated at the last table in the restaurant when I arrived a few minutes after twelve on Saturday afternoon. The huge teddy bear of a man in the camel's hair sport coat and starched white shirt stood up to greet me, towering over me by nearly a foot. "Veronica, nice to finally meet you."

"Same here," I said. A waiter came by and pulled out my chair. "Thank you," I said as I sat down and he handed me a brown leather-bound menu with a gold tassel in the middle. Natural light spilled through the windows, giving rich tones to the dark paneled walls of the old place.

The fortyish egg-faced bald producer (a dead ringer for Doctor Evil) studied me with his piercing gray eyes, probably looking to see if I had that starry-eyed look most prospective network anchors have on interviews. I smiled casually, as if this were just a run of the mill two hundred dollar lunch with a co-worker. Besides, I didn't want the job anyway. But when a network exec invites you to lunch at the city's oldest and most expensive restaurant, or even a hot dog stand, you jump, because you never know what's down the road. Don't burn a bridge before you even cross it. "So," I said, "getting any sleep lately?"

He shook his head and smiled. "You kidding? This has been the worst week of my life. Between bailing Katrina Favor out of jail in the middle of the night and dealing with the tabloids, it's been hell."

I tried to hold back a smile as I recalled the local front pages the day after she'd been arrested. "When you've got stripper name like Favor, it's a hanging curveball over the middle of the plate for the headline writers. Some of those were pretty brutal."

"Yeah, but you have to admit they were clever. We all got a kick out of *Party Favor*."

"She put you in a tough position."

"She put herself in a tough position. Pun intended."

"Hey, you could moonlight writing headlines. But seriously, I guess it must have been tough to let her go."

"Actually, it was an easy call to fire her. Thank God for the morals clause in her contract." He looked around to see if anyone in the half-empty restaurant was paying attention, then leaned forward a bit and dropped his voice. "Between you and me, we were going to replace her anyway when her contract expired next year."

"Really? After ten years?"

"Her favorability ratings were slipping, she was a bear to work with and her salary was way out of line. Then again, I'm not the one who signed her to that ridiculous deal."

"Oh, so this gig no longer pays twenty million." I playfully tossed my napkin on the table. "I'm outta here."

"It still pays a helluva lot. More than you're making now."

I replaced my napkin, took a sip of water, then glanced at the menu, which, of course, did not include prices. "Hell, I'm sure these entrees cost more than I'm making now. So what's good here?"

He looked quizzically at me, as if wondering why I was more interested in food than begging for the job. (Because I actually *was* more interested in the food.) "Uh, everything. I always get the broiled salmon with dill sauce. Save room for tiramisu."

"Sounds good. Make it two," I said, snapping my menu shut as I leaned back in my chair. "So, I'm sure people have been beating a path to your door since the news broke."

"Women will eat their young for this job. No offense."

"None taken. Hell, I agree with you. Last time we had an anchor opening we could have made a fortune with a pay-per-view catfight between a few of our reporters."

"Anyway, with sweeps coming up we need to have the replacement in the chair soon. I don't need weeks of speculation in the papers or the newsroom."

"I'm sure you have many qualified candidates."

"We do. You're one of them."

I couldn't help but smile. "I'm flattered. But I must admit I'm curious as to why you're talking to me. I mean, I'm not exactly someone with a morning show or anchoring background. And I'm not known outside of the tri-state area."

His smart phone lit up and vibrated. He looked at it, didn't answer, and turned back to me. "Well, the day after Katrina got arrested, we all sat down and threw out names of possible replacements. Yours was one that came up a few times. You're an excellent journalist, and our co-anchor said you've got a sharp wit. I had no idea you two went to college together and are close friends."

"Yeah, Scott and I go way back. We just don't see each other much because of the hours. I'm getting off work when he's coming in. Ships passing in the night."

"Well, anyway, he thought you'd be a good choice, and I think it's important that co-anchors actually like each other. Scott and Katrina were oil and water."

"So I've heard. He was about to shoe polish the toilet seat in her private bathroom and Saran Wrap the bowl. Splish-splash."

He laughed a bit. "I would have paid good money to see that. Anyway, we've been thinking of adding a harder edge to the show. So we need a real journalist as opposed to a traditional morning show host."

I sat up straight and widened my eyes, feigning interest. "Harder edge as in..."

"More political interviews, investigative pieces. We would get you out in the field to do stories, so you wouldn't be chained to the desk."

"Hmmm. By the way, you said my name came up a few times. May I ask who else thought I might make a good replacement?"

"You may ask," he said, with a wicked smile.

I shook my head as I rolled my eyes. "Typical management. You should know Jedi Mind Tricks don't work on me. Besides, I can just ask Scott."

"I figured you would. Anyway, we're doing a few tryouts tomorrow morning starting at nine when no one's around. Attempting to make the search as quiet as possible while keeping the knife throwing in the newsroom to a minimum. Scott's coming in and we're going to do a mock show with Friday's script. I'd really like you to come in if you're interested."

I wasn't, but turning down this man was career suicide. I'd never be considered for anything at the network again. I knew the "harder edge" was bogus, just a carrot to try to gain my interest. I'd just bomb the tryout and be on my way back to my real job. I forced a little excitement into my eyes and smiled. "Sure, I'll be happy to," I said, as I picked up my water glass.

"Great, I'll email you the script so you can look it over. Oh, one more thing that might pique your interest. One reason we want Katrina's replacement to do hard news is that this is the stepping stone to the evening anchor position. We see the person we hire as the heir apparent."

My glass froze in midair. Whatever attempt I was making at being casual went right out the window as my jaw dropped. That dream job I mentioned earlier? Yeah, this was it. Known as *The Chair,* the job was referred to with reverence by reporters, as if it could be spoken in italics. Gavin had dangled the ultimate carrot. "The morning show anchor will eventually replace Bill Recker?"

He nodded and smiled as he licked his lips, now having my attention and soul firmly tucked away in his pocket. Ruthless bastard. "He's retiring in three years and a half years. That's not common knowledge by the way, but he's sixty-one and tired of the grind. Wants to sail around the world on his yacht before he's too old to do it. But he wants one more presidential election, and then he's gone. So the plan is to keep Katrina's replacement on mornings till he walks out with a gold watch, then slide that person into *The Chair*. Well, actually, it would be three years on the morning show, and then..."

And then he dropped another enticing piece of produce.

"Six months covering Senator Dixon's presidential campaign."

And just like that, the job in which I had no interest was now a job I *had* to have.

***

"I forbid you to take this job."

My latest boyfriend's words out of the blue stopped me just as I was about to apply the whipped cream to his washboard abs. I sat up and put the can of Reddi-Wip on the nightstand. Obviously my plan for round two on this Saturday afternoon human dessert bar had been doused with a bucket of cold water. "*Excuse* me?"

"You heard me," said Alexander Dumont, my significant other for the past four months. He put his hands behind his head and locked his fingers. "I forbid it."

The night's dinner reservations at the city's trendiest restaurant went right out the window. I got off the bed, stood up, folded my arms in front of me and stuck out one foot like an angry teacher even though I was wearing nothing but a bright red thong. "Who the hell are you to *forbid* me to do anything that pertains to my career?"

"I'm your boyfriend, the man who is going to take care of you. And if you take this job and start getting up at two o'clock in the morning, we won't be able to continue our relationship. I already put up with you working nights."

I raised one eyebrow. "Oh, you *put up* with that, do you?"

"Every other guy I know has a girlfriend who works normal hours. Or a wife who stays home."

257

"Well, these are the normal hours for my job. And I'll never be a Stepford wife. I don't need someone to take care of me. I can take care of myself. Always have."

"You could get them to put you on the day shift."

"The eleven o'clock newscast is the station's signature broadcast, and I'm the lead reporter—"

"Yeah, yeah, I've heard about how important it is for viewers to go to bed watching your channel so that's what they're watching when they turn the TV on in the morning. Real rocket science."

"What I do for a living is important, Alexander. And I love what I do. You should know that by now."

"I just figured at some point your biological clock would kick in and this little fling with broadcasting would be over."

Now he'd crossed the line. My pulse spiked as my eyes widened. "Little fling?"

"You tell stories for a living. C'mon, it's not a real job."

Annndddd… cue the anger. "And you sell stocks to people. You're nothing more than a legalized bookie taking bets that companies will make money. Wall Street is a glorified casino."

"Don't change the subject. You're not taking this morning show job. You're not a morning person anyway."

"You don't get it. This will lead to the main network anchor job in three and a half years. You know how many people have sat in that chair in the last half century? Three. I'll be the face of the network at thirty-five. And I'll get to cover Sydney Dixon's campaign, and she's a lock to be the next President. I'll get to travel the world, have the President of the United States on speed dial, take trips on Air Force One—"

"Great, I'll see even less of you."

"It's my dream job."

"It doesn't work for me. Or my plan for us. You're not taking the job. End of story. C'mon, get back in bed."

He reached out for me and I shoved his hand away. My blood reached its boiling point, but I'm one of those people who can still think rationally even when I'm seriously pissed off. Reporters often see things in black and white, with very few gray areas. And at that moment, I knew I had to step back and look at the situation as a reporter, not as a girlfriend. I took a long look at the thirty-five year old man my friends considered to be an incredible catch. Tall, classically handsome with (ironically) an anchorman's square jaw, deep set dark brown eyes that matched the color of his short hair, a rugged face. A seriously buffed body to die for and sex that was off the charts. But the realization hit me that the man I had planned to turn into a hundred and eighty pound chocolate sundae didn't even know me.

Or didn't want to.

And just like that, I reached a decision. I knew it was time to cut my losses. "Get out."

"Excuse me?"

"You heard me. Get your underwear off the trapeze and your toothbrush out of my bathroom and whatever other stuff you've got around here and get out. You've got thirty minutes and after that anything I find that belongs to you is going down the garbage chute. We're done."

He reached out for me again. "C'mon, babe, calm down."

I glared at him. "Oh, I'm very calm. You just showed your true colors. You have absolutely no respect for my career, or for what I want to do with my life. Which, since you obviously didn't get the memo, is not yours to mold. And in case you haven't been to a wedding in a while, they took the *obey* part out of the vows, so you can't *forbid* me to do anything. You *put up* with me for the past few months? Well now you won't have to *put up* with anything. Go get yourself a nine-to-five girlfriend."

"You're serious."

I nodded. "We're done, Alexander. As you would say, end of story."